SHADES AND BLOOD OATHS

BOOKS BY KIMBERLY GRYMES

Aevo Compendium Duology Series
<u>Young Adult Science Fantasy</u>
Isoldesse
Fawness

The Red Umber Forest
(a companion novella)

◆ ◆ ◆ ◆

Three Shades Trilogy
<u>Young Adult Dark Fantasy</u>
Shade of Light
A Vengeful Shade
Shades and Blood Oaths

◆ ◆ ◆ ◆

The Four-Week Story Prep Workbook:
A Brainstorming and Outlining Workbook
for Fiction Writers

SHADES AND BLOOD OATHS

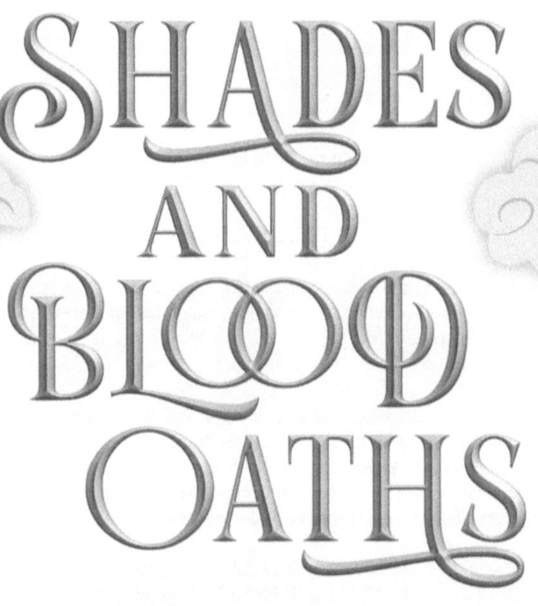

Book Three in the Three Shades Trilogy

KIMBERLY GRYMES

Tractor Beam Publishing

ISBN: 978-1-9652250-66 (paperback)
ISBN: 978-1-9652250-73 (hardcover)

ASIN: B0GF8W3326 (Kindle eBook)

Cover Design and Interior Formatting by Kimberly Grymes
Character Cover Artwork by Yves Muench | Fiverr.com/creatyves
Map by Angeline Trevena | Step-By-Step Worldbuilding

Shades and Blood Oaths is book three in the Three Shades Trilogy.
Genre: Epic Dark Fantasy
Age Category: Young Adult (14+)

Trigger warnings: Medieval fantasy world violence including death, battle scenes, and torture through mind infiltration.
Light Romance. All scenes are appropriate for teen readers 14+ years.

Tractor Beam Publishing
P.O. Box 44, Augusta, KS 67010

For more information visit kimberlygrymes.com

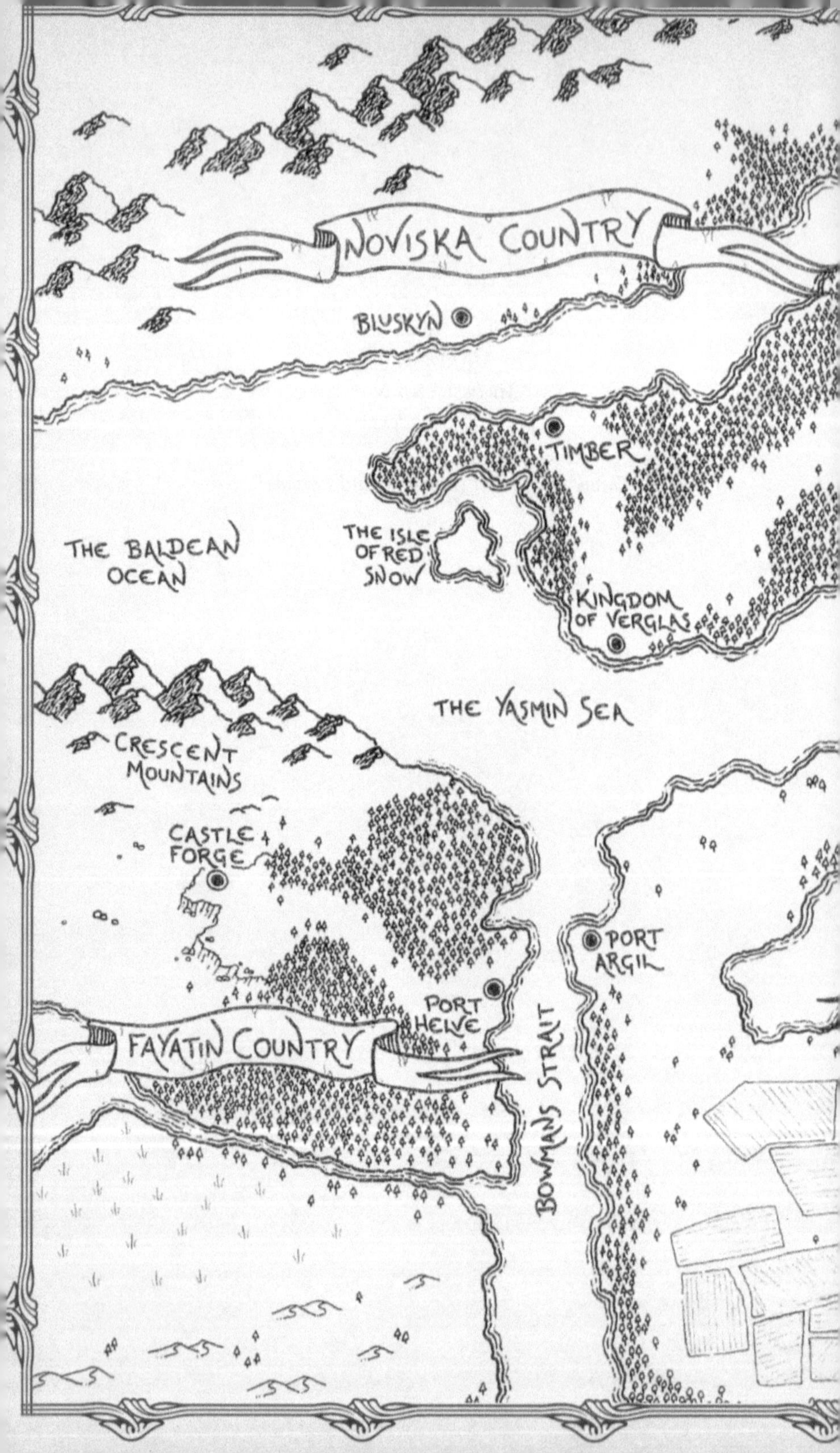

NOVISKA COUNTRY
BLUSKYN
TIMBER
THE ISLE OF RED SNOW
KINGDOM OF VERGLAS
THE BALDEAN OCEAN
THE YASMIN SEA
CRESCENT MOUNTAINS
CASTLE FORGE
PORT ARGIL
PORT HELVE
FAYATIN COUNTRY
BOWMAN'S STRAIT

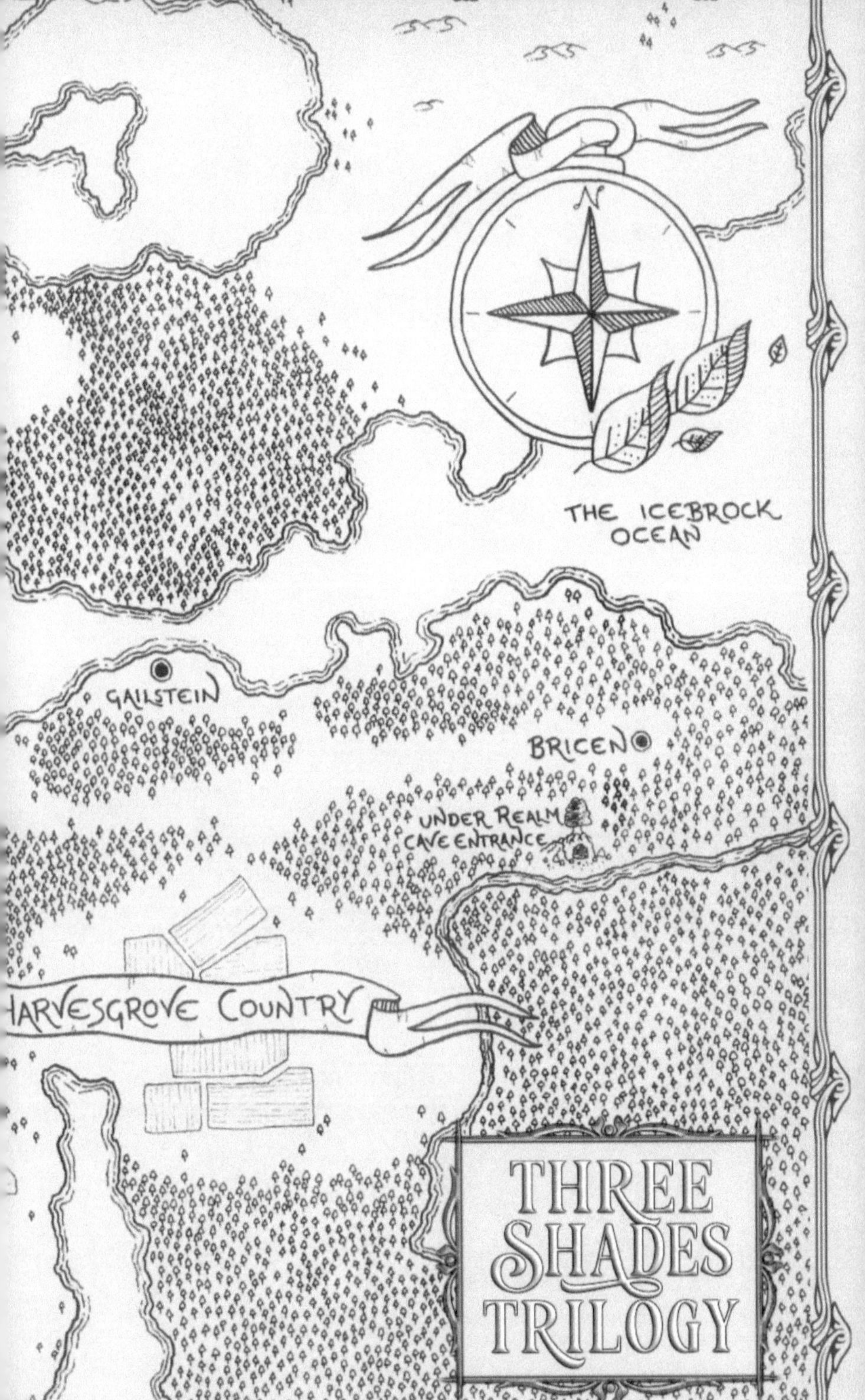

N
THE ICEBROCK OCEAN
GAILSTEIN
BRICEN
UNDER REALM CAVE ENTRANCE
HARVESGROVE COUNTRY
THREE SHADES TRILOGY

CHAPTER 1
ADELE

Through the night fog, Port Helve's docks finally come into view, and I want nothing more than to turn this ship around and sail back to Harvesgrove Country. Returning to Fayatin feels like a strange, unsettling dream, one I wish I could wake from.

An owl's screech pulls my attention from the docks to the looming darkness that clings to the land along the water's edge. I silently curse, wishing we arrived under a full moon rather than a new one. Moonlight would've helped me spot the ambush I'm certain waits for us.

Refusing to dwell on the dread churning in my gut, I keep my gaze fixed on the shadowed shoreline. The ship glides silently across calm waters, the faint scent of smoky torch flames mingling with the crisp, salty air. I can't see it, but I know it's there—the open field where I made my escape after fleeing Castle Forge. I remember how, beyond the field along the tree line, I said my final goodbyes not just to this wretched country, but to my dearest friend, Selene.

That day feels like a distant memory, as if my escape happened years ago, though it's only been two seasons. And now I return at her request, to witness her marriage.

A dockworker rings a bell at the end of the pier. We've arrived. Each *clang* of metal reverberates through my mind, a sharp reminder to stay alert. Now that the Interrogator's identity is widely known, many will want to capture me or kill me for what I've done to those they love.

I send a silent prayer to the stars, hoping Selene has sent someone to ensure our safety. It's far too late for a lady to be outside the castle, but still, I have to believe she's taken precautions. I can't allow blood to be spilled.

Boots pound across the main deck below. I peer over the quarterdeck railing. Two shipmates emerge from the shadows, striding briskly toward the bow. Hand over hand, they work together to unravel thick coils of rope pressed against the ship's wall. One ensures the ropes don't tangle while the other twists the ends into a large, looped bowline knot.

Behind me, the captain speaks in a low, flat voice. "We'll be docking any minute now."

I let my bare hand trail along the cool wood of the railing one last time before slipping my glove back on and turning to face him. An old iron lantern hangs from the mast nearby, swaying gently with the ship's motion. Its flickering glow casts a warm light over the captain's face, highlighting the deep lines etched by a life spent at sea while leaving me cloaked in shadows.

"You have your instructions," I say.

He nods, his hands hanging slack at his sides.

I take no pleasure in what I've done. I wasn't even sure it would work; I don't often command another's will. But there's too much at stake. Those who've traveled with me are in danger too.

The ship bumps gently against the dock, and shouts rise from the crew both aboard and below. A shipmate calls to the captain, but he doesn't move. His gaze stays fixed on me.

Leaning in closer so only he can hear me, I remind him, "One finger means safe. Two is for danger."

Again, he nods before descending the narrow steps to the main deck. He reaches it just as Kit emerges from an open hatch leading to the crew and passenger cabins below. She lifts an oversized basket with a matching wicker lid onto the top deck. Then, with the basket in tow, she makes her way over to the stairs leading up to where I am on the lookout level. In passing, she bumps a shoulder with the captain's arm. A fresh surge of fear twists in my gut, worried she'll uncover the truth about what I did—what I had to do. She turns to apologize to the old man, but he doesn't pay her any attention and continues toward his men holding the docking ropes.

"Hey!" I call, hoping to redirect her focus. "Did you get enough sleep?"

Traveling at night wasn't ideal, but the long journey across the Harvesgrove countryside had been exhausting. This final stretch across Bowmans Strait might've offered time to rest if the ship's cramped quarters and constant rocking hadn't made it nearly impossible to sleep.

Stretching one arm over her head, still holding the basket in the other, she yawns while scanning the deck for me. Eventually, she finds me peering down at her from the quarterdeck.

"What are you doing up there?"

"The view's better." I back away from the steps to give her room to join me.

She climbs the narrow staircase, then carefully swings the basket over the top step and sets it between us.

"They're getting restless," she says, settling beside me and resting her elbows on the railing. A cool breeze catches the loose curls framing her face as she stares at the approaching dock.

I crouch to lift the tight-fitting lid of the basket and check on Valor, Serafina, and Olive.

Three crows blink up at me, their black eyes sharp.

"I think it's safe for you to fly the rest of the way," I whisper. "Stay together and follow us from a distance as we travel to Castle Helve."

Valor flaps her wings as the others release a string of soft chirps.

A few black feathers drift into the moss-lined bottom of the basket, then land on an old shirt. Before we left Bricen, an adamant Magdala helped me prepare the crows' accommodations, wanting their trip to be as comfortable as possible. I remember being that wholesome at her age, too.

Valor lets out a tiny *caw*, snapping me from a fleeting thought about how my own childhood was stolen. I graze the top of her head and say, "We'll reunite with Barclay soon. I promise. But remember, this land isn't like Harvesgrove. Stay away from the castle grounds and the people here. Take cover at the forest's edge until I call for you."

One by one, they take flight, vanishing into the night sky.

"I still think you should've left those birds at Bricen with Sara."

After closing the basket lid, I straighten and lean against the railing again.

"She has enough to worry about. That doorway Rune opened between our realms is proving more complicated than we expected. Every day, more travelers come and go, with Bricen stuck in the middle."

After blowing into her cupped hands, she murmurs, "Well, then it's a good thing Evander's there to help her."

"Him being there does make leaving easier. But still... it's important we pay our respects to Selene and the new lord, then return to Bricen the next day, if not sooner."

"You'll get no arguments from me."

We turn our attention to the men on deck. They're leaning over the side of the ship, holding their ropes steady as they get ready to toss the looped ends to the men on the dock.

"You're late!" a burly man shouts. His burgundy knitted cap covers most of his head, the folded edge meeting his bushy eyebrows.

The man curses as he strides past his men, who work quickly to hitch the ropes over the dock's wooden posts, while keeping a keen eye on the captain. "I's expecting ya an hour or so ago."

When the captain doesn't respond, one of his men speaks up. "We had to wait out the dense fog. Rolled in and took its time passing."

Once the ropes are taut and the ship secured, the two shipmen unhook a long wooden ramp from the inner top deck wall and slid it out the gangway opening. The two dock men catch the other end of the ramp and lock it into place.

The Port Master waves a hand through the air, then rubs the gray hair beneath his cap, seemingly accepting the excuse.

Kit, not so much. "Is that true? Did we come upon some trouble?"

"The fog was enough for the captain to order a standstill until it cleared. He said he's heard too many stories about ships colliding and didn't want his boat at the bottom of the Bowmans Strait."

After grabbing the basket, I sidestep around Kit and head down the narrow stairs to the main deck. "Come on. Let's go."

"You should've woken—"

I don't let her finish. "No, I shouldn't have. You needed the rest."

I tuck the basket behind a nearby barrel, in case we need it for the ride home.

The second I turn to face Kit, who's watching the shipmen secure the ramp, a loud splash cuts through the cold air. She startles.

"What's that?" she asks, her tone sharp.

Before I can respond, a man calls out from somewhere on the starboard side, "Anchor's away!"

"Shouldn't they announce that before dropping it in the water?" Kit mutters. Her shoulders loosen slightly, though the rest of her stays tense.

Given the months that have passed since her time in the Under Realm, I thought she'd be back to her cocky self by now. But no. It's taking longer than expected.

Hoping to lighten the mood, I tease, "You've battled brainwashed angels and cult members with mystical powers, yet you're startled by an anchor splash? What happened to the girl who dared me to sneak out of the village or play tricks on her little brother?"

Adjusting her leather coat across her chest, Kit shakes her head. "I don't know where that girl is," she says, voice barely above a whisper. Slowly, she lifts her gaze to mine. "Believe me. I'm trying to find her."

I step closer, keeping my voice low. "If you want… I can try and help—you know, by…" But the words stall, unsure if I should continue my offer.

The torchlight from the dock casts warm light, barely reaching where we stand. "Sara's already tried. Whatever Merigoth did to me, she made sure I'd never forget"—Kit's voice falters, the air catching in her throat—"the feeling of her intrusion and hold over my will."

I glance over her shoulder, to where the captain stands, waiting for the docking ramp to be secured into place.

"Anyway," Kit says curtly, wiping her nose on her sleeve. "I thought Fayatin would be warmer."

Catching her subtle cue about the subject change to the weather, I don't continue pressing Kit with how she's holding up from our recent encounter with the demon queen any further. My gaze lifts to the night sky. "This will be the last new moon of the winter season. Warmer weather's on the horizon."

Once the ramp is secure, the captain descends off the ship. His boots pound against the rickety wood in a steady rhythm until he reaches the dock. The Port Master clears his throat and takes a few steps to meet the captain, but the captain walks past without a word. He eventually veers right and continues toward land. It isn't just the Port Master watching him now. The two deckhands and the rest of the crew are staring too, all of them curious to see where the old man's heading.

"What's that about?" It's Kit who breaks the silence, asking the question everyone is thinking.

Everyone but me. I know exactly where he's going, because I compelled him to check if the road is safe. *One finger for safe. Two for danger*, I remind myself.

"She won't let them imprison you," Kit says quietly.

I barely give Kit a glance, already knowing what she means. "You can't be sure of that."

"Did you ask the captain to go survey the road?"

Something like that. I don't want to lie to her, so I stay quiet, keeping my eyes on the captain in the distance. He's standing still, scanning the road.

"You're her guest, Adele. Selene's not going to let anyone harm you. Or lock you up."

I want to believe that, but I don't answer. Instead, I sidestep closer to the ramp. Glancing over my shoulder, I ask, "How about you go wake our strong man who insisted on coming to protect us?"

That gets a laugh out of her. "Our brave swordsman, whom we've yet to see in battle."

"Nathaniel's sparred with us plenty of afternoons in the Green," I say in his defense. Though I don't mention how he always shows up just before dinner, or right when his older brother, Brandulf, calls him back to the smithy. We've yet to see the sword skills he claims to have.

Needing to keep watch on the captain, I nod toward the hatch. "Go on. Wake our big, strong man."

Kit gives me that *are you serious* glare.

I respond with an eye roll. "Just go wake him." Then, quickly, I add a genuine, "Please."

She hesitates, then groans and disappears down the hatch, muttering something about why he even came.

Nathaniel's decision to join us was last minute. I believe he was waiting for me to ask him to come along, but when I didn't, he took matters into his own hands, arriving with a packed bag and ready to go on horseback. Kit argued that it would be better for him to stay in Bricen and help Sara and Evander oversee the village and the travelers passing through the realm doorway. But she also knows the real reason why I didn't turn him away.

I've come to enjoy Nathaniel's company.

When Kit returns a few minutes later, handing me my bag, bow, and quiver, we stand ready to depart the ship. Nathaniel approaches, rubbing one eye and yawning. His unkempt hair resembles the old broom we use to sweep the floors at Goslings, which has seen better days. Still, I appreciate him growing it out after I questioned why he kept it so short. The blond strands now reach past his ears.

One by one, we descend the ramp to the dock. The Port Master's attention remains fixed on the captain, who is still searching the dark road. Without looking away, the Port Master mutters, "Not sure what's wrong with the captain."

The dock boards creak beneath his boots as the Port Master faces me. The skin along his cheeks and forehead is flushed red, probably from the time under the sun, working the docks. He stands there, eyeing me over. He's at least a foot and a half taller than I am, which I'm guessing he believes is intimidating. My insides roll at the humor of his ignorance. He crosses his thick arms over his chest and continues his berating welcome speech. "I'd like to get some sleep at some point tonight, so get your stuff and be on your way."

"Aye," Nathaniel says, hoisting his bag higher on his shoulder. "I'm ready for a real bed myself."

"Adele," Kit says from behind, "what's the captain looking for?"

The burly man in front of me pushes up the brim of his cap, bushy brows lifting. "Adele, you say? As in the girl always at General Onica's right side? The infamous…" He doesn't finish his sentence, but his glare tells me he knows exactly who I am.

"Are you going to let me pass?" I ask, mirroring the intensity of his glare.

He scoffs, shakes his head, and grumbles something under his breath before turning away. A few steps down the dock, he shouts to his men, "Tie it up tight! When she's good and secure, best to head home." Shuffling to a stop, he glances back our way and adds, "Don't linger too long. The Interrogator has returned to Fayatin."

I want to lunge for him and show him just how right he is, but Kit grabs my arm the second I move. With a tense expression, she asks, "What's gotten into you?" I spin to face her, gripping the wood of my bow, unsure how to explain what this place does to me and how these people only see me as a torturer. She inches closer, speaking low enough for only me to hear. "You can't say you're worried about being locked up and then attack the first man we cross paths with in Fayatin who pisses you off."

Swallowing the anger that's swollen in my throat, I lower my gaze to the dark plank boards lining the dock. The water sloshes against the wooden posts, filling the silence between us. I let the sound of the water ease my thoughts as I inhale a deep breath.

"You're right," I say, offering her a calm, collected expression. It's getting harder to keep the dark thoughts in check, but I don't tell her that. The weight of not wanting to disappoint my family and friends is the only thing that keeps me from lashing out. I don't want to hurt anyone, yet something deep inside longs for the freedom to not be shoved into the corners of my mind. I try to imagine what my life would be like if I were both—Adele and the demon. How much control would I have over the urges brought on by my demon half?

"You good?" Kit asks, and I nod. She moves past me, but she doesn't get far down the dock. "Uh, Adele." Out on the road, the captain is now surrounded by a group of men. "Why is he holding up two fingers behind his back?"

CHAPTER 2
ADELE

Kit spins on the balls of her feet and marches over to me, her fists clenched at her sides. Her gaze bores into me, lips pursed tightly, and the slight tremble in her eyes betrays not anger but sadness. Slowly, her voice quivering with barely contained emotion, she says, "What did you do?"

Nathaniel is still standing on the ramp, keeping his distance. Though it's only been a few weeks, he's been spending more time with me and my family, and he's quickly learned that when Kit and I disagree, it's best to give us space.

"Did you—" She doesn't say the word *compel*, instead tapping at the side of her forehead.

"I needed to be sure we weren't going to be ambushed." There's no guilt or regret in my voice. Of course, I don't like doing it, but she doesn't know this country as I do. We have to take every precaution, especially since the Interrogator's identity has been unveiled. My friends are at risk of being persecuted right alongside me if one of the regional lords tries an ambush. I swore to never serve another power-hungry tyrant like General Onica, yet there's always the risk of Kit or Nathaniel—or anyone I care for—being captured and used as leverage against me. Even with that fear playing a role in my decision-making, Kit would always argue there's another way—to not compel another person's will without their consent.

There are no words to console her, so with my bag over one shoulder and my bow in hand, I continue down the dock and stop at the threshold. I focus on the men in black jackets standing around the captain, about fifteen paces from the end of the dock. His hand remains behind his back with two fingers raised. One finger for safe, two fingers for danger. None of the men glance my way, giving me a few more fleeting moments to plan out how to handle this unavoidable encounter.

I let out a sigh as I step off the wooden planks and onto the packed dirt. I'm here. I've really returned to this horrid country. I take a deep breath of the salty air, hoping the chill of the night will sharpen my senses, but my body feels the strain of the long journey, aching muscles, and growing fatigue. All I want is to climb into bed and get a well-rested night of sleep. And now we have to deal with whatever this is. I don't want to assume the worst, but my mind has overtaken my better judgment, and I can already foresee blood being spilled. Slowly, I raise my hand, ready to slip off one of my gloves, but don't when a gentle hand cups my shoulder.

"Maybe it's a misunderstanding," Kit whispers, coming up next to me. She drops her bag at her feet with a loud *thump*, yet no one glances our way. After tying back her loose tendrils of curly hair with a piece of scrap linen, she adjusts her belt at her waist, making sure her shortsword is accessible.

Adjusting my glove along my wrist, I glance at her as she readies herself to unsheathe her blade if needed. "What happened to *maybe it's a misunderstanding?*"

"I remembered where we are. The Fayatin Guard aren't exactly known for their warm welcomes." She glances behind and gives a curt nod to Nathaniel, gesturing for him to hurry and stand ready with us. He does, and something pinches inside my chest the moment I see him next to me. He adjusts his sword at his waist. Though our friendship is still fresh, I find his company invaluable, and the pinch in my chest tightens as I imagine the clash of steel and the risk of death. I don't know what I would do if I lost either of them.

"What's the plan?" Kit whispers.

My mind swarms with ideas of how we should escape, but before I can speak, the captain pivots to face us and shouts, "All is safe!"

A rush of captive air escapes my mouth, and my body relaxes. Now, the men surrounding the captain turn their attention to us, their black jackets blending seamlessly into the pitch-dark night. The captain approaches with two of the men, while the others walk away in the opposite direction, leaving three to remain and watch us with narrowed eyes.

Looping my arm through my bow, I hold it against my body, hoping to signal to the approaching men that we're not a threat. Kit takes her hand off the hilt of her shortsword and crosses her arms over her chest. Nathaniel, on the other hand, keeps one hand ready by his waist.

The captain doesn't look our way as he continues past. His boots stomp along the dock, their sound fading. Once he's back on his ship, the compulsion I've placed over him will fade as well, leaving him dazed with missing time from his memory. The two men approaching us do not continue past; they stop a few paces before us.

The man with the short dark beard steps closer, one hand casually resting on the hilt of the sword hanging from his belt. "Are you Lady Caldridge's guest?"

Guest? Does he not know who I am? And if I tell him, how will he react? The silence lingers between us for longer than he likes, and as he rolls his eyes, he repeats his question. "Are you or are you not—"

"I am," I answer, cutting him off. "Selene is an old childhood friend," I say earnestly, leaving it at that.

The broad-shouldered man standing a few feet behind straightens, his hand slowly rising until his fingers are around the hilt of his blade. When my gaze flicks to him, the man addressing us takes another step forward and quickly says, "We have instructions to escort you to Castle Helve on behalf of Lord Stolkin and his eldest son, soon-to-be regent of a united Fayatin, His Grace, Victor Stolkin. I am Second Commander Leon Pavik."

Well, that's interesting. Now I understand why Selene's uncle insisted on her union.

Kit responds, "Your escort is appreciated, Commander Pavik. Do you have horses for us?"

I sometimes forget how young we are compared to those around us. Even Nathaniel has a couple of years before reaching twenty. We've endured so much to survive this world that I feel as old as the men standing before us. I can only assume Kit feels the same, and it's evident in the confidence and exhaustion lacing her tone.

The distant sounds of chains rattling and wood creaking fill the night air. The torchlight from the port docks stretches across the dirt road, revealing a carriage emerging from the shadows. "No need," Commander Pavik says in a flat voice. His expression is hard to read in the dim light, but there's a hint of annoyance to his words. More reason to stay alert.

Kit and Nathaniel grab their bags and head for the carriage. I eye the commander as he speaks quietly with the taller man by his side. Mid-conversation, the guard's gaze lands on me, while Commander Pavik faces me. He lets out a sigh and sweeps his hand wide. "I'd hoped for a chance to rest tonight, Mistress—" He stops, waiting for me to offer my name.

He doesn't know who I am.

"Adele." It's a gamble, but what better way to see if my name and the Interrogator are tied together?

Eyes wide, the broad-shouldered guard shuffles closer, his grip tightening on his sword. One of Commander Pavik's brows rises. "Ah, I see. My Lady Caldridge forgot to mention we had a special guest attending the ceremony."

"Commander," the tall man says with a concerned tone. "She's worth—"

Commander Pavik raises a clenched fist, silencing the man. Then he steps closer, eyeing me as though I'm the monster everyone believes the Interrogator to be. His gaze dips as he assesses my appearance. When he's done, he clasps his hands together and says, "For some reason, I thought you'd be older. I mean, I'd heard rumors of your youth, but how… horrible it must've been for you to grow up under the thumb of General Onica."

"Yeah, well, it wasn't by choice." I try to sidestep around him toward the carriage, but the guard behind the commander stops me by drawing his sword and holding it across my path. I meet his gaze, unblinking, silently challenging him. Oh, how I love a good challenge.

"We aren't going to have any," Commander Pavik pauses, weighing his words carefully "problems?"

Looking at him, I reply, "I'm here to see a friend get married. That's all. Any problems that occur would be in response to someone threatening me or my friends." I hope my message is loud and clear: back off and keep your distance.

Commander Pavik seems more amused than threatened by my response. His lips purse in an agreeable expression as he nods. Then he says, "You have my word that none of my company will cause you or your friends any distress."

The tall man behind him seethes. "But, Commander—"

"Mind your tongue," he says sharply, cutting off his guard without breaking eye contact with me. Then he repeats, with calm authority, "You have my word."

We reach the carriage. Kit and Nathaniel are sitting inside, talking. I turn to the commander and say, "I appreciate that. And please know that I have no intentions to be that person anymore. I'm only here to see my friend get married. Then I'll be on my way, Commander Pavik. My home is no longer here in Fayatin."

He nods in understanding. "I will reiterate your safety to my men—unless you cause someone harm. Then, my child, you are no longer Adele, but the Interrogator once again. And many seek to either own you… or bleed you for the pain you've caused their families."

"I know. And there isn't anything I can do to mend the wrongs I've committed."

I'm about to climb into the carriage when the commander adds, "It's worth mentioning that there will be others in attendance at the wedding whom I have no control over. Keep your guard up. And come find me if you need anything. You will address me as Commander Pavik in the presence of the lord of the castle and his family—but Leon will suffice outside of court."

There's something about him that eases my concern over being arrested and thrown in a dungeon. "Thank you, Commander."

"My lord and his family are my priority. That includes Lady Caldridge."

It's nice knowing someone is here to look after Selene—to protect her from any dangers. "I appreciate you watching over her safety."

He gestures for me to step inside the carriage with a swing of his arm, and I do. Once I'm settled inside, he nods one last time to me before closing the windowed door.

Kit makes room for me to sit next to her and asks, "Everything okay?" Nathaniel sits across from us, also waiting for an update.

The carriage lurches forward, the horses' hooves clattering as we begin the ride to Castle Helve. I glance between the two of them and say, "Keep your backs to the walls. Don't wander off. I don't care what that man says about trusting him or going to him for help. I trust only the two of you—and Selene."

They nod, understanding.

I lean back in my seat, stretching out my legs. Tomorrow is about the wedding—paying our respects to Selene and Victor—then heading back to Bricen. That's the plan.

I close my eyes and pray to the stars this will be an easy in-and-out visit.

Then again, who am I kidding?

Nothing's ever gone easy in my life.

CHAPTER 3
RUNE

Staring up at the clear blue sky, I imagine my mother looking down at Stellara from beyond the stars, filled with pride. A warm breeze brushes against my wings, carrying with it the faint scent of blooming trees from the forest beyond the city walls.

My gaze lowers to the sprawling view of our city. There's still a great deal of work to be done, but we've come so far in just a few weeks, especially with the influx of help from the human world. Those who crossed over, eager to explore the Starlight Realm, have all agreed to do their part in restoring it.

Stellara may never be what it once was, but it *will* be saved. The city is becoming a place that welcomes both angels and humans.

"There you are," Elijah's voice calls, warm and familiar. He bounds up the steps of the old empty citadel, two at a time, until he reaches my side. The sunlight catches in his dark hair, making his eyes shine as he slips his hand over mine, intertwining our fingers. "What are you doing up here?"

Straightening my shoulders, my wings arching slightly, I point to the garden area off to the left. "I heard something exciting is happening."

His face lights up, eyes beaming with excitement. "Oh, well I did hear whispers about the girls making a breakthrough." He gives my hand a gentle squeeze. "Your city is coming back to life. You did it, Rune. You saved the city and the angels."

My heart swells at his words. "*Our* city," I say, correcting him, because it wasn't only me. It was him too.

Without Elijah's love and encouragement, I never would've dared to open our world to outsiders. Now, things are good. The laughter of children mixes with the sound of hammers and saws. Angels and humans work side by side, smiles etched across their faces.

The city is alive again, bound by a shared purpose.

Sudden cheering erupts from the garden below. A group of people rushes across the cobblestone courtyard to see what the fuss is about. Elijah tugs my hand, already making his way down the steps, calling to me, "Let's go see what's happening!"

His excitement is infectious, and I can't help but smile as I follow him.

Everything feels perfect—almost *too* perfect, I think. A fleeting thought, quickly pushed aside as we reach the crowd.

They've formed a circle around three girls kneeling at the edge of the garden soil. Aleksandra sits in the center, and my heart swells again. She no longer wears her green cloak or hides her horns beneath a hood.

Here, in Stellara, everyone has come to accept and love her as part of our community. Gardening has become her passion, and I'm thrilled she's chosen to work with the others to explore new ways to grow vegetation.

I crouch beside the girls, my gaze landing on a tiny green stem with two delicate leaves sprouting from the rich brown soil. Pointing to the small miracle, I ask, "What have you got there?"

Aleksandra continues to write in her journal, focused, while the other two girls—one angel and one human—talk over each other, their voices full of excitement. They laugh at their synced words before Cameron gestures for Jordana to go ahead.

The human girl scoots closer to the plant. "Oh, Rune! We're going to be able to grow our own crops now!"

I glance up from my crouched position to Elijah, whose face, like everyone else's, mirrors the overwhelming excitement of this milestone. His gaze meets mine, and I smile before turning back to the girls. "And you think we'll have a full harvest this sol season?"

Cameron answers this time, her light brown wings trailing behind her like a cloak of feathers. "Oh, most definitely. Isn't that right, Aleksandra?"

Still concentrating on her journal, Aleksandra softly repeats the last of what she's writing: "Exceeding my expectations." She closes the small leather journal and focuses on the tiny sprout, pushing more fresh soil around the stem's base.

"The soil here has different nutrients than in the Human Realm," she explains, gently grazing the underside of a leaf. "We weren't expecting anything to sprout for at least another two weeks."

"Hurray!" a man in the crowd cheers.

"We should plant more gardens!" someone else suggests.

"Oh, yes!" a woman chimes in, her voice bubbling with excitement. "I can send extra food to my sister's family in Noviska!"

Elijah steps forward and raises his hands to settle the growing excitement. "Let's focus on feeding the community here in Stellara first. Then, maybe down the road, we can talk about what to do if we have extra."

A rumble of voices rises, many agreeing to wait while many others loudly plead for their loved ones still struggling in the neighboring realm.

I rise from my crouch and raise my hand to quiet the crowd. When the voices settle, I speak clearly, letting my tone carry reassurance. "I know everyone's excited about this wonderful accomplishment. And we will celebrate the girls' hard work during tonight's supper with extra wine from the storage."

This has everyone cheering once again, and the sound fills my heart with joy. Once the clapping fades, I continue, "But Elijah is right. We must consider our own community before deciding what we can share with those outside of Stellara." A few of the older residents wrap an arm around the individual standing next to them, offering them some comfort. It pains me that we can't help everyone in need, but one day we'll get there. One day we will be able to welcome more humans and send our surplus food out to those in need.

Not wanting to ruin the mood, I tell them, "I'm so proud of what we've accomplished these past few weeks. Our progress has given me a great hope that the new Stellara will be even better than what it used to be."

"All right, everyone! Let the girls get back to their gardening. We'll celebrate their milestone at supper!" Elijah calls, his voice barely reaching those at the back of the crowd.

While he continues to usher everyone away from the gardens, I turn to the girls again. "Thank you. You really have done something wonderful today."

Jordana and Cameron giggle with excitement. The two of them were instant friends shortly after Jordana and her family crossed over from the Human Realm. Aleksandra took a little more time to warm up to them, and others. Now, the three of them are always together. Although Aleksandra wasn't asleep for as long as Adele and Sara were in that enchanted sleep, the girl is still in her youth. I'm happy she's living a free life where she can make her own decisions about her future.

"We're going to clean up," Cameron tells Aleksandra. "We'll meet you at the library when we're done, yes?"

Aleksandra stands, holding her small gardening journal in one hand. "Sounds good to me."

Her two friends spin away with a bounce in their step and hurry out of the garden area and across the cobblestone courtyard. When they've disappeared down the line of restored homes, I look back to Aleksandra.

Her gaze is on the sprout. "So fragile and helpless."

I'm caught off guard by her words. Instead of assuming the worst, I suggest, "Yes. We'll need to put up some boards or fencing around the raised beds."

Elijah returns, still wearing his proud smile. "Marvelous work, Aleksandra! You'll have to share your secrets with us at supper about how you finally got the plants to grow."

"Of course," she says, snapping out of whatever reverie holds her attention. She then gives Elijah and me a quick smile before tucking her journal under her arm and wiping her hands on her apron. "I'm going to head home and clean up. I'll see you later." Without waiting for us to respond, she makes her way out of the garden area. Those who lingered in the courtyard congratulate her as she weaves through them.

Once she's out of sight, I bend over, wanting a closer look at the sprouting plant, marveling at how far we've come. Angels don't need food to survive—we thrive on the sun and natural elements. It was the humans who insisted on planting seeds when they first arrived. For weeks, they couldn't get anything to grow.

Aleksandra found a way to get the soil fertile enough for the seeds to grow.

I remember her early days here—hidden away in her room, hood drawn tight over her horns. Only when she met Cameron and Jordana, who saw past her guarded exterior and accepted the kind, intelligent girl beneath, did Aleksandra begin to gain confidence. Then, it didn't take long for her to interact more with the community, eventually finding her calling here in the gardens. Now, seeing her coax life from soil that was resistant to taking water fills me with pride. She truly has become part of the community.

I move to Elijah's side. "They did it."

He's beaming with a toothy smile. "I never doubted them. The three of them have been determined to grow something in this garden for weeks now." He wraps one arm over my shoulders and pulls me in, planting a soft kiss on my forehead. I no longer fear judgment from the other angels about my relationship with Elijah. Our love might have been forbidden back in the day, but those times are gone. We're building a new future where anyone can love whomever they choose.

"Have you seen my bracelet?"

Both Elijah and I turn around to see Jordana has returned and is searching along the beams of the raised garden beds.

"I took it off because I didn't want it to get muddy, and then I forgot about it."

Parting, we help Jordana search for her lost item. Elijah makes his way farther down the row while I search the dirt around the young plants. While sifting through the soil, I praise our young gardeners. "You three really did something amazing here. It'll make life easier for the humans who want to stay and build a future here."

Jordana finds her charm bracelet under the gardening tools spread out on a nearby potting table. She shakes the dirt from the silver links while explaining, "Oh, no. Cameron and I had nothing to do with reviving the soil. Aleksandra was the one who figured out we needed to bring in better dirt if we were going to grow anything."

"Is that so?" I say, warmth blooming in my chest. The girl who once seemed so lost now stands at the center of something meaningful. And how smart is that—to bring in healthier soil.

Elijah's brows pinch together as he cocks his head. "And where did you find the dirt?"

"Well, uh…" Jordana stutters, as if she isn't sure she's supposed to tell anyone.

"It's okay, Jordana. You can tell us." Intrigued, I gently rub her arm to reassure her she can confide in us, while hoping she'll reveal what's on her mind.

"It was Aleksandra. She had the idea to get healthier soil from a place that's already growing healthy plants and trees."

"Trees," I repeat, concern lacing my tone. I silently pray to the stars this conversation isn't going in the direction I think it's going.

The young human reacts quickly and offers an explanation in Aleksandra's defense. "We know we're not supposed to go beyond Stellara's walls—"

And there it is… Exactly what I'd hoped she wouldn't say. The girls snuck out beyond the city walls.

"You could've gotten hurt out there!" Elijah snaps, his voice harsh as his excited expression sinks. His eyes narrow at the young girl while he rubs a hand over his chin. "This is bad," he says to me. "We can't have people wandering off."

His concerns are justified. And it's in moments like this that I admire how he's taken on a leadership role alongside me, Evander, and Gianna. The girls should've known better than to have ventured outside of the city without telling anyone. It's something the leaders adamantly stress to those who cross over from the Human Realm to live here in Stellara.

What's done is done. And now we have to take this experience and learn from it.

Holding Elijah's gaze, I explain in a calming tone, "We'll speak with Aleksandra about it later. For now," I look to the human girl, "going forward, please, don't leave the borders of Stellara. The forest may seem harmless, but there are many dangers in this realm, and since our absence for over a hundred years, those dangers could have spread. One day, when life within Stellara has returned to normal, meaning we have the numbers to defend ourselves if needed, then we can discuss sending out explorers. But for now, we mustn't go beyond the wall."

Jordana nods. "Yes, ma'am."

I gesture with a wide sweep of my hand toward the courtyard and say, "That'll be all for now. I'm glad you found your bracelet."

"Thank you!" She hurries off, a bounce in her step.

"I'll talk with Aleksandra," Elijah says, already turning away from me.

I grab his arm, stopping him. "She doesn't need to be watched every minute." When he turns to me, I add, "I know we had our doubts—wondering if she came here just to escape her past and Sara. But I think she's found her place."

"But she snuck outside of the city." The disappointment shows in his saddened expression.

"I know, but she did it so we could grow this…" I point to the first of many crops to be grown. "She solved the problem. We can't reprimand her for that."

He inhales a deep breath and slowly exhales. "You're right."

"I think it's time we gave her a little more freedom." It's probably not what he wants to hear. He's been caring for Aleksandra these past few weeks as if she were his responsibility. But she's around the same age as him, and her time with the Order proves she can take care of herself.

"I think it's time we ask her if she's ready for a place of her own. Maybe move into one of the smaller homes with Jordana and Cameron?"

His pursed expression softens, and a small smile blooms. "Yeah. I think that's a great idea! A place she can make her own. There's a vacant home a few houses down from our place."

Oh, Elijah, I think to myself. Then, to him I say, "See what she says about the idea, and then let her decide where she wants to live. There are plenty of empty homes she can choose from."

He pats my hand before heading down the narrow alley that leads toward our home. Watching him walk away, eager to talk to Aleksandra, has me thinking about what a wonderful father he'll make one day. Every morning fills me with joy and anticipation for what the future holds for our relationship, the community, and our beautiful city.

Not wanting to burden him with more tasks, I silently add to my list of things to do: find out where the girls were able to sneak out through the wall, because we can't have them or others wandering off and explore the Starlight Realm. This realm may seem beautiful on the surface, but my mother and the other Star Leaders worked hard to keep the dangers out and angels safe.

And now it's up to the new leaders to do the same.

CHAPTER 4

ALEKSANDRA

"You were right," I whisper, my lips brushing the cool, smooth surface of the black sphere. Though its coloring resembles spilled ink, its texture is anything but wet. Some days, it almost feels alive. Its temperature constantly shifting, its surface trembling when agitated, and once, it even rolled off the bed as if trying to escape. "The fertile soil we needed to restore the garden was exactly where you said it would be."

A tendril of heat snakes across the surface beneath my hands.

"I'm curious," I say, voice low. "How did you know what would revive the soil's health, if you've never been to Stellara or the forest lands beyond?"

There's a long stretch of silence. For a moment, I think whoever—or whatever—is on the other end of this mystical sphere isn't going to answer.

Just as I lean forward to repeat the question, the voice finally responds in its usual eerie tone. *"Dirt is dirt, here or there. We know much about death, and much about life. One does not exist without the other. And there is always time that fills the space between. We only provided you with the knowledge to revive and extend the soil's life a bit longer."*

The riddles are becoming easier to decipher. I'm not sure if that's because we've grown more familiar over the past few weeks, or because I'm learning to tune into its nature, its way of speaking.

"Well, it was exactly what the dried-up dirt needed—fresh, healthy soil from the forest."

"So, you were able to leave the city undetected?"

I scratch the top of my head, fingers catching in the thick curls, grazing the tender spot from earlier. On more than one occasion, I've slipped out of the city unnoticed, yet during my latest outing, I accidentally struck my head on part of the stone along the top of the narrow break in the city's barrier wall. Elijah had told me, after I'd asked about security, that most of the broken section had been patched up. But I'd found one gap they'd missed. It was a tight fit, and I don't plan on bumping my head again, but in the end I made it out.

"It wasn't easy," I admit with a wince, "but manageable." Keeping the mysterious entity talking, I press on. "How do I know you'll keep your promise and give me what I'm owed?"

Suddenly, a sharp prick stings my finger, and I jerk my hand back as blood wells up and spills onto the surface of the stone. While I try to figure out where the needle came from, the voice speaks again, *"We vow through a blood oath to grant your request of an audience with the one you seek power from. You must find the Bocnite first."*

I return my hand to the stone, letting the blood oath proceed. My blood sinks into the black surface, vanishing without a trace. "Can you tell me where they are? How I can find you?"

Along with gardening, I've been painstakingly trying to decipher Merigoth's journal, but the strange language is hard to interpret. One thing I was able to figure out from the illustrations of creatures with horns is that the demons are referenced as Bocnite. So, I know that much at least. Figuring out the rest has been a struggle.

"How can I find you?" I repeat my question. I almost drop the thing when a waft of black smoke rises from all over the stone's surface. I'm expecting it to float off into the air, except it doesn't. Instead, it enters my nose. The cold air tickles, causing me to gasp and breathe it in instinctively.

A surge of energy hums through me, and it thrums in my chest like a second heartbeat.

"That is but a taste of what you can expect when you arrive. We are two of one, and will soon be one of more. You will have your power, and we will have our freedom."

Great. More riddles.

I don't understand what that means, but I don't dwell on it. Not when the power still pulses through me. It feels amazing. Addicting. I want more.

"We will be one of more," I repeat, the high already beginning to fade. "What does that mean?"

"All will be right in due time."

Before I can demand more answers about the Bocnite, a familiar and endlessly irritating voice floats up from downstairs.

"Aleksandra? Are you up there?"

With an eye roll, I quickly return the sphere to my nightstand. Two weeks ago, I stopped hiding it altogether. I told Rune and Elijah it was sentimental, something like a toy Sayen and I used to play with while we had been imprisoned under Master Ebenus's rule. The lie was easy to sell.

A shiver skates across my shoulders at the memory of that horrid, power-hungry man. He let admiration turn him into a tyrant. Good riddance.

"Aleksandra, you in here?" The door creaks as it opens. Elijah notices the noise and glances at the hinges. "Oh, right. I said I'd fix that annoying sound," he mutters. Spotting me on the bed, he adds, "I'll grease them later tonight, okay?"

"Yeah, sure. Thanks."

He steps farther into the room, then flashes me that idiotic smile of his. "I wanted to talk to you alone, if that's okay."

I kick off my boots, clumps of dirt dropping onto the hardwood. Then I lean back against the headboard and swing my legs up onto the bed.

"It's been a long day," I say, stretching slightly. "I thought I'd rest before meeting Cameron and Jordana at the—"

"Library," he finishes. "Yeah, they told us."

Us. Of course. He's rarely more than a few feet from Rune. At least their constant proximity makes it easy to track their movements, giving me room to explore.

Besides the crack in the city wall that lets me slip into the forest, I've also found Rune's abandoned childhood home where her mother, once a leader of this city, housed many archives. That includes a hidden bookshelf filled with journals from various Realmwalkers, which will be useful once I'm granted the power needed to rule every realm ever visited by the angels. I also find the abandoned home has been the best place to read Merigoth's journal without any prying eyes wondering what I'm reading. It took a few weeks, but I eventually deciphered enough to know what I'm here for was outside the city walls.

"I wanted to talk to you about sneaking out of Stellara," Elijah says. "It's not safe. You not only put yourself at risk, but Cameron and Jordana too."

"There's no danger out there."

"There is, or supposedly there is… But that's not the point," he replies, shifting his weight from one foot to the other.

"Have you even been outside the city?" I ask.

He shakes his head.

"Then how would you know? The woods are healthy and thriving with wild berries, mushrooms—"

"It's not your call to make," he interrupts. "You, me, and the other humans—we're new to this realm. If Rune hasn't left the city yet, there's probably a reason." His shoulders lower slightly as he perches on the edge of my bed. The mattress dips under his weight. "Look, I get it. The freedom is exciting, and I know you want to explore."

"I do."

He holds up his hands, smiling. "I know—I know. Just… pace yourself. And don't put yourself—or others—in unnecessary danger."

He's in danger if he doesn't get out of my room soon. This place is starting to feel worse than the Human Realm's cages.

Then he grins wider, and I nearly lose it, until he says, "Rune and I think it's time you were given a place of your own."

This unexpected statement has my insides humming with excitement. I mean, I don't think I'll need a place of my own for very long… but still, to have some peace and quiet without Rune or Elijah constantly asking what I'm doing, if I'm okay, or if I'm hungry… It will make it much easier for me to accomplish my goal.

Reeling in my excitement, I play the heartbroken response so he doesn't think I'm too eager to separate myself from them. I blink a few times, clear my throat, and ask with a sad tone, "You want me to leave?"

"Only if you want to," he quickly clarifies. Then, when I don't answer right away, he dips his gaze and finds mine. "You're not as happy as I thought you'd be. What's wrong?"

I don't know why, but I dart my attention to the black stone on the shelf. He doesn't miss it.

"Are you thinking about Sayen? Because I think she would've wanted you to live a happy life."

"Yeah, probably," I say with a sniffle, even though Sayen was more of a pet than a friend. I would've disposed of her months ago if I hadn't discovered the black sphere. The voice on the other side told me to keep her around, and to bring her with me when we finally met. She was to be payment for the power I seek.

Too bad that imbecile Reborn stormed Sayen's home, killed her family, and left her so injured she was no longer of any use to me. It was a small setback. I was pleased to discover that this place is full of naïve people desperate for new friends, and they don't care that I'm a girl with demon horns.

"I'm sure your friend is smiling down from the stars at the new life you've got and the new friends you've made," Elijah says, continuing his efforts to comfort me.

I wish he'd stop and leave me be. Maintaining my ruse, I say, "Cameron and Jordana are nice. Regardless of…" My words trail off as I graze the rough surface of my horn with my fingers.

Elijah gives me a playful jab in the shoulder, like some encouraging father figure he thinks I need or something. He's probably younger than I am, for stars' sake. Responsibility wears on us all. He feels bound to care for the city alongside Rune.

My responsibilities, however, are much grander, and will stretch across every realm once I'm granted the power promised to me.

"Just like Adele, you chose your own path. Demon blood, human blood, or whatever other kind of blood—you make your own choices now."

Damn right I do.

Hearing the name of my so-called sister makes my insides recoil. Adele—the one sibling from our messed-up trio who got the fairy-tale childhood. Bedtime stories. Games. Laughter. She wasn't tied up like livestock, poked and drained of blood. She spent most of her life blissfully unaware that demon blood coursed through her veins.

What infuriates me the most? She wasn't even born with the physical likeness of Merigoth. No horns. No jagged reminders of what she was. I silently snarl.

"I should head to the library," I say, standing from the bed and slipping my boots back on. It's clear the rest I was hoping for isn't going to happen. "Cameron and Jordana are waiting for me, and then we're all going to the doorway to help receive this week's rations from Bricen."

He doesn't move out of my way. Instead, he pulls me in for a hug.

I resist the urge to push him off. To scratch his face. To spit in the gouges. I hate all this community love.

Still, I make a mental note *not* to kill him—not yet. Not until I'm the almighty, powerful queen ruling the realms.

"I'm glad you decided to move to Stellara with us," he says. "You're going to do amazing things here. I just know it."

That's one thing we can agree on.

The things I plan on doing *will* be amazing.

CHAPTER 5
ADELE

The moment I wake, the unusual comfort jolts me fully alert. The room is dim, heavy curtains blocking most of the sunlight, but enough filters through to confirm I'm *not* in my bedchamber at Castle Forge. Panic prickles under my skin. But as it slowly ebbs, I sink deeper into the plush mattress, the soft sheets and thick quilt cocooning me in warmth.

When I roll to my other side, my gaze lands on the second bed across the room. A sliver of morning light slices across Kit's face, resting just below her nose. With no urgent need to get up, I close my eyes again, letting the comfort hold me a little longer.

It doesn't take long for Kit to stir. She yawns and stretches, arms arching over her head.

"You awake?" she asks softly.

"Mm-hmm," I murmur, still groggy. I crack one eye open to see her curled under the quilt, only her face peeking out.

Tightening her makeshift cocoon, Kit pulls the edges of the quilt up over her mouth and mumbles, "Can we bring these beds home with us?"

I chuckle, because honestly, if I could, I would. Tossing back the covers, I swing my legs over the side of the bed. The borrowed nightgown, left out for me last night, slips down to my ankles as I stand. My toes sink into the plush rug beside the bed, a welcome buffer from the cold stone floor.

Despite it being early spring, winter's chill still lingers, especially in the early hours before the sun warms the land. I grab clean clothes from my bag and step behind the privacy partition to change.

From the other side of the room, Kit groans, stretching her arms out from under the quilt. "I could use another hour or two in bed."

Sliding my tunic over my head, I tell her, "If you think these beds are good, wait until you see the spread of food these people feast on."

I emerge from behind the partition, holding my leather vest, just as three sharp knocks sound at the door.

When I open it, a young man in a crisp castle attendant's uniform stands tall, chin slightly raised. "Lord Stolkin requests your company for breakfast in his private dining hall," he announces.

I narrow my eyes. "Do we have a choice in the matter?"

He exhales, clearly annoyed that I've asked. "No. He's expecting you within the half hour." Then, apparently finished with his task, he pivots neatly and walks away.

"Hey!" I call after him.

He pauses and glances over his shoulder.

"Where exactly is this private dining hall?"

His shoulders sag, and even without seeing his face, I can *feel* the eye roll. Slowly, he turns to face me again. "At the bottom of the main stairs, take a right and follow the corridor past the great hall. At the end, you'll see a set of double doors on your right. That's Lord Stolkin's private dining hall. He'll be expecting you to dine with him and his company for breakfast."

Before I can ask *what* company, he spins around and walks away briskly, clearly eager to escape.

I close the door with a muttered curse. "Charming."

Typical Fayatin behavior. It's not just the nobles who act superior, but the common folk tend to, too. They think they're entitled to the best of everything. And if they can't afford it, they'll take it from anyone too weak to fight back.

Ugh. I hate this country. I'd rather be back in Noviska, trudging through knee-deep snow and frozen mud, than deal with another smug, arrogant Fayatin.

Slipping on my leather vest, I tell Kit, "We've been summoned to dine our morning meal with Lord Stolkin and company."

Kit sits up in bed, her nightgown bunched at her waist. "What company?"

I shrug. "No idea." Then after tying the leather laces of my vest, I open the door. "I'll go wake Nathaniel. You get dressed—and make haste. I don't want Lord Stolkin and his guests waiting on us."

She groans, and I shut the door behind me, giving her some privacy.

Two doors down is where Nathaniel sleeps. I knock, but there's no answer. I knock again, louder. Still nothing. A third time, I knock and call out, "Nathaniel! It's me, Adele."

Silence.

A flicker of unease sparks low in my chest. My thoughts immediately jumped to the worst—that he's been taken to use as leverage to get to me. My gloved hand curls around the iron ring of his door, and I twist it gently. The latch clicks, and the door creaks open.

I step inside.

The tension in my shoulders eases when I hear his heavy breathing, deep and easy. He lies shirtless on his back, the quilt twisted just below his waist. Despite the morning chill, the sunlight streaming through the window warms his pale skin, casting a soft glow across his chest. His muscles have benefited from his work at the smithy.

Still, something sharp lingers in my mind. I don't like how quickly my mind assumed violence. To vengeance. The darkness stirs with disappointment, hungry for a threat that isn't there.

I approach his bedside. "Nathaniel," I say, nudging his shoulder.

He swats my hand away without opening his eyes, then rolls onto his side, facing me. The defined lines of his muscles catch my eye, and something entirely different stirs inside me, and it has nothing to do with danger.

"Nathaniel," I snap, louder now.

He groans, shielding his face from the sun. "Adele?" His voice is rough, thick with sleep. He licks his lips, wipes the corner of his mouth. "What are you doing in my bedchamber?"

"Waking you. We've been summoned to dine with Lord Stolkin."

He rolls over again, tugging the quilt over himself. "I'll eat later. This bed is too comfortable to leave."

I almost laugh because he's not wrong. These beds are divine. And though we're far from intimate, the idea of sharing a bed with him doesn't rattle me as it used to. Not after the past few weeks.

After Marcellus kidnapped me, things changed, especially with Nathaniel. We've gotten closer. He's seen more of me than I ever intended anyone to. I've told him about my past. About who I used to be. About the girl General Onica tried to mold into a weapon.

And he's never judged me. Always reassures me that anyone in my place would've done the same.

He called *her* the monster. Not me.

And yet… I'm not sure I believe him.

Because part of me wonders if I was made to wound, not heal. Mum brings comfort. Me? I stir the deepest fears, drag trauma to the surface as though it's a gift. My reach doesn't soothe. It's best at inflicting pain and trauma.

Nathaniel abruptly sits up, propped on one elbow. "If they have those sausage links, can you pocket some for me?"

Crossing my arms, I narrow my eyes and smirk. "I will do no such thing. Who stuffs breakfast meats into their pockets?"

He rolls back into bed with a groan, the quilt swallowing him whole. "I would," he mutters.

"They'll stop serving breakfast soon, and who knows when we'll be fed again?" I try one last time, hoping that'll get him moving, but his stillness says otherwise.

"Adele," he grumbles, half turned toward the wall, "I will find food. I'm a grown man."

Something else has changed about Nathaniel these past few weeks. He's grown more comfortable around me. He's no longer nervous about speaking to me. Our early conversations were mostly him fumbling through his words. His intentions regarding me are clear. And since I'm the one still holding back, he's poured his focus into becoming close with those I care about. More of a gentleman's gesture in showing he's a patient man and is willing to win the approval of my friends and family. It didn't take long for Kit, Elijah, Rune, Evander, and Mum to welcome him into our circle. Even Selene, though she hasn't seen our courtship unfold, would no doubt approve of him as a mate.

"Fine." I don't have the time or energy to argue.

Back in Kit's and my room, I find her dressed and staring out the window.

"I've never seen the ocean before," she says quietly.

I join her, gazing out at the endless stretch of deep-blue water. The sun casts long golden streaks across the waves, and off to the left, the docks at Port Helve are already alive with movement with ships coming and going, their crews unloading and loading cargo. High above, white birds soar, their calls far higher-pitched than those of my feathered friends.

It should feel peaceful. Freeing, even. But the weight in my chest won't lift. Not with guests we haven't met who may ask questions I'd like to avoid.

"Come on," I say. "We don't want to keep Lord Stolkin waiting."

Taking a deep breath, Kit nods, her gaze lingering on the horizon. "Or his guests."

CHAPTER 6
ADELE

Dodging busy castle staff setting up the great hall for the event, we finally find the double doors at the end of the corridor. Hopefully, Lord Stolkin's private dining hall lies beyond them.

Two guards flank the entrance, stiff against the stone wall. They wear midnight-blue coats marked with the white *F* of Castle Helve, encircled by stars. All six Fayatin regions have their own color schemes, but the insignia stays the same.

As we approach, I slow, narrowing my eyes. The guards are identical. Brothers, maybe. Same light brown hair, same stubbled jaws. I squint, trying to catch what sets them apart.

Kit leans in and murmurs, "The one on the right's missing his pointer finger."

My gaze dips. Sure enough. The stub's been healed, but that kind of mark usually carries a meaning—thief.

The guard with all his fingers lifts a hand. "This is a private hall. Not for commoners."

I bite down on the instinct to bristle, clenching my gloved fists instead. "We were invited. By Lord Stolkin."

The guards exchange a knowing glance, silently agreeing not to argue. Instead, each guard reaches for the closest iron ring of the double doors, twists, and pulls them open.

We step into a warm room with a long table stretching the length of the space, flanked by eight high-backed chairs. Though there are no windows, the room is brightly lit, creating a secluded and intimate atmosphere. A lively fire crackles in the hearth, complemented by a large wood-and-iron chandelier and numerous iron wall sconces that illuminate the room in a warm golden glow.

At the head of the table sits Lord Stolkin, his chair built in the same style as the others but with a higher back and ornate carvings curling across the mahogany. He stops mid-conversation the moment he sees us. He raises his hand, and the man at his left—Selene's uncle, Lord Caldridge—falls silent.

Across from Caldridge sit Victor Stolkin and Commander Leon Pavik. All four men turn their attention to us, eyes sharp and assessing.

Lord Caldridge shifts in his seat and offers a genuine smile, though a subtle concern lingers in his expression. He was always kind to me during my time at Castle Forge. Though, back then, I was just an orphan girl under the care of a cruel woman. An unfortunate situation. But now, he likely knows the truth. And that truth has probably changed his opinion of me—not as a victim, but as a pawn. Worse still, that the Interrogator has been close to his niece all these years.

Clearing his throat to break the awkward silence between us, he gestures toward the empty chair. "Adele. You've arrived just in time to settle a dispute Lord Stolkin and I were having."

I take long strides, aiming to project maturity and confidence, not just the persona of the Interrogator. General Onica used to warn me that timidity invites predators, especially power-hungry men eager to assert dominance. My slender frame and feminine features already paint me as weak and small, but even in a room like this, with so much authority gathered at one table, they know better than to underestimate me.

I sit beside Lord Caldridge, shoulders straight, chin high. Kit slides into the seat on my other side, quiet but present, her posture just as purposeful.

I keep my eyes on Caldridge, the man who arranged this union for Selene. At the edge of my vision, across the table, Victor Stolkin is watching me. He's pretending not to hear Leon Pavik murmuring beside him. Victor's gaze isn't polite. It lingers with a calculated intensity, and I can't tell if he's a man too used to getting what he wants… or if he sees me as something to acquire.

Caldridge picks up his goblet, then after taking a sip, he sets it down and asks, "Tell me, Adele. In your time at Castle Forge, did General Onica ever speak of uniting the regions under one rule?" His snowy curls peek out from beneath his maroon velvet beret, a white feather tucked neatly into the band.

His question catches me off guard, and my stomach tenses. Silently, I remind myself conversations like this were going to be inevitable. Even though I'd rather not talk about my days at Castle Forge, I knew someone would be curious.

Lord Caldridge was present at many of General Onica's council meetings, and he knows exactly her opinion on uniting the regions of Fayatin. Except, if he's asking me this now, then perhaps he didn't know General Onica as well as I thought. The irony amuses me, and I quickly hide my laughter, picking up the tongs to serve myself some ham. "You're not being serious, right?"

Caldridge turns smugly to Stolkin. "I told you. Onica had no interest in uniting the regions. You wouldn't believe me."

Lord Stolkin studies me as I quietly add cheese and fruit to my plate. Kit mimics Lord Stolkin's overflowing dish— ham, bacon, biscuits, cheeses, fruit, poached eggs. I can almost feel her excitement beside me as she savors the rare indulgence of a noble feast. Nathaniel's missing out on a delicious spread of food.

Eventually, Lord Stolkin gestures toward me with his fork. "And why not? Uniting the regions would bring Fayatin under one rule. That's strength. That's legacy."

I take a bite of cheese. It dissolves quickly, feeling rich and smooth in my mouth, yet the taste turns my stomach. The luxury feels wrong. Too much like Castle Forge. Too much like *then*. I reach across the table, grab a biscuit, and begin picking it apart. Bread is regarded as a common food, and its simplicity helps settle the memories trying to surface.

The lord of the castle continues. "Because one ruler means everyone else must kneel. And General Onica feared that ruler wouldn't be her."

He's not wrong. The general was often paranoid about the regional lords rebelling against her. That's where I came in. They all knew she had the Interrogator in her pocket.

I glance at him, my voice level. "She used to say 'You can force a man to bow, but that doesn't make him loyal.'"

Lord Stolkin's grin creeps up one side of his face before he releases a loud, booming laugh. His shoulders shake with the force of it, sending biscuit crumbs tumbling from his beard onto his stretched doublet. The seams strain around his belly, tugging the gold buttons taut.

"That woman feared nothing—or so we thought!" he says, turning toward Victor. His son's intense gaze hasn't let up from staring at me.

With a collected tone, Victor leans back into his chair and asks me, "What's your opinion on the matter?" The young lord's already showing signs of a well-fed man. Give it a few more years, and he may be bursting from his doublet like his father.

"I have no say in the politics of Fayatin." The dry biscuit takes more effort to swallow than it should, its bland taste and dry texture is a poor substitute for the savory and fluffy biscuits Aunt Lauren used to make. The thought stirs a pang of grief, but I quickly push it aside, needing to stay focused on the conversation.

The young lord isn't satisfied with my answer. After exhaling a deep breath, he says, "Oh, but your insight would be greatly appreciated. You were privy to many of the country's decisions while sitting in on General Onica's meetings and," his next words come slow and deliberate, "being the once-feared Interrogator."

Once feared, I say to myself. *Huh. I don't know whether that's a good or bad thing.*

"Fine." I set my fork on my plate and share my thoughts on the matter. "Uniting the regions would be a step in the right direction, that's for sure. But it's not going to happen. General Onica made sure of that. She manipulated the lords, feeding them lies to keep them complacent and bound to her will—even if it meant deceiving them at every turn."

The dining hall's heavy doors creak open again, iron hinges groaning in protest as the twin brothers step inside and take their posts. A third guard rushes in behind them, urgency written all over him. This time, I catch the twins eyeing the mounds of food laid out across the table. Their mouths part slightly in awe. Judging by their expressions, they either haven't eaten in some time or are unaccustomed to such luxury—likely both.

A sharp kick under the table jolts me back. Kit's foot connects with my leg, snapping my attention from the guards to Victor. One of the soldiers leans in, whispering something in his ear. Lord Stolkin, unfazed by the interruption, continues devouring his plate as if nothing has changed.

Victor tosses his napkin onto his plate and shoves back his chair with a scrape against stone. Leon Pavik is at his side in an instant. Victor gives me a small, unreadable smile. "Thank you for coming all this way to witness the ceremony between Selene and me. I hope we have time to speak more after the festivities and before you return to Harvesgrove. I have something of importance to discuss with you."

I tilt my head, about to ask what it's regarding, but he cuts the moment short with a curt nod and follows the guard out. Commander Pavik trails behind him. The twins, still eyeing the feast, hesitate before finally closing the doors.

"You've given me much to think about, girl," Lord Stolkin says mid-chew.

Lord Caldridge leans over the arm of his chair and beckons me closer. "Have you seen my niece yet?"

I shake my head. "I figured I'd see her later, after the festivities."

"Ah, yes." He straightens, then adds, "You should go now. I imagine her nerves are bouncing about. Seeing you again might help her settle."

"I can do that."

He places a hand on the table near my plate instead of reaching across to touch me. He knows me well enough not to try, but I assume out of habit because touching me was prohibited by the general during my time at Castle Forge. Old habits combined with new realizations. *Smart old man.*

The two lords resume their conversation, no longer interested in us. I wait as Kit picks through the mountain of food she's claimed, tasting bits of everything. Meanwhile, I pile a few biscuits and slices of ham onto a napkin, hoping the two old men don't notice.

Once Kit is satisfied, we rise to leave.

As if waiting for that very cue, the twins open the double doors the moment our chairs slide back from the table.

"Thank you for the lovely meal," I say to Lord Stolkin. "Though I don't plan to return to Fayatin again, it was nice to have met you, sir."

Playing the pleasantries hand might be the only safeguard I have against his authority, both here and maybe one day in Harvesgrove.

"Yes, yes. You are more than welcome to return to Castle Helve anytime. You and your friend," he adds, pointing his fork toward Kit.

We both bow and exit the dining hall.

The door shuts behind us. While Kit heads down the corridor, I hand one of the twins the napkin full of food. "It's not much, and you deserve more. You, the guards, and the rest of Fayatin."

They exchange glances before one quickly snatches the napkin. Both guards return to their posts, alert and attentive, one concealing the food behind his back.

I catch up to Kit, who's been watching the exchange. Together, we head toward the great hall, where servants bustle about. A quick glance over my shoulder shows the twins devouring the food as fast as they can before anyone notices. One of them looks up and gives me a small, grateful nod.

Kit groans, pressing a hand to her stomach. "I'm so full, I don't think I'll be able to eat for days." A loud hiccup follows, and she covers her mouth to muffle the burp that escapes.

"You should go and rest before the ceremony. I'm going to find Selene."

At the end of the corridor, the noise and bustle grow louder. Out in the great hall, the castle attendants are still setting up for the post-ceremony celebration. Weaving through the constant traffic of servants and decorators proves harder than expected.

Somehow, we get separated. Kit calls out, "I'm going for a walk, to check out the castle grounds."

I nod, understanding. Kit is a creature of habit, and her perimeter walks have always grounded her.

She heads toward the kitchen corridor just as I slam into someone behind me. "Oh, sorry." Being touched always sets me on edge, but I manage to remain outwardly calm.

The castle worker scowls, readjusts his grip on the vase full of cascading flowers, and hurries on his way. The press of so many bodies in close quarters is beginning to fray my nerves. I pivot, spot the staircase across the room, and hurry to escape the great hall.

Now, it's time to find Selene.

CHAPTER 7
ADELE

Avoiding eye contact with those meandering about the castle, I hug the stone walls as I navigate the second floor. Whenever a guard passes by, I drift toward the nearest window, pretending to be captivated by the ocean view. The guards at Castle Forge were always on high alert whenever outsiders visited. At Castle Helve, however, their demeanor is reserved rather than aggressive, exhibiting a more refined composure. Nevertheless, to avoid unwanted attention, I avoid eye contact, despite the difference in how the guards act.

The cozy atmosphere of Castle Helve is shaped not just by its disciplined guards and attentive staff, but also by the stark contrast to General Onica's cold, unyielding stronghold. Here, Lord Stolkin's welcoming decor is impossible to miss. Artistic tapestries drape the walls, their rich colors matched by plush rugs softening the hard stone floors. Mirrors, positioned with deliberate precision, reflect beams of sunlight that chase away the usual gloom that plagues most castles.

Everything on the surface appears well and pleasing. From the decor to the mannerisms of the staff. Yet, beneath it all, I can't help but wonder: does this warmth truly reflect Lord Stolkin's character… or mask something deeper? Is his desire to unite the regions truly for the good of the country, or is there an ulterior motive?

I'm about to turn a corner when a hushed conversation catches my attention. Staying close and out of sight, I pause to listen.

"It's unnatural—having that *thing* here inside the castle," a man says, his voice a throaty croak.

"You're not wrong. Yet there's nothing we can do about it. Young Lord Stolkin wants it to remain," the second man replies, his voice deeper, slower with a lazy drawl.

"I've got a bad feeling about this," the first man mutters. "What if it brings a curse?"

"A curse? You think?"

Before I can hear more, the heavy *thud* of boots startles me. A guard appears so suddenly behind me that my hand instinctively flies to the hilt of my dagger. I was too focused on the voices to notice his approach.

"You two. Report to the stables and assist with the incoming carriages. The regional lords are arriving," the guard barks.

Two men in uniforms step into view and hurry down the hall. One glances my way but says nothing. I stay put and watch them disappear around the corner, frustrated I didn't hear more about this *unnatural thing*. Were they talking about me—the infamous Interrogator of Fayatin, returned with her cursed ability to trap minds?

"You there."

The guard who gave the orders steps fully into the hallway, his stern gaze pinning me in place.

"Are you lost? Commoners don't belong inside the castle."

Ah. Finally, a guard who would've made the general proud. Still, it's vexing how often people assume I'm a commoner. Why? Because I'm a young woman and not parading around in lace and jewelry? I *like* my look. It's practical.

"I'm a guest attending the ceremony."

He narrows his eyes, the midnight blue of his coat marked by Castle Helve's insignia, his expression drawn in scrutiny. He's not convinced.

Before he can speak again, I cut him off. "I'm a friend of Selene's." That gives him pause. He's taking in my appearance again, but this time with more judgment. As if he's heard the rumors that Selene's friend is also the Interrogator.

The darkness within me stirs, eager to rise and remind this man who I really am. I close my eyes, drawing in a steady breath. And another. Then I force the darkness back into the deep crevices of my mind, where it belongs.

He straightens his shoulders, one hand tightening around the hilt of his sword. "The Interro—"

"I'm not that person anymore," I cut in, sharper than intended. "It's just Adele now."

But even as I say it, my reach surges against the barriers I've built in my mind. Denying its existence only seems to provoke it further. A sudden, stabbing pain explodes behind my eyes. I flinch, pressing the heels of my palms against my temples as I ride out the wave.

"Are you ill?" the guard asks, his gaze dipping to meet mine.

The pain fades as quickly as it came. I straighten. "I'm fine. Just a slight headache."

That was new, and unsettling. The darkness has never lashed out like that before, not physically. It's growing stronger by the day, hungering for release. I'd hoped compelling the captain last night to investigate the road for ambushes would've satisfied it. Apparently, it wasn't enough.

"Right." He hesitates, eyes narrowing once more before he turns and walks down a narrow corridor off the main hallway. I step closer, hugging the wall as I peer around the corner, watching. Two doors down, he knocks three times, standing rigid with one arm folded behind his back. When the door opens, he speaks briefly to the woman inside. She glances in my direction, then nods and closes the door.

The guard returns to me, his face unreadable.

"Follow me."

When the door opens again, the woman inside gestures for me to enter.

"Thank you for helping me find my friend," I say, offering a kind smile, trying to soften his perception of me. If the castle staff are already whispering about some *unnatural presence*, which I can only assume is me, then I'll do what I can to show them I'm no longer the person they fear.

"Leave us!" Selene commands, sounding more like a noblewoman than the girl who used to run from her tutors and court responsibilities. The roomful of maidens quickly set down whatever they're holding and scatter from the bedchamber, leaving me and my friend alone.

This room is a step up from what she had at Castle Forge. From corner to corner, floor to ceiling, everything is swathed in luxury—ornate mahogany furniture, fine linens draped across an oversized canopy bed, oil paintings, and gold-framed mirrors reflecting soft candlelight.

Seeing her in her beautiful white dress, standing so proudly and joyfully in the center of the room, I decide against teasing her about the lavish display. It is her wedding day, after all.

She wiggles her fingers and holds out her arms, wordlessly inviting me in. I oblige, letting her embrace me, something I wouldn't have ever done a year ago. I'm proud of my progress, how my circle of trusted people has slowly grown. My thoughts briefly drift to Nathaniel.

After releasing me, she gathers the layers of satin and lace in her skirt and lifts the hem so she doesn't trip as she crosses to the bench before her dressing table. It's ironic, how the grace and poise she once wanted to shed are now defining characteristics. Even before she speaks, I can tell something within her has changed. I only hope it's a change she chose.

"What has your tongue?" Her mouth curves into a smile. "Do you not approve of Castle Helve? I find it much more pleasing than that stark, cold dungeon of a castle we used to live in." Her fingers find a loose thread in the lace of her dress, fiddling with it, trying to tuck it back in.

I kneel before her, forcing her to meet my eyes. Her dark gaze lifts to mine, but even then, I can't tell if she's truly happy.

"Please tell me this"—I swing an arm wide, gesturing to the lavish room—"is what you really want. You've never wanted this life. So why now?"

Her gaze goes distant, and for a moment I think she'll finally let the mask slip. But she doesn't. She places a hand on my cheek, and I tense. The heat from her palm spreads through me, and my fear of hurting her recoils inward. Only my hands serve as an outlet for the darkness.

She smiles gently. "My time in Bricen made me realize I belong here, with these people and in this life." Her hand falls away as she exhales. "I felt like a burden in Bricen, to you and everyone else. But here… here, I'm not a burden. I'm a future queen. People are honored to serve me."

I can barely believe the words coming out of her mouth. My awe shifts swiftly into suspicion, focusing on one word in particular.

"What do you mean, *queen*?"

Her smile curves, slow and teasing.

"Selene," I say, standing. "Is Lord Stolkin in talks with the other lords to unite Fayatin?"

"Not exactly." That coy smile says she's hiding something. She shifts on the bench, turning from me to face the mirror, picking up a silver-plated brush. Her eyes meet mine in the reflection.

"It's not the Lord Stolkin you're thinking of who's uniting the country."

She means her betrothed.

"Victor? But he's not even the lord of Castle Helve—*not yet*, anyway."

"Formally, no." She brushes her hair, looking far too pleased.

"You're okay with all of this?" It's a ridiculous question. She's clearly basking in the attention and pampering, but I still have to ask. "And you feel safe here?"

Her hand pauses mid-stroke down her long hair. "Of course I'm happy." Her smile flattens, and her gaze sharpens. "If I weren't, then I would leave."

Crossing my arms, I scoff. "Oh, so if you decide you don't want to marry Victor, then you're free to go?"

A long silence follows as Selene looks away and resumes brushing her hair.

I clear my throat. "Well?"

"It wouldn't be that easy."

"So, no. You don't have any say in the matter. Victor needs a queen, and you're it."

Abruptly twisting in her seat, not caring how her gown bunches beneath her, she waves the silver brush at me. "We're trying to do something good for this star-forsaken country. There are people barely surviving in the villages and townships. General Onica encouraged the regional lords to be vigilant. *Don't give them too much because they'll just want more.* I know this because my uncle is one of those lords! He's the only one who ever went against that monster's orders and showed compassion to his constituents."

"Selene, you don't need to tell me. I was here, remember?"

"Then why are you questioning what we're trying to do? You, of all people, should be praising Victor, Lord Stolkin, my uncle, and me for what we've planned for Fayatin."

My rebuttal sits on my tongue, but I swallow it. If her vision truly brings hope, who am I to stand in the way? The people of this country deserve better. My doubts have nothing to do with Selene. They're rooted in Victor's and his father's intentions once they gain the power that comes with uniting the regions.

I relax my arms and lean against the canopy bedpost. "You know all I care about is your safety. I wouldn't be a good friend if I didn't ask questions about the company you now keep and something as monumental as you becoming Fayatin's first queen."

Slowly, her icy expression softens. The warm glow highlighting her cheeks returns. "You're my closest and dearest friend. You always will be." She stands, sets her brush on the dressing table, and approaches me. "There is nowhere safer than here, in this castle, under the protection of my betrothed." She reaches out and takes my gloved hands in hers, and I don't resist. "He has plans for this country, and he cannot accomplish his goals without me. I'm tasked with growing our family, the first generation of royal blood of Fayatin, while Victor starts to rebuild the country."

My brows pinch as I process the weight of her words. She's to *grow* his family. Not dwelling on what that entails, I ask her, "And when exactly is this coronation happening?"

Gently patting my hand, she answers, "Today! Our union not only binds us in marriage, but is a coronation, crowning us as King and Queen of Fayatin." Her hands drop from mine, and she spins in place, giddy with excitement. When she faces me again, her hands are clasped to her chest. "The regional lords have already pledged their allegiances and signed the decree uniting the country."

I push off the bedpost, scratching the nape of my neck. "Well, then. It sounds like you all have everything planned out. I guess I'm happy for you. And you're right about how this country deserves better."

Selene nods. "It does. Victor and I are to set sail in a fortnight to the Kingdom of Verglas to formally introduce ourselves to the King and Queen of Noviska."

Caw, caw!

The familiar call catches my attention, and I spot Barclay nestled in a makeshift nest beneath the window. I cross the room and crouch beside him. "Hey, there you are. Believe it or not, you little troublemaker, I've missed you." I brush my gloved fingers across his feathered head. He responds with a string of low chirps, nudging the top of his head into my palm.

"He's been wonderful company," Selene says as she comes over and unlatches the iron clasp to the window above and pushes open each of the slender window panels. A cool gust of fresh air sweeps inside. My feathered friend hops onto my forearm. His talons curl over the white linen of my sleeve, poking into my skin. Standing next to the open window, I hold him up to eye level.

"Your siblings are somewhere in the forest along the edge of the castle," I whisper. "Go and find them—and stay together." Barclay gives me one last *caw* before leaping off my arm and flying out into the open sky, then disappearing beyond the battlements.

Selene reaches out and pulls in the two panels of the window, then turns to face me. "Do I have your blessing now?"

"Do you need my blessing?"

With a slow shake of her head, she replies, "No. But I'd like to know that I have it. That my dear friend is happy for me and approves of our plans to do better for Fayatin."

I stare into her glossy eyes. "If you're happy, then I'm happy. I trust you. And you know I'll always come whenever you need me."

Her smile returns, warm and radiant. "Promise."

I take her hands in mine and give them a gentle squeeze. "I promise."

CHAPTER 8

ALEKSANDRA

Lying on my bed, I silently enunciate each word from Merigoth's journal. One phrase continues to elude me: *Orie-nima Halvyn*. It's scrawled on nearly every page, a haunting refrain. It has to be connected to those Bocnite-demon creatures that infected her. Why else would she keep mentioning it?

Frustrated, I slam the journal shut, the soft leather cover bending at the corners. I've come so far. It's maddening to know that somewhere out there, all that power is just waiting for me to claim it.

I get up from the bed and return the journal to its hiding spot behind the canvas painting above my dresser. The oil painting was a gift from one of the angels. I can't remember her name, only that she thought I'd appreciate the forest scene—warm sunbeams breaking through treetops, melting the snow below. She claimed the snow represented my past, and the sunlight symbolized the future. The trees, she said, stood for the people who cared about me, offering shelter and a sense of community.

That fool couldn't have been more wrong. All I saw was a clever place to hide the journal.

After slipping on my canvas shoes, I head outside. The overcast sky is growing darker, heavy with the promise of rain. A welcome relief for the gardens. Most of the community has retreated indoors, keeping busy, waiting to see if the storm hits.

I spot Cameron and Jordana talking with a few older women and a man by the edge of the garden area. Taking my time, I cross the courtyard toward them. Cameron spots me first, and they all turn to smile at me.

Their smiles make my stomach turn, but I keep that feeling buried.

"Good day, everyone," I say, forcing a cheerful tone. "Do you need me to set out the water barrels? Looks like the rain may come sooner than expected."

"Already done!" Jordana replies brightly. "Elijah came by earlier and asked us to add two or three more barrels, just in case."

I keep my grin in place and choke down the urge to spit. "He's so smart. We're lucky to have him."

"Oh, that we are," Cameron says, looping her arm through mine and tugging me closer. She does the same to Jordana with her other arm. "And I wouldn't want to be without you two either!"

"Well, we'll leave you to it," says one of the older angels, gray feathers mixing in with her brown ones. She ushers the group away from the gardens. "See you three for supper later."

"Thanks again for the exciting news!" Jordana exclaims, leaning away from Cameron's linked arm hold.

But Cameron clings tighter, pulling her even closer, almost knocking us over into a nearby bush. Once we regain our footing, I have to stop myself—*twice*—from shoving them both away. Every brush of Cameron's body against mine feels like claws raking across my skin.

Untangling myself from her grip, I say, "I want to check on the sprouts." I grab the garden journal from inside the cupboard under the gardening table and make my way to our newest crop beds.

They seem to be doing well, and I inspect each row with quiet pride.

Jordana moves to the table and begins filling small pots with fresh forest soil while Cameron kneels beside me. Her wings are tightly tucked against her back. Trowel in hand, she digs a narrow trench straight down the center of the long, raised bed for the new watering hose we're installing today.

Using a charcoal stick, I record the progress of the plants and vegetation. I don't even realize I've been mumbling that insufferable phrase from Merigoth's journal—*Orie-nima Halvyn*—until Cameron asks, "Why do you keep repeating the word 'Shadowlands' under your breath?"

Sitting up straight, I slowly turn to the young angel, eyes wide. "Is that what 'Orie-nima Halvyn' means? 'Shadowlands'?"

She nods, then shrugs. "I believe so. I'm a little rusty when it comes to the primitive language of the ancient ones, but yeah… I'm pretty sure that's what it means."

I scoot closer. "What are the Shadowlands?" I press.

Cameron stops digging and rests the small shovel in her lap, puzzlement in her gaze. "I guess no one's told you about it, huh?"

I shake my head, fully focused on whatever she's about to reveal.

"The Shadowlands are a dark place in the Starlight Realm—far from the city, so don't worry. We're not allowed to go there. It's dangerous, and it's the only part of the realm that sunlight doesn't reach."

"What's out there?" I ask, my curiosity ravenous.

She shrugs again and resumes digging. "It's not the kind of place anyone *wants* to visit. From what I remember, no one who went out there ever came back."

How exciting. That's exactly where I need to go. The demons who infected Merigoth must be hiding there.

I reach over and wrap my fingers around Cameron's wrist, pressing into her skin. Using the darkness within, I compel her mind to obey. "Come with me. Don't say a word to anyone."

The trowel slips from her hand, and she rises without question.

As we head out of the garden area and into the courtyard, Jordana calls after us, "Where are you two going? We've only just started our shift."

"Be right back," I shout over my shoulder, not slowing down, Cameron right behind me.

Once we're in my bedroom, I slam the door closed and lock it with the imbued necklace. Cameron stands there like a statue, awaiting my next command.

A light sprinkle of rain started moments after we left Jordana in the gardens. Before showing her the journal, I quickly strip off the wet sweater I'm wearing and toss it across the room. Then, after grabbing a dry sweater, I pull it over my head, stretching the neckline as I guide one horn through, then the other.

Cameron still stands where I left her, hazy eyes staring straight ahead. Water drips from her fingers and feathers, pooling at her feet. I toss her a used towel and say, "Dry off. I can't have you ruining the journal with wet hands."

While I retrieve the journal from behind the canvas painting, Cameron obeys, patting her arms and body, then running the towel gently over her wings and through her hair. When she's done, she stands at attention again, damp towel clutched loosely in one hand.

I take the towel from her and add it to the pile of wet clothes. "Sit," I instruct, pointing to my bed.

She crosses the room and sits at the edge of the mattress.

I hand her the journal. "You will tell no one about this. Understand?"

She nods and takes the journal, but her eyes remain unfocused, staring straight ahead.

"Look through it and tell me if you can read it."

Slowly, Cameron's gaze drops to her lap. She flips through the pages, her eyes scanning the foreign script. In a flat voice, she says, "I can read some of it." She turns a few more pages. "It appears every entry is written in the primitive language of the ancient ones."

"And you *can* read it, right?"

"Yes. My linguistic ability translates the words in my mind." She closes the journal and hands it back to me.

I take it, then clasp my fingers over her hand, sending a sliver of darkness into her skin—along with new instructions.

"I want you to go home and pack an overnight bag. Tell your family you're staying here with me. Say nothing about the journal or the language inside. Bring something to keep your clothes dry—we'll be out in the rain."

When I draw my hand away, I sever the darkness. After removing the necklace from the door, I open it and say, "Go, and meet me by the gap in the wall, the one we use to get out of the city."

Cameron stands and leaves the room.

When I hear the front door close, I get to work packing my own bag.

Cameron and I are going on a little midnight hike.

CHAPTER 9
ADELE

Although the ceremony is beautiful and full of spectacle, the proceedings drag on far longer than expected. The minister's voice is so low, barely coherent, from our seats at the back of the hall. I'm not the only one struggling to stay focused. The man in front of me stretches his shoulders, cracking the stiff silence, while a woman across the aisle rolls her neck with a faint groan. Sitting on these wooden benches for over an hour is terribly uncomfortable. Even Nathaniel, usually steady as stone, is drooping beside me, his head bobbing toward my shoulder more than once.

The ceremony takes place in Castle Helve's second hall, which is smaller than the great hall we walked through this morning on our way to breakfast, but no less impressive. My gaze trails up the navy velvet curtains draped behind the dais, their folds catching the faint sunlight streaming through narrow eastern windows. White and blue flowers, arranged in huge stone vases along the dais, fill the hall with a soft, sweet scent.

I tug at one of the long sleeves on the dress Selene gifted me for the event. The deep green color suits my taste and reminds me of the forest treetops of Harvesgrove. But I'm not enjoying the snug fit of the bodice and sleeves—or the fact that I'm not wearing pants. Just a simple undergarment that wears like pants but is half the size and made of fabric that breathes like my white tunic. It's all strange to me.

Kit, on the other hand, mentioned how she missed wearing dresses and was thrilled to dress up for the event. Her gown, a vibrant blue, matches mine in its fitted style from the waist up, then flows into a skirt that covers her feet. She tied most of her short curls into a bun, leaving a few loose to frame her face. I braided my own hair, politely turning down the maidens Selene sent to help.

And here we are, an hour later, sitting in our dresses while listening to the minister drawl on about how lucky Fayatin is and the stars' blessing on the happy couple. One. Long. Hour to say all of that. I shift on the hard bench, wishing the ceremony would end before the sun warms the hall into a stifling oven.

The choice to hold the ceremony here instead of at Port Helve's chapel puzzles me at first. But the pieces fall into place as a boy in a white robe steps onto the platform, carrying a red pillow with a golden crown resting elegantly atop it. I forgot this isn't just a wedding—it's a declaration of power. A coronation meant to mark Victor Stolkin as more than just the new lord of Castle Helve, but as Fayatin's first royal king. Whether this will be Fayatin's salvation or its downfall is still unclear.

When Nathaniel's breathing grows heavier, I elbow him in the side. Not too hard, but enough to startle him awake. He clears his throat and wipes the side of his mouth, blinking as he straightens.

"What'd I miss?"

"Like the entire ceremony," I whisper, then add with a teasing edge, "How are you tired? You said the bed was the most comfortable you've ever slept in."

He leans in a little, voice low. "I'm not tired. I'm bored out of my skull. The man's voice could put a dragon to sleep."

I press my lips together, fighting a smile. "Well, try not to snore next time."

"Can't make any promises if this drags on much longer."

He offers a small, tired smile before yawning and shifting his focus back to the ceremony. I try to do the same, but my gaze drifts over the crowd. None of these nobles and lords would survive a day without their servants or the comfort of their fortified castles.

Selene's time in Bricen was a welcome change, a life far from the trappings of nobility. But even though she embraced it, she ultimately missed the noble life. Now, she's stepping into it completely—with a crown, no less. Everything will be handed to her tenfold.

Everyone's watching the ceremony. I glance across the crowd, my gaze catching on a man three rows up. His eyes sweep the attendees, but when they land on me, they don't move. My stomach tightens. A second later, he turns away, but the unease lingers, growing sharper when I catch another man across the hall, staring.

I turn to Kit on my left, about to ask her a question when I spot another guard, this one standing in line with the others against the hall wall, staring in our direction. He momentarily falters in his duty of holding up the large flag bearing the Castle Helve insignia. When our eyes meet, he stares at me for three long breaths before he finally averts his gaze.

"I feel like we're being watched," I whisper to Kit.

She doesn't look concerned, but her gaze sharpens as she leans closer, scanning the crowd without moving her head. "No one's going to attack us right now," she says, her tone deliberate. "But we need to talk about what I saw outside—beyond the castle grounds."

A woman clears her throat behind us, followed by a sharp *shhh*. My nerves jump, and I glance over my shoulder, scowling at the old noblewoman. Kit might be right about us being safe for now, but there's always the chance someone will figure out who I am and try for my life. Or worse, Kit's or Nathaniel's.

Up on the dais, the minister finishes crowning Fayatin's new king, and then proceeds to announce the new queen. "By the will of Fayatin's people and its stars, I present Queen Selene."

My friend stands so poised, I almost think someone stuck a wooden board under her dress to keep her back straight and stiff. She lowers gracefully without bending, and the minister gently places the gold crown upon her head.

Behind the royal couple, the blue velvet drapes part, revealing a large throne of polished stone. It's beautiful and daunting at the same time. Flanking the king's throne are two smaller stone chairs, like oversized wooden seats turned to stone.

The orchestra begins a robust chord as the minister steps aside, allowing the new royals to take their seats. Victor sits first, followed by Selene. Then the new king nods to someone in the front row. Commander Pavik climbs the dais and claims the second smaller throne.

The minister raises his arms high. "You are now obliged to pay your respects to our new king and queen."

The front rows stand, then file out into the center aisle. One by one, they approach the king and queen, bowing, offering praises, and murmuring their gratitude. When our row's turn comes, I catch a familiar face passing by—Lord Houfston of Castle Nautica. His much younger wife loops her arm through his, oblivious to me. She's too focused on smiling at the crowd, basking in the attention, her over embellished gown nearly swallowing her whole. The neckline plunges lower than every other noblewoman's, a deliberate flaunting of wealth.

I should've expected the squabbling lord of Castle Fishrot to be here. His smirk grows wicked the longer his gaze lingers on me, as though he knows something I don't. This has the darkness within me excited for action. I silently calm the energy, but should the necessity arise, I will allow it to have its way with him.

"Is that what's-his-name? From Gailstein?" Kit whispers.

"Yup," I reply, keeping my voice just as low.

"Do you think he'll try again?" she murmurs, leaning behind me to keep an eye on the heavyset old man as he ushers his wife out of the throne room.

I shrug, unsure. I wouldn't put it past him to try and capture me again, but with a new king on the throne, I doubt he'd risk it, especially without his full Fishrot guard. Still, I can't shake the sight of that wicked grin. He knows something I don't, and that doesn't sit right with me.

When it's our turn to approach King Victor and Queen Selene, Nathaniel and Kit both bow politely before turning away from the dais. I, however, step closer than the others and do something I wouldn't normally dare: I open my arms.

Selene's regal expression falters for just a second before she waves me in for a hug. The stiff fabric of her gown presses against my soft velour dress, and I'm careful not to knock the crown from her head as my cheek brushes hers.

There aren't many I'd allow this close, but Selene's friendship means everything to me. I have to trust she knows what she's doing, and that Victor will protect her in my stead.

"Darling, people are starting to gawk," Victor whispers, a slight edge to his voice.

Selene steps back, her hands dropping to her sides as her composed, queenly demeanor returns. "I appreciate you making the trip to Castle Helve. You are always welcome to stay."

I nod at her kind offer, then step toward Victor. "I trust you'll care for her as if she were your most prized possession."

He tilts his head slightly, meeting my gaze. "I can promise she'll be well cared for. Though, I do still hope we can speak in private sometime after the festivities. There's a proposition I'd like to discuss with you."

I hesitate, the weight of the moment sinking in. "Please don't ask me to revive that old life. I don't—"

"Adele," he cuts in, calm but firm. "I have great respect for you and your abilities. But I would never ask you to be… that person again." He straightens, his smile returning. "We'll talk more later. For now, enjoy the festivities. Drink, eat, and celebrate this glorious inauguration of a new era for Fayatin!"

I take a slow breath, knowing now isn't the time to press him further. With a final nod, I turn and step away from the dais, letting the next patron take their turn. Following Kit and Nathaniel out of the smaller hall, I can't help but wonder—what could the new king of Fayatin need from me?

CHAPTER 10
ALEKSANDRA

I don't bother leaving a note for Rune or Elijah. I'm not their ward. And while I may look close in age to Elijah, he's much younger. More than just power, the demon blood in my veins sustains my youthful appearance. Dear old Father, Master Ebenus, woke me a few years before Mother and Adele ever stirred from their timeless sleep.

"Watch your step! You're no good to me if you twist your ankle and can't walk!" I call ahead, watching Cameron stumble over a tree root. She catches herself on a nearby tree, falling halfway into a small bush, the leaves sprinkling her with raindrops leftover from the recent rainfall. She shakes them off before she continues moving through the forest. Though certain trees have a golden shimmer to their leaves, it's not enough light to see the ground. We use the soft glow of the sunstones I threw into my pack before leaving to light the way.

I released her from my control once we were far enough from the city, but before I did, I placed one of my imbued stones around her neck, preventing her from using her wings or seeing the necklace. I explained to her that if she tried to run, I'd take her will again. And then I added, for good measure, how I'd command her to follow blindly until she was no longer useful, and then leave her out here where no one could find her.

She didn't like the sound of that and agreed to behave.

That was hours ago. Since then, we've barely spoken. Fine by me.

Something skitters across our path, and she shrieks, hopping from foot to foot. "Oh, Aleksandra, please can we go home? We shouldn't be outside the city. Not this late."

"Keep going," I say, jabbing the space between her wings. She shivers and spins to scowl at me.

"I thought we were friends," she says, hurt and angry.

"Well, we're not. Now move."

She hesitates, whimpering as she walks. "Where are we going?"

"You know exactly where we're going," I snap. "And stop whining about the dark. It's exhausting listening to you angels harp on about how dangerous it is outside the walls. First of all, Stellara isn't as fortified as you think. That barrier wall of yours? A single, strategic strike with a battering ram would breach the defenses, thereby exposing your city to the nightmarish creatures you fear."

Cameron slows, pressing a hand to a narrow tree trunk as she glances back at me. "The demons are real, Aleksandra. They're not just myths. The Bocnite are real—and so is their bite."

I adjust the pack on my shoulders and study her. Her face is hidden in shadow, lit only by the soft sunstone glow that touches the curve of her chin.

"You know of the Bocnite?"

She scoffs and turns to face me fully, dead leaves rustling beneath her feet. "Everyone knows. We may not recall every detail, thanks to Merigoth's enchantment, but most of us remember enough to remain within the city limits, especially at night."

She brushes her hair back, tucking it behind an ear. "I remember the stories. All of them. For decades, the angels of this realm fought the Bocnite—beasts that dwell in the deepest caves and tunnels of the earth. The Dark War only ended after Rune's mother sealed them underground, locking them away from the surface."

She pauses, and her voice softens. "It's why Stellara built the wall around the city."

That information could be useful. Feeling a flicker of obligation, I share, "They're the ones who infected Merigoth."

"Is that right?" she asks.

I nod. "It's all in her journal." Then I remember: I compelled her to forget translating it. "Never mind. This way."

I pluck the sunstone from her hand, leaving her in darkness. She scurries after me, boots rustling through the undergrowth, until I stop in a small dirt clearing surrounded by trees.

"We'll make camp here," I say, scanning the space. "Gather firewood. I'll find some stones."

She doesn't argue. Good. She knows running is pointless. I have the sunstone, and without it, she'd be blind in the dark. Staying with me is, apparently, the lesser evil.

When she returns, arms full of kindling, I have her toss it into the shallow pit I've dug. I ring it with stones, and she arranges the sticks. Once she's done, I kneel beside her. A few strikes of flint later, the fire catches.

As flames rise, she inches closer, curling toward the warmth. But her eyes stay fixed on the shadows between the trees. Despite the golden light filtering through the leaves, deep, shadowy crevices remain between the branches, the air growing still and cool, giving our little campsite an ominous surrounding.

"Lay down your blanket and get some rest," I order while unstrapping my own.

She hugs her knees instead, wings draped over her shoulders like a feathered shield. "How can you sleep? We don't even know what lives out here."

I pause, blanket in hand, and gesture toward the extra stones placed around the clearing. "I created a barrier. As long as the stones stay connected by the natural lines of the trees and roots, the magic I infused will keep anything from getting in." I narrow my eyes. "Or out."

She scans the stones again, her posture softening, wings pulling back slightly. "You can do that? Use magic on rocks and stuff?"

Before I can answer, she presses on, voice lighter now, almost hesitant. "I mean, I knew Adele had that whole mind-entering thing, which… I guess isn't so unique, is it?" She peers at me, curious, as if I'm a riddle she's only just begun to solve.

The sound of my dear sister's name sends a surge of rage coursing through me, my ears ringing with it. The darkness within stirs—flaring hot in my mind and prickling just beneath the skin of my fingertips. I grit my teeth and force the words out. "What my sister, brother, and I can do is unique. We were created with the purpose of serving Merigoth as her Shades. But I refuse to be anyone's tool. I plan to uncover the origins of my abilities and become my own master."

I don't mention the rest. That I plan to trade Cameron for more power. That I will rule this realm and every other. For now, it's better to win her empathy than drag her in chains.

She pulls her blanket tighter, the tension easing slightly as the spell settles over her. Her gaze flicks to the horns on my head. "I'm sorry," she says softly. "You must have so many questions about your existence." The firelight dances across her face. "But… isn't there another way to find the truth? I don't think going into the Shadowlands to find the Bocnite is the answer. You're risking both our lives."

"I can handle whatever we face," I say flatly, lifting my gaze to the stars between the branches. "My destiny is tied to the Bocnite. Through them, I'll find what I'm looking for."

She doesn't reply. The fire crackles in the silence between us. After a long moment, I glance over. She's curled on her side, blanket pulled to her chin, her pack tucked beneath her head. Her eyes, half-lidded, catch the firelight like twin sparks.

"Good night, Aleksandra," she murmurs.

I don't respond.

I can't bring myself to offer kindness in return.

She is not my friend.

She is a pawn in this game of power.

I sit and watch the night sky for a long time before reaching into my pack to retrieve the stone sphere. The polished surface is cool in my hands, its weight familiar and oddly comforting. Across the fire, Cameron has rolled onto her other side, facing away from me, her loud snores breaking the otherwise quiet night.

Gazing at the stone, I whisper, "You never mentioned the Dark War or how the Bocnite are dangerous."

The voice within the stone is unpredictable. Sometimes it answers quickly; other times, the silence stretches on and on. Tonight, the reply comes sooner than expected.

"The Bocnite are not to be trusted." The voice pauses before continuing, *"You are close. Keep moving forward. You have your offering, yes?"*

"I do," I say quietly, not wanting Cameron to hear. Then I add, "After hours of walking, we're still in the forest. The angel girl says the Shadowlands aren't far once we're out of the trees."

"Hurry. We are but two of one, and will soon be one of more. You will have your power, and we will have our freedom."

"What does that mean?" I ask, and then stare, waiting but the stone falls silent.

I shake it in frustration, hoping to force the voice to return. Nothing. Only the occasional rustle of a wild animal in the leaves and the flutter of wings above disturb the night.

With a sigh, I tuck the stubborn, silent rock back into my pack and pull out my extra blanket to cushion my head. Stretching out on my back, I stare up at the stars. Their light shimmers between the leaves above, and eventually, I drift off to sleep.

CHAPTER 11
ADELE

A few hours later, my stomach is full and my head swims from too much wine. Kit and Nathaniel are nearby, laughing and deep in conversation, reenacting a story about Elijah tumbling from a high rock as a child. I suspect they've had a bit too much to drink as well.

Throughout the evening, I've caught several people eyeing me, and I can't help but wonder if they're plotting against me, maybe even waiting for me to let my guard down so they can throw a sack over my head, drag me away, and punish me for the lives I've destroyed.

Lively music fills the great hall as guests take to the dance floor in a synchronized, unified performance. Someone bumps into me while I sit at the dinner table, mumbles a brief apology, then staggers off. The noblewomen's extravagant gowns and the lords' perfectly tailored jackets make them seem like an entirely different breed. I miss the simple hues of village life—browns and ivories stained with garden soil, sweat from building homes, and soot from the smithy fires. These people have never gotten their hands dirty, and probably never will. Yet they all stare at me as though I don't belong here.

"Adele, are you feeling all right?" Kit's voice cuts through my thoughts as she plops down in the empty seat beside me. "You're looking a bit paler than usual."

"I'm fine. I just miss Bricen."

"We'll be heading home soon enough," Nathaniel chimes in, coming around to lean against a stone pillar. "I, for one, am looking forward to some normalcy. And the smithy is probably falling apart without me."

"I'm sure Brandulf is managing," Kit says with a low chuckle.

More eyes are on me now, from every corner of the room. Everyone here knows what I did for General Onica, and they blame me for it. They want me to pay for her governing decisions. But I never would've tortured anyone if she hadn't ordered it. They must know this. With more eyes glaring at me, I'm fooling myself to think they'd ever take pity on me. I'm fairly sure they'd celebrate a victory with me rotting away in a holding cell or hanging from the high battlements along the castle walls.

Too many eyes. And it's so hot in here. Scratching at the fitted sleeve of this insufferable dress, I jump to my feet and mutter, "I need some air."

I hurry through the crowd toward the corridor leading to the kitchen and Lord Stolkin's private dining hall. The dress, with its wide skirt, catches underfoot and nearly trips me. I gather the fabric and lift it just enough to move swiftly without catching the hem, then slip into the kitchen. The servants are bustling about, and I sidestep out of the way but inevitably collide with one poor man carrying four bottles of port wine.

"I need air," I rasp, my voice catching with my shallow breathing.

He spins on his toes, one hand still clutching two bottles as he gestures toward a dark hallway in the back corner of the kitchen. I nod in appreciation and weave my way over to the archway into the corridor beyond. Warm torchlight stretches in along the stone floor from the opening at the far end. The double doors to the outside are propped open, letting the cool night air drift into the stuffy kitchen.

The adjoining bailey isn't for stables or training but is more of an enclosed space with animal pens, vegetable and herb gardens, and a small waterwheel for fresh water. There are a few torches lit and staked along the main path of the enclosed space.

I head straight for the long wooden bench affixed to the outside of the goat pen. A few goats gather near a hay pile on the opposite side, while two others sleep beneath a modest shelter. I rest my elbows on my knees, press my heated face into my gloved hands, and focus on breathing.

"Hey, watch out!" Nathaniel shouts as a chicken clucks and flaps its wings, taking a short flight before landing inside the goat pen. "There you are." Approaching, he emerges from the shadows, his features more visible as he comes into the torchlight.

"Where's Kit?" I ask. I sometimes find myself speechless in his presence, a feeling that leaves me uncomfortably exposed and vulnerable.

"Selene waved her over. So, I'm guessing she's off chatting with Fayatin's new queen."

I inhale a deep breath and sit up straight, staring at the night sky. The darkness from the moonless sky comforts me with an unsettling familiarity.

Nathaniel sits beside me on the bench. "Not one for crowds, huh?"

"What's that?" I shift slightly on the narrow wooden plank.

"You rushed out of the great hall like it was on fire or under attack," he says. "And since we're not facing any immediate threats, I'm going to assume it was the crowd."

I say nothing, but my blank stare must be enough to prompt him to keep going.

"I know coming back to this unforgiving country—and facing its people—isn't easy for you. But I think you're overthinking things. No one's out to get you, Adele."

I might've believed him, but it would be naïve to underestimate my value to the lords of Fayatin, especially after seeing Lord Houfston earlier. If any one of them had the opportunity to force my hand into doing their bidding so they could obtain more power, they'd seize it without hesitation. And if they succeeded, it wouldn't just be me they'd control. It would put Selene in danger too, now that she and her new husband are at the top of the power chain.

Wanting to change the subject, I ask, "Why did you leave Fayatin?"

He stretches, clasping his hands behind his head and extending his legs. A few chickens peck at the dirt near his boots, then wander off toward a patch of thick grass by the opposite pen.

"My story's boring," he says. "You don't really want to hear it."

"Nathaniel, I've been trying to get you to tell me your story since I let you into my close-knit circle."

The torchlight softens his features, and a grin tugs at his mouth. His eyes glint as he says, "Oh, so you *let* me into your circle?"

"You know what I mean. I'm not the type to trust people easily."

He drops his arms and leans forward with a smirk. "That's for sure. Took weeks of me chasing you down to get more than a few minutes of your time."

The thought of Nathaniel putting in that much effort to win me over makes my heart pound and my stomach flutter. Yet I cannot find it in myself to let him get close. I fear the darkness within me will harm him, and it's the reason I keep him at arm's length.

"Well, I want to know more about you and why you left."

He shakes his head and murmurs, "You don't want to hear it. I don't want you to think differently of me… once you know the truth."

I open my mouth to argue, but he sighs, already giving in.

"Fine. But you have to promise you won't think any less of me."

"I'm not making that promise," I say, firm. "If you want to be honest, then let me be honest too. Just tell me."

Voices drift from the dark corridor, and two young boys rush out carrying wooden buckets. They run to the waterwheel, fill the buckets quickly, then disappear back inside Castle Helve. The festivities must still be going strong.

I glance at Nathaniel. My nerves have finally settled, and I'm glad to be out here—with him.

Until he says, "I was one of General Onica's guards, posted at the north mine in the Crescent Mountains."

I shoot to my feet. "Wait—what? Have we met before? Back when I… when I lived at Castle Forge? Did you seek me out? Is that why you came to Bricen?"

"Whoa!" He lifts his hands, palms out. "Slow down. Let me explain." One hand gestures to the bench. "Please, Adele. I've been rehearsing this conversation for weeks. Let me tell you everything, then you can decide how you feel."

From everything I've come to know about him, Nathaniel doesn't strike me as someone who wants me dead. And if he ever did… maybe he changed his mind.

Curious, I slowly take my seat, but with some distance between us. "Fine. Talk."

"Brandulf and I were forced into the general's guard about four years ago," he begins. "I was a scrawny fourteen-year-old who could barely lift a broadsword. The guards who came to our village only wanted the strong men. But since our parents died when I was a baby, Brandulf had always looked after me. He refused to leave without me."

He pauses, then in a solemn voice he continues. "For a long time, I resented him for dragging me into the guard. I wasn't ready for that kind of harsh life. But later, after seeing how the villages in Fayatin were falling apart—people dying from starvation and disease—I realized I wouldn't have survived on my own. In a messed-up kind of way, he saved my life. Brandulf has always put me first, even when I don't deserve it."

I can appreciate that brotherly bond. They value family, and that resonates with me. Refocusing on the story, I ask, "They posted you, a child, at the north mine?"

He shrugs. "They were filling numbers, Adele. They don't care who. I'm a body and they needed more guards."

I know exactly *why* the numbers needed replenishing. The north mine wasn't some gentle hollow at the base of the mountain, shielded from the deadly Noviska winds. No, the barracks sat atop the tallest peak. Its conditions were exposed, treacherous, and brutal. But it was valuable to General Onica because it was the largest pocket of untouched iron ore compared to all the other mines throughout the Crescent Mountains. The general didn't care how high the mining entrance was, how dangerous the climb was, or how many would die guarding it. She only cared about the ore within.

"Did you know the miners weren't allowed a second pair of boots when theirs wore through?" His voice is solemn, the memory of his time there weighing on his words.

I shake my head. I know the miners at the primary sites along the base of the mountains were barely given anything, basically what they arrived with. To hear that the general supplied boots and clothes to the north mine in the first place surprises me.

Nathaniel continues his story, and I pay close attention to every word. "Over time, the harsh weather and treacherous conditions wore through many of the boots and garments. The miners took it upon themselves to trade and mend what they could, but often it was the older men who ended up with the worst of the worst. Eventually, I started using my personal leave after shifts to travel down the mountain to a small depot. It was a supply post specifically for the guards—replacement gear, extra food, clothes, boots. I started using my rations to buy whatever I could afford. Then I'd return to the north mine barracks and hide it away until a miner needed a new shirt… or boots… maybe some extra food."

"That's not a reason to be ashamed of your time in Fayatin." I look at him earnestly. "Why would you think your kindness would upset me?"

He scoffs. "I haven't finished my story."

"Oh."

"Brandulf eventually figured out what I was doing and forbade me from going to the depot again. He said if I needed something, he'd get it for me. We shouted at each other half the night. Me trying to explain that we had to help these people, and him trying to convince me that I wasn't helping them, I was dooming us."

Nathaniel stares off toward the distant shadows near the castle wall, voice quieter now. "For weeks after that, my heart cracked every time one of the miners approached me. Begging for help because their boots were worn through. Or because they'd lost their winter cap and their ears were turning black."

"What did you do?" I ask, leaning in. His story reminds me of the old tales Mum used to tell me—grim but hopeful, the kind that made you hold your breath until the very last word.

"One night, I snuck out of the barracks. Brandulf had confiscated my rations, hoping it would deter me from sneaking off."

"But it didn't keep you from going to the depot, did it?"

Nathaniel shakes his head. "Nah. And because I didn't have any way to buy the rations, I resorted to stealing."

"Did you get caught?" The thought of getting caught stealing sends a wave of panic, but then I settle my nerves, telling myself that if he was sent to the Interrogator for his crimes, he wouldn't be sitting here with me right now.

"I did. The guards manning the depot beat me to where it hurt to breathe. They were trying to force a confession out of me, wanting to know who else I was collaborating with in helping the miners. No matter how many times I swore I was working alone, they wouldn't stop kicking and punching." His voice remains steady but raw as he continues, "As my vision blurred and I started slipping into unconsciousness, one of them told me it didn't matter. Said by first light, I'd be taken to Castle Forge… and the Interrogator would rip the truth from my mind."

"Oh, Nathaniel." I cover my mouth. "That's horrible."

"Yeah. So I guess we were bound to meet one way or another."

"What happened next?"

He stands and stretches his arms and then rolls his neck, releasing a few stiff *cracks*. "Brandulf happened. When I didn't return that morning, he guessed where I'd gone. Lucky for me—otherwise, well… who knows what *you* would've done to me."

I answer honestly. "I would've done whatever the general told me to do."

He frowns. "And why was that? You could've taken her out with a simple—"

"There's nothing *simple* about what I can do," I cut in, looking up at him from the bench. "Besides, I had no family and nowhere else to go. Not leaving Castle Forge earlier than I did was about self-preservation." The many faces I'd seen in that windowless room surface in my mind. A room known throughout Fayatin, and possibly all three countries. Those who go in, don't ever come out the same. I pray to the stars that he fully understands my next words. "I hated every minute of every interrogation, but I also didn't want to be out there—homeless and starving. And even more so, after befriending Selene, I couldn't leave her at Castle Forge. Not with General Onica prowling the castle, ready to take her anger out on anyone who crossed her path, including my friend."

He sits beside me again, closer this time, so close our knees touch. Then he reaches over and wraps his fingers around my gloved hand. "I get it now. But you have to understand that no one knows that about you. They only know what the Interrogator can do. Maybe if people knew your side of the story, they'd be more open to having you around."

He's right. All they see when they look at me is that insufferable title. A threat to anyone in my company. But they're wrong. I know that now. And I need the people of Fayatin to see the true *me*. Releasing a sigh, I curse, thinking about how connecting with others isn't one of my strengths.

"Should I finish my story?" he asks.

Gently, I place my other hand over his. "Yes. You were caught, beaten, and restrained. Then—"

"Then…" He squeezes my hand and picks up where he left off. "Brandulf came charging in, sword swinging. Cleared a path through the entire depot to find me. When he finally did and cut me loose… I couldn't believe the wreckage he'd left behind."

"Well, I guess Brandulf is the amazing swordsman you always claim to be!" I tease. This gets a soft chuckle from him. I reign in my attempt to amuse him, and apologize, "Sorry. Please, go on."

"As I was saying," he repeats, trying not to smile, "he got us out. We couldn't return to the north mine, so we fled deeper into Fayatin. We spent months moving from village to village. Then we caught a break, eavesdropping on a conversation between two men talking in a tavern about General Onica mobilizing her army. She was planning to cross Bowmans Strait into Harvesgrove Country. It was our chance to blend in and disappear."

"And that worked? No one recognized you?"

He shakes his head. "Nope. We slipped away from the marching guards once we reached Harvesgrove's shoreline. And though we had our freedom, we followed Onica and her guards."

"Why's that?" I ask, curious to know why they didn't seize the opportunity to get as far away as they could.

"Well, while aboard the ship, we overheard some of the guards discussing the general's plan to retrieve a missing person." He gives me a meaningful look. "They were going after you."

I stare at him, breath catching. He's talking about the attack on Bricen, right after we returned from the Under Realm. Instinctively, I rub the area above my heart and below my shoulder, where Marcellus stabbed me with his spear.

"So," he continues his story, "I told Brandulf we should follow from a distance. Learn everything we could about the person they feared so much."

"You chose to stay and spy on me?"

He hesitates, then says, "Yes, but please hear me out. And this is going to be the part where you have to promise you'll forgive the old me… and remember we're friends."

Again, I shake my head. "I can't promise that. Not until I know everything."

He sighs, dragging a hand through his tousled hair—the same hair he's been stubbornly growing out because I requested him to. "Fine." Then, while staring into my eyes, he confesses, "I wanted to find you so I could kill you."

Somehow, I already knew that's what he'd say. Why wouldn't he? The Interrogator was a monster—a walking nightmare capable of ending lives with a single touch.

"I'm guessing you saw what happened between me and General Onica at Bricen?"

He nods. "Brandulf and I watched it all. We remained out of sight, but had a good view. We saw that sickly-looking second-in-command of hers—Alister, I think that's his name—bury an axe through her shoulder and halfway into her torso. Then… flying people with birdlike wings showed up, fighting him off. One of them opened some kind of magic hole in the ground and tossed the sickly giant through it. Craziest thing I've ever seen."

There's a sharpness and an almost excessive amusement in my laughter.

His brows rise in surprise at my outburst. A soft blue light from the moon illuminates his face. "Why are you laughing?"

Inhaling a deep breath, I try to steady my nerves. "I'm not laughing because it's funny. It's just… you saying *that's* the craziest thing you've ever seen, especially after the day we'd had? We'd just returned from the Under Realm with demon spirits and Reborn creatures, passed through a wasteland filled with thousands of open graves for sleeping holes in the earth, all under a sky without a sun. And then we faced off against an evil demon queen who used to be one of the Starlight Realm's leaders. So yeah, there's a *lot* more unbelievable things out there than flying warriors and a magic hole in the ground."

"And now, you must know I'd stand by your side and fight any evil that comes to Bricen's gates, or wherever our friends reside." He slips his hand from mine. "I'm ashamed of the thoughts I had then. I wanted to end your life, Adele."

"But you didn't."

"No. But Brandulf was determined to. Once he had a face to the name, he believed that if we were to rid you of this life all would be right in the world. The only thing I could do to keep him from charging out that day when the threat had left was plead with him to be patient and wait. Plus, I wanted to know more about what you were doing in Harvesgrove—why you'd left Fayatin."

"So you *stalked* me?"

He hesitates. A slow nod, then a reluctant shake of his head. "We settled in a village a few hours west."

"Gailstein," I say flatly.

"Yeah. Brandulf got work at the smithy while I went east every day to Bricen. To watch you."

A cold knot twists in my stomach. "You watched me for *weeks*?"

He scoots closer, eyes steady. "I didn't just decide to spare your life, Adele. I decided I wanted to be part of it. You weren't the monster everyone made you out to be. You weren't the Interrogator."

"No," I whisper, my voice brittle. "I wasn't. I wanted a new beginning. To build a better life where others didn't fear me."

With a gentle touch, he tucks a strand of hair behind my ear. "I saw that. And once I convinced Brandulf to move to

Bricen, which took a *lot* of convincing, I knew you and I were going to be friends. I saw your kindhearted nature, even though you rarely show it. You're a good person, Adele. That's what I want everyone else to see—the real you. They'll come to understand you're not the Interrogator. The Interrogator was a tool… and that tool doesn't exist anymore."

"It does if one of the other lords forces my hand."

"We won't let that happen."

He shifts in his seat on the bench, his knee brushing mine. He reaches for my hand but pauses, fingers flexing before he sighs and lets it fall to the bench between us. Something stops him. Actually wanting to be touched is something entirely new to me.

"I care for you, Nathaniel," I say softly, offering a little peace of mind.

"You do?" He stumbles over his words. "I mean… you care for me as in a close friend, or—?"

I take his hand in mine. I'm not ready to touch him without my gloves, but I want him to know that this… whatever it is Selene and Elijah keep talking about—this love-and-romance stuff—is something I want too.

"Considering everything I've said, including my desire to end your life, you still care for me?"

I nod. But in case he can't see it from the low torchlight behind us, I add, "If you're okay with us taking our time… I'd like to get to know you better as a suitor."

He cups his free hand over our clasped ones, giving a gentle squeeze. "I'll never rush you. I won't ever ask more of you than you're willing to give. You're a beautiful person, Adele. Inside and out."

He leans in, and my heart pounds in my chest.

Am I ready for a kiss?

What if I'm wrong and my hands *aren't* the only way to use my reach?

I don't move. Then I feel his warm breath brush against my lips.

This is really going to happen. I'm about to experience my first kiss.

Suddenly, this dress feels too tight. My heart is beating against the velour fabric.

"Hey! There you two are!" Kit's voice cuts through the air as she walks out from the castle. "Since you're out here, I've got something to show you. Something you're gonna want to see."

Leaning away, I put some space between us. I don't know whether I want to punch Kit or thank her. I'm ready to explore these feelings I have for Nathaniel, but I still don't want to hurt him.

"We'll pick this up later, okay?" he whispers, then stands. His hand is still in mine, and he gives a small tug until I rise and walk beside him.

"I'd like that. To talk more later." And I do. I want to open up. I want to tell him everything, especially the fear I carry about hurting him. It's strange, because I don't tell *anyone* everything. Not even my closest friends. My heart feels at home when I'm with Nathaniel.

With our hands still clasped, we walk side by side out of the bailey toward Kit. We stop at the top of the hillside, looking out over the land. The night stretches far and wide, and in the distance, on every hilltop and in every valley, are tents and encampments, their fires glowing like stars scattered across the earth.

My body tenses, and my hand slips from Nathaniel's.

"Oh, Kit. This is bad. This is very, *very* bad."

CHAPTER 12

ADELE

The fire in my core, ignited moments ago by the thrill of sitting close to Nathaniel, of almost kissing him, suddenly extinguishes, replaced by a cold, icy pit of dread.

This is *not* good.

This is *not* what I was expecting to see.

How could I have been so naïve to think the regional lords wouldn't bring their full guard?

I recall how our bedchamber window overlooks the ocean. Not once did it occur to me to check the other side of the castle. I assumed the endless stretch of hills rolling out beyond the grounds as far as the eye can see were empty.

"I wasn't sure if this was normal… for one of these grand weddings," Kit says.

"This is *not* normal," I reply, my voice flat, barely above a whisper. "Not even for a royal wedding."

"There must be thousands of them," Nathaniel murmurs, his gaze sweeping over the view before us.

Beyond the castle walls, the countryside is blanketed in camps. One after another, encampments sprawl across every hillside, outlined in flickering torchlight. Their fires glitter like fireflies beneath the night sky, and banners whip in the wind, each flag representing a different region of Fayatin.

The regional lords didn't just arrive with their traveling parties. They brought their entire armies.

"This isn't good," I mutter under my breath. "Why would the lords bring their full guard to a wedding?"

"I think that's a question for the new king," Kit says pointedly.

I nod, my stomach knotting. "Then let's go ask the new King of Fayatin."

Weaving between servants, I hurry toward the great hall, drawn by the lingering sounds of laughter and music. But the moment I step through the archway into the hall, everything changes.

The air stills.

The noise fades into an eerie silence, distant and hollow, like the echoes of a party long gone.

Dirty plates remain scattered across the tables, goblets left behind. Some are half-full, others completely drained.

Where has everyone gone?

I move cautiously toward the center of the great hall, my shoes scuffing against the stone floor. Ahead, the dais looms, with the royal family's long, decorated table stretched across it. Victor's and Selene's oversized chairs sit empty at the center.

Cool night air drifts in through the open windows, causing the floor-to-ceiling blue velvet curtains that line three sides of the great hall to sway gently. Candle flames flicker, casting restless shadows across the room. The tables are lined with them, and tall iron candelabras stand in each corner, their flames dimming. Then, eventually each one snuffs out one by one. Even the wall sconces, positioned high along the stone walls, sputter and fade until they, too, die out.

Then come the chandeliers. Three hang from the vaulted ceiling, and in a procession, their candles go dark, plunging the hall into thick, uneasy shadow.

The only light that remains is the dying glow of the fireplace. Above the hearth, where I swear was a portrait of Lord Stolkin, is now an enormous mirror. Stepping closer, I stare at the reflection, which mirrors the emptiness behind me.

Turning to face the empty tables again, I call out, "Hello? Did the party move outside or something?"

Where are Nathaniel and Kit?

"Alone once again."

The voice echoes through the hall—or maybe it's only in my mind.

But, regardless, I know that voice. A shudder of fear attacks my senses, and I search the darkness for the source. "Show yourself!"

I slide off one glove, then the other, and tuck them into the front of my vest. My fingers flex, ready.

"Don't play games with me!" I warn. "I promise it won't end well."

"Ah. Is that what this is? A game?"

A low, sinister chuckle curls out into the vacancy of the cold room. It echoes deep into my head, along with an icy chill that seeps into the core of my bones.

This can't be happening.

There's no way.

It *can't* be her.

I locked her in her own mind, and Rune has her body hidden somewhere safe in the Starlight Realm.

So, this cannot be her.

"And why not?" she answers, entering my thoughts. *"You really think so highly of yourself? You actually believe you could trap the most powerful being to ever exist?"*

The laughter rises, louder by the second, building to full hysteria.

I grip my hands into fists, needing to steady the trembling fear running through me. *She's not really here*, I silently remind myself. "Yes! I did trap you in your own mind!"

"Oh, you are such a naïve child," she says between cackles. *"You've done exactly what I needed you to do. You are, and always will be, a child of malice and destruction. It's in your blood."*

Her words cut through my defenses, like daggers laced with venom.

"No," I whisper, then louder, *"Where are you?"* I shout into the shadows of my mind. *"I did what I had to do—to stop you!"*

When she speaks again, her voice sounds as if she were standing right behind me. I spin toward the fireplace—but no one's there.

I must be imagining this. I must be dreaming. Though I don't remember going to bed… it's the only explanation that makes sense. Then, from above the hearth, something shifts. A shadow moves in the mirror. The closer it creeps to the surface, the more the firelight reveals.

Thin white strands of hair drape over a skull stretched tight with pasty skin. Black horns twist from the sides of her head, identical in shape, though not in size, to Aleksandra's. My sister's horns were never this large.

Merigoth.

It's her.

Somehow awake and… watching.

I turn, scanning the vast emptiness of the great hall. I'm still alone. That means she's only in the mirror. I face her again. "What do you want? I'm assuming this little chat is happening inside my mind, so just tell me, what's your next move?"

Within the mirror, her gaze widens, and the skin where her eyebrows should be cracks open, flaking off into the air like scorched ash. She lifts a bony gray finger, the nail curling to a thick, sharpened point. "If it's a game you wish to play," she says through the mirror rather than inside my head, "then it is a game we will play."

"No! I don't want to have anything to do with you!"

"Shhh," she says, letting her smile momentarily drop. "It's not polite to interrupt." Reviving her happy mannerism, she offers me some praise. "You've done well, my child. You've played your role exactly how I'd hoped. And my offer still stands. Pledge your loyalty to me—willingly. I won't enchant you or force you to join my cause. It must be your choice. Just as it was for your brother."

"No." My answer comes out with an unbendable tone.

"I will be watching," she says, staring at me with those soulless dark eyes.

"Watching?" I ask. "How?"

Her devious smile returns. "What fun would it be if I told you the answer? I thought we were playing games?"

She laughs, her mouth opening and revealing sharp, jagged gray teeth. She begins to slowly back away, retreating into the shadows of the great hall reflected in the mirror. Then, as if the shadows themselves have arms, they creep over her body, embracing her from top to bottom.

"You can't keep secrets from me," she says in my mind. *"Even when locked away, I see and hear everything."*

Then she's gone, swallowed by the darkness.

She's been watching us this whole time. But how?

And she made it seem as if she wanted me to trap her in her own mind. I played right into her plans. Even the memory I used to imprison her… she had it all picked out and waiting. She wanted me to see that memory. The day she was turned away by the angels.

"Oh, stars," I say with a sigh. "I let Rune take her to the Starlight Realm without protest. To the one place Merigoth has been trying to get back to."

What's done is done. I can't change the past. Right now, I need to wake up and then do two things. First, I need to get in touch with Rune and have her check on Merigoth and make sure the demon queen is still locked away.

Then, I need to figure out how she's watching us.

And stars help me, I think I already know.

There's only one way to find out for sure.

Kit's going to be pretty pissed off with me.

CHAPTER 13
ADELE

Nathaniel's voice rises out of the darkness, pulling me back to the real world. The shadows fade. The guests reappear, laughing and talking as though nothing happened. Some sit and eat, nodding along with full mouths.

"Adele!" Nathaniel clasps my shoulders and gives me a gentle shake.

"I'm okay," I say, brushing his hands off. "Where's Kit?"

I glance behind him, searching the crowd. No sign of her. I lock eyes with him and lower my voice. "Nathaniel. Where is Kit?"

He swings an arm out, almost smacking an old woman in a pale blue gown. She stumbles on her hem, nearly falling before Nathaniel catches her.

"Excuse me!" she snaps, hitting him with her cane. "Keep your filthy hands off me, you mongrel!"

He clears his throat, trying to apologize, but she's already moved on, wedging herself into a nearby group that includes one of the lords and his wife.

Nathaniel exhales sharply, then checks over his shoulder before pointing again, more carefully this time, toward the master table.

Kit's there, hunched beside Selene, whispering in her ear. Selene nods, then rises and follows her. Kit catches my eye and gives a quick wave, motioning for me to come.

I grab Nathaniel by the sleeve and weave us through the crowd toward the open hall, where Kit and Selene are waiting.

"We need somewhere quiet to talk," I tell them, urgency tightening my voice.

"This way," Selene says.

She leads us down a corridor, her gloved hand raised in a graceful wave. The gloves are white and elegant, reaching all the way to her elbows. They match the rest of her gown— soft, royal, refined.

This life suits her. And while I'm happy for her, proud she'll have a hand in healing the country, I can't help but feel a little sad. I already miss her.

She opens a heavy wood door, the iron hardware groaning as it swings wide. Once we step inside, she closes it behind us and turns to face us.

We're in a small library. A wall of books stretches across the far side of the room. Adjacent to the door we came through, a fire crackles in the hearth, casting a warm flicker across the stone walls.

Selene leans against the arm of a long blue sofa, careful not to wrinkle her dress. "This better be important. My place is by Victor's side now. I have a duty—"

"A duty?" I cut in, torn between finding out what Merigoth meant and unveiling Victor's plans for the country. "Do you even know what being by his side involves? Has Victor told you what his plans are for Fayatin?"

"I don't appreciate your tone," she snaps, and then starts for the door. "If this is why you pulled me away—"

"Did you know the lords have their full guard stationed in the rolling hills for as far as the eye can see?" Kit asks, cutting Selene off before she has a chance to storm out.

Selene sighs with defeat. Then she looks at each of us, her gaze finally landing on me. "Do you trust me?"

Of course I trust her. It's her husband I don't trust, not yet. I choose my next words carefully. "If you say there's no ill intent behind the lords bringing their entire armies to Castle Helve's backyard, then I believe you." I step closer and meet her gaze. "But I've seen how power changes people."

A small smile appears. "Yes, Adele. That's something you should know all too well."

The quip hurts, coming from her.

"Sorry," she quickly apologizes. "That was uncalled for."

It's Kit who answers, "Yeah, you think? Adele has done nothing but look out for you."

Selene's pale cheeks flush, and she reaches for the door handle. "I trust Victor, his father, and my uncle. They're not like those who lived at Castle Forge under General Onica. They're good people." Then, without another word, she opens the door and storms out, slamming it shut behind her.

Stunned by her behavior, I turn to the fire. I've never seen Selene so agitated or hostile toward me. I shouldn't have upset her.

"She's preoccupied with the festivities," Kit says gently, cutting into my guilt-stricken thoughts. "Maybe we should talk to her tomorrow, before we leave."

I wish we were leaving tonight. Looking to Kit, I try and hide the unease in my gut, knowing I'm about to upset another close friend. I need to verify my hunch about how Merigoth has been watching and listening to every move we've made.

As I turn to Kit, I slip off my gloves and let them fall to the floor.

"Adele?" she asks, confusion crossing her face as she eyes my hands.

Before she realizes what's happening, I press my fingertips to her temples.

"Adele, what—" She doesn't finish her question.

The darkness in my mind pours into hers, slipping easily through the cracks of her mind. Power hums beneath my skin, rushing through me as I thread myself into her memories. It's effortless. Familiar. What's disturbing is that the feeling is slightly reminiscent of the warmth I felt during my near-kiss with Nathaniel. The two moments couldn't be more different—one laced with violation, the other with longing—yet both leave behind a stillness that feels more like a trap than peace.

"Adele!" Nathaniel shouts, alarm piquing his voice.

Without breaking contact, I keep my eyes on Kit's face. "Don't touch me," I instruct. "I need to know something. I promise I won't hurt her. Just… back away."

He hesitates, swallowing hard. His gaze briefly flicks to Kit's frozen expression and then back to me. "What are you even looking for? It's Kit. She's on our side."

"I know. It's not her I'm worried about, but someone she encountered. Just let me concentrate, okay?" That's all I say. Then I close my eyes and push deeper.

Visions flood my mind. Memories she thinks about often, the ones that weigh the heaviest. Saying goodbye to Elijah before he left to live with Rune in the Starlight Realm. The battle with the Hoods in Noviska when Kit drove her sword through that Hood's back. It was her first kill.

And then—

I gasp.

Aunt Lauren.

My breath catches in my throat, horrified at the memory. My aunt lies there, her hair completely burned down to her scalp, skin melted to reveal red flesh in patches along her arms, neck, and face. And her wings are gone, glowing magma dripping from the exposed bones where they'd connected at her back. The image of her pleading with Rune to embrace change has my knees weak. I should've been there. I should've destroyed Alister when I saw him in Noviska. If I had, she'd still be alive.

"Adele, what's wrong?" Nathaniel's voice cuts into the memory, pulling my attention from the horrific scene.

I wasn't expecting to see her again. Not like this.

Tears break loose, spilling down my cheeks and dripping off my chin. I try to inhale and calm my upset nerves, but watching Aunt Lauren take her last breaths tightens my chest with unbearable grief.

"Adele! Why are you crying? What—what's happening? Please, hurry. This is taking too long!" He's right. I'm here for a reason. Shoving aside the memory of my aunt's death, I refocus the darkness and continue diving deeper into her past. I push through layers of visions until I reach the moment Kit was trapped—under Merigoth's enchantment, a prisoner in the Under Realm.

This is what I came for.

I slow the memory, playing it back moment by moment. Two Reborns drag Kit into the throne room and force her to the foot of Merigoth's throne of bones.

I remember this day, though I wasn't inside the chamber yet. I was probably still climbing out of the hole where I first found Kit, or trying to break through the mountain's entrance, heavily guarded by brainwashed angels.

The demon queen descends the decaying dais toward Kit. "Ah, so this is the child who cares so much for my granddaughter. Perfect."

Her cracked lips purse tightly as she hums.

Strange how Merigoth's enchantment from a time long past gives me the same bliss as when I stood before her in the Under Realm. My muscles slacken and a fog creeps into the corners of my mind. But the darkness within me reacts like a protective parent. Its tendrils snap at the fog like whips to jolt my awareness, keeping me focused.

The memory continues to play out as Merigoth lifts a bony hand and cups Kit's chin, forcing her to look up.

With her other hand, she drags a sharp nail beneath Kit's jawline, slicing the skin. Blood wells instantly.

Then, with that same nail, she cuts her own palm. Black blood drips from the wound. She presses it against Kit's fresh cut, humming all the while. Her dark blood enters through the open wound along Kit's skin.

"You are now nothing more than a bridge between me and the world," she whispers. "I will see and hear everything you do, sweet child."

As she releases Kit's face, my friend's head goes limp.

Then Merigoth turns away from my friend. With no one else in the room, as the Reborns left the second they presented Kit to their queen, Merigoth stands facing… me. Her smile is wicked. Somehow, she knows I'm watching. Or she knows I will be watching at some point in the future.

My suspicions are confirmed when she says, "You are weak, and easy to manipulate, granddaughter." Her smile widens and part of the dry skin along her top lip splits, dark liquid filling the crack. "You may believe that what you are about to do here is a win, but what you are actually doing is helping me."

Her laugh explodes like a scream inside my skull. It echoes, deafening and sharp, until I can't think anymore.

I pull my hands away from Kit's face and withdraw my reach. She stumbles backward, dazed, and collapses onto the sofa. Merigoth's laughter lingers in my ears for a few agonizing moments before finally fading, leaving only dread behind.

"She's been watching us this whole time," I whisper, breathless.

Kit stands suddenly and swings.

Her fist slams into my cheek. Pain flares through my jaw and rings in my ear.

"Stop!" I yell, raising my hands. "I had to see for myself!"

"See what?" she snaps. "Whatever it was, you could've asked!"

"No, I couldn't." I pant, holding my aching face. "Merigoth… while you were under her spell, she cut herself and smeared her blood into a wound on your face."

Kit freezes. "There's no cut. She never made me bleed."

"She did. I saw it—under your chin." My voice softens. "She came to me earlier… in a daydream or something… told me she's been watching. I didn't understand how. Then I remembered—she was alone with you."

Kit frantically searches the room until she finds a freestanding mirror and rushes over. She lifts her chin. The moment she spots the scar she touches it with her fingers. Abruptly, she turns to face me. Eyes trembling, her voice shaky, I cannot even imagine the emotional pain Kit's feeling right now. A single tear slips free, and she asks, "Are you sure that evil monster's demon blood is inside me?"

I hesitate… then nod. "I believe so."

"Am I going to die?"

The question hits hard. I didn't even think about the long-term effects. I won't lie to her. "I don't know," I admit. "All I know is Merigoth is using your eyes and ears. She's watching everything."

"Ugh," Nathaniel groans from the floor.

I crouch beside him. "I'm sorry you had to see that."

"A little warning next time, okay?" he mumbles, pushing himself up into a sitting position. He searches the room until he finds Kit. "Are you okay?"

She's trembling, pacing back and forth in front of the freestanding mirror. Flashes of the deep red fabric of her dress come and go in the reflection. "I don't know. I've felt fine all these weeks. But knowing she's been… watching and listening?"

"Who?" he asks.

"Merigoth," I say, stepping closer to Kit. "I'm sorry."

Kit's fists tighten at her sides. "You should've asked."

"Would you have said yes?"

She doesn't answer at first. Her shoulders sag, and her fists unclench. "No."

"We would've argued for hours. Kit, I am your friend. I may not be the most compassionate one, but I would do anything to protect you. I needed to know if your life—and ours—was in danger."

She lifts her gaze from the floor. "You are compassionate… in your own way. You do the things no one else wants to so we don't have to carry the weight."

It's not one of my finer qualities, but she's right. I'd rather bear the guilt than let someone else live with it.

"So," I ask quietly, "we're good?"

Her shrug shifts into a nod. "Yeah. At least now we know more about Merigoth's plan."

"Well, not really," I say, then gnaw on my lower lip. "But knowing she's watching and listening through you tells us she's at least aware. We still don't know if she has control over her body."

Nathaniel steps up beside me. "I think we need to—"

I reach up and press my gloved hand over his mouth. "We need to be careful what we say in front of Kit." He nods, and I lower my hand.

Turning to Kit, I say, "I'm sorry, but you can't stay here. You need to go back to Bricen."

"I figured you'd either lock me in the bedchamber or send me home," she says with a huff. "And here I thought all that Under Realm mess was behind me."

"It *is* behind you," I reassure. "You're not in danger. But we can't have you here. It makes it hard to plot our next move and keep everyone safe, especially if she's watching and listening."

"We should head back to the party," Nathaniel says, gesturing to the door. "Later tonight, I'll escort Kit to the docks, where she can catch a boat to Harvesgrove. Then I'll return, and we can figure out a plan together."

I appreciate his offer. It'll give me time to talk to Victor about those armed men gathering to the west of Castle Helve out in the hills and this mysterious proposition he wants to discuss with me. Looking to them both, I say, "I'll have Barclay fly ahead and send word to Mum and Evander that we need to speak with Rune."

"I want to help, Adele," Kit says, scratching her forearm through the velour fabric of her dress.

Shaking my head, I tell her, "The only thing I need you to do is to return to Bricen and lock yourself in your home. Mum will make sure you get food. But we have to cut Merigoth off from seeing and hearing anything else." I dip my head, trying to catch her gaze. "Promise me you won't do anything that puts more people in danger."

Her head snaps up, eyes blazing. "I would *never* intentionally put anyone's life in danger! You know that!"

"I do," I say quickly, holding out my hands in a calm-down gesture. "I'm only saying this because if someone were in danger, you'd be the first to run in and try to save them. I'm asking you to sit this one out—for now. Please."

"Adele's right, Kit," Nathaniel adds. "Once the demon queen is dead, you'll be free from her tether for good."

Kit inhales a shaky breath, then nods. "I hate her. If I ever made an exception about being okay with ending someone's life—it'd be hers. She's taken so much from me, from Elijah, from our village. I want her gone from our lives for good."

"And that's exactly what I plan to do," I say, hoping to reassure her that's our endgame plan. "Once we're done here, we'll follow you back to Bricen and deal with Merigoth."

I turn to follow Nathaniel to the door. But the second he opens it, Kit lets out a cry. We whip around just as she clutches her hand into a fist. He slams the door shut, and we both rush to her side.

"What's wrong?" I ask, panicked and unsure of what's happening.

Blood drips from between her fingers, falling to the stone floor in steady drops. She's crying out, stumbling backward until her backside hits the arm of the sofa. Nathaniel and I flank her, helpless.

Kit slowly opens her hand.

I blink, trying to make sense of what I'm seeing.

Some invisible force is slicing her skin open—right before our eyes. The cut keeps growing, a thin red line etching down to the base of her thumb before it finally stops.

"Adele!" she screams. "What's happening to me?!"

Nathaniel untucks his shirt and, with haste, tears at the bottom hem. He holds the long strip of fabric out to Kit. "Wrap this around it."

She obeys, tears spilling down her cheeks. Her face has gone pale—so pale her warm brown skin looks ghostly.

Then her whole body tenses. Her eyes go wide, unblinking, as if she sees something we can't. She starts trembling, shaking her head over and over.

"No. No, please. No, no, no! This can't be happening—not again!"

"What? What's happening?" I grab her shoulders, then gently shake her until she blinks and finds my eyes. My voice breaks. "Kit!"

She sobs, her voice small and shaking. "I hear her—in my head. She's talking to me."

"What's she saying?" Nathaniel asks, his gaze flicking between Kit's face and her bleeding hand.

Kit holds her palm out, the strip of fabric already stained through the wrapping layers. My poor friend is barely keeping it together, sniffling and choking back sobs. "That evil maniac wants you to know that she's enchanted a blood bond between us. My life is bound to hers," she whimpers, then adds, "If she bleeds, then I bleed."

"Oh, Kit." I don't have the words. This is worse than I ever imagined. How are we supposed to kill the Queen of the Under Realm now?

The only comfort I can offer is to pull her into a hug. It's awkward, and I stiffen at the contact, but I force myself to hold her.

It's what Elijah would do if he were here.

"We'll figure this out," I whisper. "I promise."

CHAPTER 14

ALEKSANDRA

We break camp at first light. Though, *light* is a generous term. The Starlight Realm's southern regions rarely get full sun, so a perpetual twilight casts an eerie golden glow through the trees, the faint shimmer on the leaves illuminating the forest floor. Though this realm bears some similarities to the Human Realm, it's anything but the same.

As we trudge through the dense woods, I think about how difficult it was to get the seeds from Harvesgrove to take root here. From a distance, the forest might resemble those back home, but up close, the differences are undeniable—especially the leaves. Their green surfaces sparkle, releasing golden dust motes into the air when disturbed. The magic-like foliage intrigues me, but deeper study will have to wait—at least until I secure my rightful place as ruler of this realm and every other.

A few hours into our morning trek, we finally reach the forest's edge. Without stopping to rest, we press forward into the flat, open field covered in ankle-high yellow grass. The shift from lush, shimmering woods to dry, brittle terrain is jarring but satisfying. We've left the forest behind, making our destination one step closer.

Cameron still hasn't spoken a word to me. The only sound between us is the soft *crunch* of grass beneath our boots.

What I first mistook for a distant mountain range slowly reveals itself to be something far stranger—a vast expanse of narrow black rocks, jutting from the earth at irregular angles. The sides of each one are smooth and cut like long gemstones. There have to be thousands of them. As we advance, the golden grass thins, giving way to cracked dirt and a forest of towering obsidian spires.

"We shouldn't be here," Cameron murmurs, her voice barely louder than the breeze. Her gaze darts nervously across the formations. There are some as wide as oak trunks, others as slender as my arm. The unsettling shadows, stretching out long and sharp with an unnatural, shifting quality, disturb me far more than the faintly gleaming surfaces do.

"How are there shadows without sunlight?" I ask, peering at the closest one.

"It's part of the Shadowland curse," Cameron answers. "And another reason we shouldn't go out there."

Adjusting my pack, I study the strange landscape. Each monolith has a chiseled edge, as if shaped with intention— sculpted, not weathered by time.

Cameron takes a step back.

I tsk a warning, snapping her attention to me. Her trembling eyes have no effect on my decision. Placing my hands on my hips, I ask, "And where do you think you're going?"

She drops her bag at her feet and shakes her head. "There are stories… warnings… about these stones. They aren't safe."

Curious, I step closer and press my palm to the smooth surface. Cold. Unyielding.

"They look like regular old rocks to me."

But the second the words pass my lips, I realize they aren't just regular rocks. A slow, rising heat seeps into my skin, and beneath my palm, a faint tremor stirs. My fingers flex, feeling a subtle pulse thrumming beneath the surface.

"Cameron, you have to feel this." I keep my gaze locked on my hand until something flickers in my peripheral vision. It's the shadow of the pillar, and it's moving toward me.

It curls inward, coiling with a deliberate, serpentine pace, inching closer to where I stand. The vibration beneath my skin intensifies, and my hand begins to tremble from the heat. The surface is getting hotter, pain searing my skin, yet I can't pull away.

Something is holding me here, forcing me to watch as the shadow creeps closer.

"Aleksandra!" Cameron shouts, lunging forward and grabbing my wrist. The moment she yanks my hand free, the stone falls still. The shadow snaps back to its original position so fast, I almost think I imagined it.

Almost.

I step back, heart pounding, the realization settling in like ice through my veins—the girl I kidnapped might have just saved my life.

"What was that?" I ask, rubbing my palm where it still burns.

Cameron swallows, then speaks, her voice unsteady. "All I know is what the stories say. The Shadowlands are only safe to pass when the stones sleep. Wake them, and their shadows will attack. This is their land."

"The rocks are alive?" I ask, incredulous.

"I only know what the stories say." Her gaze drops to my hand. "You couldn't pull away, could you?"

"No."

"It's not a good feeling, is it? Having no control over your own actions."

My curiosity twists into irritation. I don't need a morality lecture, especially because my entire life has been controlled by everyone but me. What I need is power. And that's what I aim to get. Narrowing my eyes, I grab a fistful of fabric from the front of her shirt and yank her close.

"You're not in a position to lecture me," I growl. "I could wipe your mind clean and leave you here to die slow and alone. You do what I say if you want to survive this."

The flicker of nervousness in her eyes shifts. She glares and I can see the anger rising within her.

"One push," she says quietly. "That's all it would take to bring you down. You think you're powerful? Out here, you're one stumble away from death. Not even your special powers could save you." She gestures wide to the field of towering black stones. "So, yeah. Let's go out there and see who lasts longer."

This side of Cameron has my insides laughing, and eventually, I can't hold it in. A short chuckle slips out. "Okay. You got me there. We're in uncharted territory."

I brush past her and pick up her bag, then turn around and hand it over. "My whole life's been about survival. Looking out for me, and me only. You can't blame me for being a little defensive… and closed off."

Her shoulders ease, and the tight lines around her mouth soften. Taking her bag, she says, "I can't imagine what kind of life you've lived. But I've never given you a reason to think I'd hurt you or treat you any different than anyone else in Stellara."

I extend my hand. "Okay. Going forward, I'll try to be less threatening… if you try to be more helpful in figuring out what's out here."

Her brows lift, and she lets out a dry laugh, shaking her head. "Oh, no! I'm not touching your hand. But fine. Since we're already out here, I'll be more supportive. Deal."

I drop my hand and nod. "Good enough for me. And all you need to know for now is that we're looking for a mountain—specifically, a cave."

Her brow furrows, curiosity in her expression, but she doesn't press. She just hoists her bag over her shoulder and starts walking beside me.

It's the least I can tell her, for now, especially if she's going to help me find the entrance to where the Bocnite are hiding.

The deeper we go into the Shadowlands, the denser it gets with more spires jutting up from the earth. Weaving between them without contact becomes taxing. I accidentally graze one, and the second my knuckles touch its smooth edge, the shadows surrounding it curl inward, closing in around me.

For a brief moment, I wonder what would happen if I let the darkness swathe over me. What would it do? How much damage could an intangible shadow cause?

Cameron's hands clutch at my arm, pulling me from danger, seconds before I find out. Reluctantly, I offer her a genuine smile. "Thanks."

She steps away, maintaining an arms-length between us, with a sunstone in one hand, the light bright enough to help us maneuver through the deadly field. Searching her surroundings, she checks to make sure she's not too close to one of the stones, and then says, "Well, as much as I dislike you right now, I don't want you to die out here."

We sidestep around the rocks, careful not to touch them. Once again, we fall into a silent trek. Some time passes, and my eyes are growing weary when Cameron stops and shouts, "There!" Her magically bound wings rustle with excitement. "Do you see it?"

I shuffle closer and follow her line of sight. I can't be sure of the time since the sun doesn't reach this far into the Shadowlands, but it's dark out, like middle-of-the-night dark. Even with the sunstone, it's still hard to see whatever's got her excited. My sight isn't as sharp as the angel's. After staring off into the distance for a long moment, giving my eyes time to adjust, I see a low collection of the rocks, like a bird's nest, except this has a hole at the base. Looking to my prisoner, I tell her, "That can't be the cave we're looking for. Shouldn't there be a mountain or something?"

"No, this is it. Come on," she insists, waving for me to follow.

We approach the cluster of black stones piled crisscross like a stack of kindling in a giant campfire.

With her hands on her waist, she stares up at the cluster of pillars. "I recognize it from one of Merigoth's illustrations in her journal."

I swing my backpack around and pull out Merigoth's journal. Cameron walks over and holds her sunstone high over it. Flipping through the pages, I stop when I see the illustration.

"That's the one!"

Her excitement is sweet, and I mirror her enthusiasm by saying, "We did it! We found it!" I gesture to the dark space in the center. "No turning back now."

Cameron takes the lead, holding out the sunstone, and as we get closer, we see a hole in the ground, wide enough for both of us to fit through.

"Angels first," I insist, nodding toward the entrance.

"Uh. How about we go together?" she counters.

I don't argue, because either way I'm going down the hole. "Fine," I say and swing my pack to the front so I have a better hold of it. Cameron does the same, and then we sit on the top edge, which appears to be more of a smooth slide along dark rock. Not the same rock as the pillars, this is more level with the ground.

"Ready?" she asks me, holding out her hand.

"Oh, now you want to hold my hand?" I say with a little sarcasm.

Cameron rolls her eyes before saying, "You've dragged me out here against my will, but now I'm actually curious to see what we find. We're in this together. You and me. There's no one out here to help us, so might as well work together." She shakes her hand, emphasizing her impatience.

Slipping my fingers over hers, I reel in the darkness, commanding it to stay put. "Let's go," I say and scoot forward. We both slide into the darkness, and we both scream from the steep descent. When we land, our boots hit the ground at the same time. Breathing hard, we look at one another before bursting out laughing.

"That was actually fun!" she says between chuckles.

"It was, yeah." And I'm not lying to her, either. It's been a long time since I've laughed like that, and I'm tempted to climb the rock to do it again. But we're here to find the Bocnite, so fun will have to wait.

After dropping her hand from mine, Cameron stands and adjusts her pack onto her back while holding up the sunstone, taking in the small cavern. I do the same with my pack and follow Cameron. We search the small cavern that's comparable to my bedroom at Rune's place. There's nothing but rocky wall. That is, until we come upon a narrow tunnel.

"I guess we go this way," I say, and instead of insisting she go first, I grab the sunstone and take the lead. Holding the light up, we follow the tunnel as it curves to the right, and then the left. Each bend makes it hard to see what we're walking into. When I step out into another small cavern, we're met with a giant flat wall with a door carved into it. The height of the door is at least two of me, while the width is five or six of me standing shoulder to shoulder. There are carvings all over the thing. Cameron will have to translate them for me.

Holding the sunstone up above the tunnel entrance, I call out, "Hey! Are you coming?"

Silence.

"Hey! Cameron?"

No answer.

Fury boils inside me. I shouldn't have trusted her to—

"I'm here." The angel girl coughs, stepping out of the dark tunnel.

"What happened?" I ask. The question leaves my mouth before I realize I don't actually care what happened. I need her alive as my offering. But there's a tiny part of me that's starting to wish I'd found someone else.

"My wings got caught in the tight gaps of that insufferable tunnel."

Tucking a lock of curls behind one ear, I look to the sunstone in my hand and ask, "These things can die?"

She nods. "I mean, they aren't alive or anything, but yes… the energy within can be used up."

Good to know. I wave for her to check the door out. She immediately starts trailing her fingers over the engravings, muttering words I can't hear.

"Do you know how to open it?" I ask.

She ignores me and continues looking over the symbols and words. She does grab the sunstone from my hand and holds it closer to the stone carvings. "Here! Yes! It says this door leads to the Bocnite."

Excitement swells in my core. We're so close to all that glorious power.

"So, how do we open it?" I ask again.

She drags her fingers along the curves and lines of the stone until she's over at the far side. "Here!" She holds the sunstone over a small cubby that's next to the door. "It's a lock. You need the sunstone used to lock it… to open it."

I grab the sunstone in her hand and stick it in the cubby, resting it on the shallow bowl deep inside the cubbyhole. Nothing happens.

"That's not the right sunstone. Those are my family's sunstones that work on *our* home. You'll need to find the ones used specifically for this door."

Releasing a guttural scream, which startles Cameron, I then shout, "You mean we have to go back to Stellara?"

Her tone is small and scared. "I'm sorry."

Pulling my hand out, removing the sunstone we brought, I stare up at the slab. "Where are we going to find a sunstone that opens this door?"

The girl shrugs. "Not sure." We both stand there and stare at the mysterious door. "I can only think of one angel that might know where a sunstone as important as this might be."

She doesn't need to say the name out loud. I already know exactly who she's talking about. I guess we're heading back to Stellara after all, because I need to have a conversation with Rune about a key.

CHAPTER 15
ADELE

It's the middle of the night, and I've called the crows into my bedchamber. They sit perched on the footboard of my bed, wing to wing, waiting for my attention. I stand in front of Barclay. His body is slightly larger than the others. "I know it's cold, but I need you to fly as fast as you can, only resting when absolutely necessary. It's important to get this message to Mum or Evander."

Barclay ruffles his silky black feathers and briefly spreads his wings, releasing a series of chirps. It's his way of saying he understands. Once I've secured the parchment inside the small leather satchel tied around his neck, I hold out my arm in front of his chest. He hops onto it, his black talons gripping my forearm, pinching the white fabric of my tunic against my skin.

"I promise I'll ask Rune about a better way to communicate over long distances, okay? This back-and-forth is getting tiresome—for both of us. I miss having you around," I say, gently petting the feathers along his back, between his wings.

He caws twice, seemingly pleased by my words. Then, as I open the window and cold night air rushes inside, I extend my arm, and he takes flight, diving out into the dark.

Turning to the other crows, I say, "He'll be fine, and will be at home in Bricen, waiting for us when we return. I need you three to stay close and stay together. I have a feeling peace isn't exactly on King Victor's agenda."

Three sharp raps knock at my bedchamber door, startling the crows. Before answering, I whisper to my feathered friends, "Go. And be safe."

One by one, they fly out the window. I cross the room and crack open the door. Nathaniel stands on the other side.

Giving him more space to speak, I open the door wider, and he says, "Kit's on the boat. Not a ship, but more like a fishing boat. It'll take her longer to cross the strait, but she'll get there."

"And over in Harvesgrove?" I ask, hoping she remembers where the livery is where we kept Bessie and the other horses.

"She'll be fine, Adele."

I'm tempted to invite him in. Almost kissing is one thing. Actually doing it—or other things—is something else. If my reach found a way to slither into him earlier, while I was searching Kit's mind, then I can't trust it not to try again. Just thinking about the darkness stirs it, as though it's laughing at me. Some days I wish I were fully human. Other days, when the reach serves a purpose, I'm grateful for it.

He inhales a deep breath and his gaze dips to my mouth. Nodding, as if agreeing to something I haven't said yet, he takes a few steps away. "She'll get home safe, and she knows to make sure someone reaches out and tells Rune that you need to speak with her."

"I also sent Barclay with the same message. He should arrive there a few hours before Kit. Which means, we should expect to see Rune by midday tomorrow."

A smile spreads across his face as he combs his fingers through his hair. "I'm going to go." He gestures to his door down the hall. "I need a bath before bed."

The image of him bathing floats through my mind. Heat blooms under my arms and up my neck.

He then steps closer, so fast my feet stumble about. He reaches up and caresses the top of my arm. I'm about to give in to the impulses and deal with any consequences should the darkness attempt to slither its way into his mind. But then, the smell of fish and salt fills my nose as I lean closer to his face. Covering my mouth, I say, "Oh, you do need a bath."

A smile cracks, and then he's laughing. "I was hoping it wasn't too noticeable."

Pushing him away, my gloved hand pressed against his chest, I shake my head. "Go and take your bath. We can *talk* more tomorrow."

Then he says something that melts my insides. "I was hoping to kiss you tonight, Adele."

Swallowing the lump that's formed in my throat, I softly answer, "Yes, that would be nice. But…" He steps closer, and I laugh, pushing him away again, "Not tonight, and not while you smell so awful!"

He joins me in laughing. Then, eventually, he moves down the hall to his own room. "Fine, fine. You are worth the wait, my lady."

"Oh, I'm no lady," I say teasingly. Which has me thinking, what has gotten into me? Where is this flirtatious need for physical contact coming from?

After closing the door, I press my back to it. Understanding dawns on me about why Elijah always longed to see Rune and how Selene must feel about Victor. Even Kit, whenever she tells me about the occasional tryst she has with the young man in Gailstein. These feelings aren't just moments of happiness, but something deeper in my core—something that needs to be satiated almost as much as the darkness wishes to be free. How will I find the balance between the two, especially if I want to be closer to Nathaniel?

I take my tonic and let my thoughts of exploring more of this romance with Nathaniel carry me off into a deep, relaxing sleep.

I wake feeling as if I had the best night's sleep in a long time. Today is the day I confess everything to Nathaniel. He'll be understanding, reassuring and patient with me.

After dressing, I hurry out of my bedchamber and down the hallway toward his room. The door is slightly ajar. I push it open. "Hey! Are you ready for some breakfast?"

No answer.

I step inside, hoping to catch him still asleep and without a shirt again, but his bed is empty. He must already be dining with Lord Stolkin and the new King and Queen of Fayatin.

Leaving his room, I close the door behind me and then head down the stairs toward the dining hall.

Empty.

I keep walking, making my way to Lord Stolkin's private dining room. Also empty. Frowning, I stop a young girl in a brown dress with a darker brown apron. "Where is everyone?"

"Oh, miss. You haven't heard the screaming?"

"What screaming?" I ask, my words slow and heavy with suspicion.

She shakes her head, then shrugs. "I don't know what it is, but Master Victor—I mean, His Grace, King Victor—has commanded everyone to vacate the castle, except for his guard."

I eye her from head to toe. "Then why are you still here?"

"I was just on my way to the kitchen. We're to stay in there until we've gotten word that it's safe to come out."

She darts off before I can ask anything more, disappearing into the empty corridors. I glance around the great hall, from which most of the wedding embellishments have been cleared out. Meanwhile, a strange sensation awakens the darkness within. It stirs, concurring with my suspicions that something feels wrong.

Then I hear it.

A loud, guttural cry.

It sounds more beast than man.

A fearsome sound from my past.

Two guards rush out from a side corridor near the castle entry, swords at their sides. I move to intercept them.

"Where are you coming from?" I ask, blocking their path.

"Miss, you should vacate the castle. For your own safety." One gestures toward the double doors. "Everyone's been sent to the church in town while…" He clears his throat. "While King Victor and Lord Stolkin handle the situation."

"I can handle myself," I say, gaze flicking toward the dark corridor behind them.

There's no way it could be who I think it is.

My reach stirs in the back of my mind. It's ready, eager to help. I try to suppress it, but the more the darkness builds, the less I want to stop it. I slip off one glove. Then the other. Tuck them into the front of my leather vest.

The guard is still talking, trying to guide me toward safety. But I don't hear his words. I raise my hands. With just a touch of my fingers to their faces, the reach releases— instantaneous and unrelenting.

When I searched Kit's mind, I had control. I held back.

Not this time.

This time, I let the reach take over.

It's like coming up for air after being underwater too long. I don't search their memories or fears. I just send one command: *Sleep*.

Both guards crumple to the stone floor, their swords clattering beside them. Stepping over the unconscious guards, I don't bother putting my gloves back on. My strides are wide, purposeful, as I make for the dark corridor. From the corner of my eye, I catch a glimpse of the kitchen girl, frozen in place, staring at me with horrified eyes. I press a finger to my lips. *Shhh*. Then I disappear into the dark corridor.

The stone staircase spirals downward, one level, then another, and another. The air grows colder. A sharp scent of sea salt rises with each step. We must be near the water's edge of Bowmans Strait. There must be an exit to the ocean somewhere down here in the bowels of the castle.

Another roar rips through the silence. Closer now. Louder. More guttural. Torches line the long, windowless corridor. Their flames flicker against damp stone walls. There are several wood doors, worn and sturdy at the same time. Each one has a small, grated window at eye level.

This must be the dungeon.

Two doors down, a guard bursts out, stumbling into the hallway. He doesn't even glance my way as he rushes past. His face is pale, his eyes wild with fear. Whatever's in that room has completely shaken his confidence.

Quietly, I approach.

Peeking into the open door, I see Commander Pavik. He stands at attention, flanked by two guards on either side, their swords drawn and trembling in their hands.

I can't see what they're facing—but I hear it.

A low, guttural growl that reverberates through the floor, like thunder trapped beneath the stone.

A rational part of me knows I should turn away. This isn't my place. I shouldn't intervene.

But curiosity and instinct override reason.

I take one step inside.

Then I see it.

And my heart races while the salty air gets stuck in my throat.

No.

The creature's eyes lock onto mine. Every muscle in my body seizes. My feet refuse to move. Its skin is slick, gray, stretched tight like rotting leather over a swollen frame. Bloated, deformed—but unmistakable.

Even with his bloated deformities, I know exactly who and what it is. And my fear turns to rage.

CHAPTER 16
ADELE

Alister's attention snaps to me. His bulging eyes, glazed over with a ghostly white haze, fixate as though seeing nothing else. He sways on bloated legs like a walking corpse that's washed ashore. But he's not dead. Not yet. And judging by the tension coiling in his fists, he's just as furious to see me.

With a wet slosh, he takes a step forward and roars. His jaw unhinges in an unnaturally wide, monstrous way. The second his bellows cease, his jaw snaps back into place with a sickening crunch.

One of Commander Pavik's men tries circling wide, sneaking behind the creature. I force myself not to look his way, not wanting to hint to the Reborn about the man's approach, but Alister turns anyway. He faces the guard and releases another guttural roar, stunning the poor fool long enough for Alister to swing a meaty fist into his chest. The guard slams into the stone wall with a sound like broken branches. His sword clatters to the floor, followed by his lifeless body.

I seize the moment and run at Alister.

He's quick to return his attention to me, somehow sensing the attack. His bloated arm swings toward me like a battering ram. I duck under it, every nerve burning with purpose. In one motion, I snatch the guard's sword, pivot on the balls of my feet, and drive the blade toward his neck with a scream lodged in my throat.

The steel bites deep, slicing through swollen flesh with a wet squelch. His throat is thick, bloated with seawater and decay, but I don't stop. I can't.

Not for the years of cruelty I suffered at Castle Forge under Alister's command.

Not for the dozens he tormented.

But *for her*.

For Aunt Lauren.

For the woman who loved me like her own, and who died screaming in agony because of this thing.

Alister starts to turn toward me—but he's too slow.

The blade breaks through, and his head severs clean and falls to the ground with a thud. The uneven stone floor causes it to roll toward the door. His dead eyes stare up at me, his lips frozen mid-snarl.

A moment of silence follows, broken only by the creak of his body slumping backward, crashing into a thick oak door behind him.

Pavik stares. "What have you done?"

A faint howl of wind whispers from the cracks in the door behind the corpse. The scent of brine lingers beneath the heavier stench of decay. The ocean is close.

I drop the sword, and it clangs against the stone. Breathing heavy, I glare at the commander. "You're welcome." My voice comes out hoarse, laced with all the fury I've carried for years. Wiping the sweat from my brow with my sleeve, I nod to the monster's twitching body and ask, "How the hell is he here?"

"You knew this beast?" Pavik sheathes his sword. The lingering guard follows suit, though his face remains tight with unease.

"Of course I knew him," I snap. "He was General Onica's second-in-command."

Pavik exhales sharply, rubbing a hand across his mouth. "I know Alister." Then, pointing at the head and what's left of the body, he says, "And *that*… isn't him."

"Ah, but it was. Maybe not the Alister you knew, but it was him." I stare at the head lying ten paces from where I stand. It'll please Mum to know the brute is dead-dead. A sick satisfaction coils in my gut.

I step around Alister's body and approach the commander. "There are things in our world that have crossed over from other worlds. It's hard to explain, and much easier when Rune is here to show you. Anyway, the demon spirit that killed him and took over his—" My words are cut short when a thick black smoke snakes out from the severed part of Alister's head.

"Stand back!" I shout, throwing my arm out and waving for the men to move. "*That's* the demon spirit that possessed Alister. If it gets inside you, it will end your life and claim your body for its own use. The creatures they become are called Reborns."

Pavik and the only guard remaining by his side draw their swords again, ready to strike at a moment's notice. I grab the blade I used to bring Alister down, ready to defeat this evil phantom creature from the Under Realm once and for all.

The air above the decapitated head collects into a large plume of darkness, like a thundercloud ready to rain pain and suffering. Slowly, it reshapes into its original demon spirit form and frantically flies around the room. The birdlike creature, with beady red eyes, circles the group. I duck low, as do the guards in the room, wanting to avoid any contact. It releases an ear-piercing shriek before disappearing out the door and into Castle Helve.

"We can't let it escape!" I shout, bolting after the screeching shadow. My boots slam the stone floor, each step fueled by my determination to end this vile creature's existence. Pavik and his men follow close behind.

"If it finds another body to control, there's no hope in saving that person," I call over my shoulder. "Remember, the demon spirit will turn the person into a Reborn!"

"A what?" a guard who joined us out in the hallway of the dungeon asks, breathless as he keeps pace beside me. "What's a Reborn?"

We take the stone stairs two at a time until we reach the castle's entryway. There, we huddle together, back-to-back, swords ready, ears straining for screams. Anything to reveal which direction the demon fled.

In a low voice, I say, "They're phantom spirits from a dark and evil realm called the Under Realm. General Onica captured one last fall in Harvesgrove while hunting me. I was at Castle Forge helping Selene when I saw the demon spirit forcefully enter Alister's body through his mouth. It twisted his face—*changed him*. That was the day Alister died and his Reborn took over."

We stand perfectly still and listen. There are no screams. No cries. Just an eerie silence.

Pavik turns to his men. "Search the castle," he orders.

I step forward, blade raised. "Don't wait for orders. If it moves, strike. And if you miss, you swing again—*and again*—until it dispels into the air."

The men scatter in pairs, going in all directions of the castle.

The commander grabs one lingering guard by the collar, fear trembling in the man's eyes as he searches the hall. Jostling the man until he's got his attention, Commander Pavik commands, "Go find the king, queen, Lord Caldridge, and Lord Stolkin, and get them to the tower. You guard the chamber room door, and don't let anyone else in until I get there. Tell Victor: *there's mold on the bread*. Do you understand?"

The guard nods and rushes off.

"What does that mean… *There's mold on the bread*?" I ask, my grip still iron-tight around the sword hilt.

He gives a faint smirk. "Ah, we have little phrases that we use to communicate to one another. It was something my brother and I did as kids. Lord Stolkin may run the castle, but Victor and I have worked hard to earn the loyalty of the guards. A few key phrases were taught to some high-ranking guards to assure the men that any orders not coming directly from us had our implicit approval."

I'm impressed, but I don't tell him that. I might just steal that idea for my own family—especially with Rune and

Elijah off in the Starlight Realm, Selene here in Fayatin, and the rest of us scattered across Bricen.

"This has to be reported to the king. Queen Selene should be with him. If you want to check on her—"

Shaking my head, I cut him off. "I need to find Nathaniel. He should be around here somewhere. I trust you to make sure Selene is safe."

"I swear to it," Pavik replies, solemn. "She won't be touched by whatever that unearthly phantom is."

He dashes up the stairwell.

I tighten my grip. I have to trust him. I have no other choice because I can't be in two places at once. But if that demon spirit finds Nathaniel first… I don't know how I'll handle taking the head of the man I think I love.

CHAPTER 17
ADELE

After looking for over an hour, I'm unable to find Nathaniel inside or outside along the castle grounds. The bloody demon spirit has been quiet as well. Now, I stand at the top of the hill just beyond the kitchen bailey, taking in the sight of the rolling hillsides covered in encampments. From up here, the soldiers bustling about resemble tiny ants. If King Victor is uniting the regional armies into one royal guard, I worry I may not stand a chance if he decides to turn on me.

"Oh, there you are."

"Commander," I say as he steps beside me. "Are the king and queen and lords all safely tucked away?"

"They are. And please, call me Leon."

"I'd prefer one or the other, and since I must call you Commander for formalities, let's stick with the formal title,"

I say coolly. "So, how can I help you, Commander Pavik? Have your men spotted the demon spirit?"

On the hill closest to the castle, men form tight circles, training in hand-to-hand combat. I hold my gaze on their activities while he answers.

"No. We're still searching the grounds. I've sent a small company to Port Helve to ask the townsfolk if they've seen anything… unusual."

Brushing my long braid off my shoulder, I ask, "You're not going to warn them about the potential danger?"

He shakes his head. "Why cause a panic?"

"They deserve to know."

With a deep, throaty hum, he says, "King Victor wants to see you."

I take one last look at the encampments before turning to follow him inside. As we climb the stone staircase from the great hall, I ask, "Have you seen my traveling companion, Nathaniel?"

"Not recently. He and your other friend left last night."

We reach the second-floor landing of the tower staircase we've started climbing. I have to assume we're heading up to the secure chamber room where Selene and her new husband are being kept.

"Kit had to return to Bricen," I explain. "Nathaniel was escorting her to the ship. He returned right after. I spoke with him last night before heading to bed."

We reach the top of the stone tower and walk out into the small round landing. The only light comes from a single iron torch posted near the door. Two guards straighten at our arrival, flanking a single door. Commander Pavik lifts a hand, signaling them to stand down.

"The king and queen are expecting us."

The guards nod in unison and then step aside. Before entering, Pavik glances over his shoulder and asks, "Did you see your friend this morning at breakfast?"

"No. And he's not on the castle grounds. I've searched. I'm worried he went down to get a closer look at the encampments."

Pavik frowns. "I would advise against that. The regional lords aren't exactly thrilled with King Victor's decision to unite the armies. I wouldn't want to provoke them into a fight."

"I have no intention of fighting them," I reassure him, in case he believes I'm foolish enough to confront the entire armed guard from every region. "I'm ready to return home. Selene's well-being is my priority. But the demon spirit in your castle? *That's* the more pressing reason I've stayed."

Then, he asks, "So… you wouldn't charge down there and fight your way through all those men if your friend was being held against his will?"

He's testing me. I speak my next words slow and deliberate, so he fully understands. "I don't have a problem doing *whatever it takes* to protect—or save—those closest to me."

I don't ask if he understands because I can see it in his eyes.

He gives a small nod and gestures to the door. "Come on. Let's see what the king and queen want."

Twenty minutes have passed, and I remain persistent in my refusal of His Highness's request. The large room I'm in, a simple, safe space for the lord of the castle and his family, feels suffocating. The walls, lined with dark wood paneling, close in around me. It might be a sanctuary of sorts, designed in case of an attack, but right now the chamber feels more like a cage. Lord Stolkin, Lord Caldridge, Victor, and Selene sit in upholstered armchairs around a small table, the atmosphere heavy with expectation.

Victor, now king, stands while I remain seated. He's persistent, but so am I. The sound of the wind outside only adds to the silence between us. Commander Pavik stands at the rear of the room, casting an occasional glance out the window, always alert.

"Adele, this is an opportunity for you to—" my friend states, but I cut her off before she can finish.

"For me to what, Selene?" My voice is sharp, betraying the frustration I can no longer hide. Selene lowers the book she's reading, her eyes narrowing as she gives me a familiar glare. The one that says she's warning me to tread lightly. But I'm too upset to care right now.

"How are you—of all people—okay with this absurd proposal?"

"Your friend cares about your well-being," Victor says. It's a low move, trying to use Selene to get me to agree to this insanity.

My gaze shifts from Selene to him, our eyes locking. I hold his stare, unblinking. I refuse to back down. He needs to understand I will not—cannot—agree to this. No one will ever control me or what I can do.

"It wouldn't be like before," the king says, his voice softer, more measured as he submits to the intensity of our brief clash.

"You're asking me to leave my family in Harvesgrove and come live here to be your Interrogator." The words sound wrong coming from my mouth, as if they don't belong.

Victor quickly holds up his hands, eager to rephrase. "That's not what I said. The Interrogator died with General Onica. You're not that person anymore, Adele, and I'd never command or ask you to use your"—he gestures toward my hands—"abilities. You do whatever you see necessary as Fayatin's—"

The word slips from my tongue before I can stop it, souring the air between us. "General. You want me to be your general."

Commander Pavik, who has been watching from the window, gives me an approving nod. His gesture of consent feels like a weight pressing on my chest. The responsibility that Victor's offering isn't just to lead Castle Helve's army of guards, but to command the united army of all the regional lords.

"Yes," Victor says, "but if the title is troubling, we can come up with something else. This is a new era... a new beginning for Fayatin."

Selene abruptly stands from her seat. Her blue satin dress swishes against the wood of the table as she steps closer, holding a small leather book in her hands. She doesn't speak at first, but the urgency in her eyes is clear.

"You're the most powerful person in all three countries—Harvesgrove, Noviska, and Fayatin," she says, her voice unwavering. "We need your presence to unite the armies. To bring them together without the lords rebelling and starting a conflict. If we fail, it could set our plans for a better Fayatin back by decades. Maybe longer."

I shift uncomfortably in my seat, crossing my arms over my leather vest. My eyes lock with Victor's, a challenge in my gaze.

"I thought you said the lords were in agreement about handing over their forces."

Victor shakes his head, his face tense. "Not all of them. A few say they will comply, but I can see it in their eyes. They're plotting resistance."

The king's usual neat hair is disheveled, a sign of his growing unease. His white tunic is untucked, his appearance suggesting either a rushed dressing or that he's been pacing and running his fingers through his hair. The truth stings. I hoped they were all aligned. If not… this could be worse than I imagined.

I look at Selene again. Her expression is one of concern, her eyes pleading with me to understand.

"I need time to think about it," I say, the words leaving my mouth like a reluctant surrender.

Victor exhales heavily, his frustration barely contained. "Yes, of course. That's all I ask for."

I lean back in my chair, my mind racing. There's no easy choice here.

"I'm a reasonable man, Adele. I have no intention of using you for your abilities."

"So you say." My words are cool, skeptical. "If Selene trusts you, then I'll try. But trust isn't given freely. You'll have to earn it."

Commander Pavik moves toward the door, signaling the end of our conversation, but before he opens it, Victor calls to me once more.

"Adele," he says, his tone more serious.

I pause, turning slightly toward him.

"Trust is earned—not given. You may not trust me, and I have no reason to trust you. Keep that in mind as you ponder your decision."

His gaze is steady, unwavering.

"Accepting the offer gives you immense power over an entire army. And in return, I'll expect your full loyalty—to maybe even prove yourself loyal."

The weight of his words hangs in the air, but I offer no response.

Unsure of his complete meaning, and eager to leave this room, I agree only to get out of this space. "Duly noted. I'll have my answer for you by end of day." Commander Pavik opens the door, and we're immediately met with the shrieks of the demon spirit. "Close the door!"

CHAPTER 18

ALEKSANDRA

The walk back to Stellara is much faster than the hike out to the Shadowlands. Not wanting Cameron to be seen, I compel the angel to sit by a tree far outside the city walls and wait for me in the forest while I go retrieve the sunstone and restock our supplies. I can't risk losing my offering.

It's dusk, and I'm hoping everyone's gathered for dinner. It'll be much easier to sneak around. I slip through the gap in the barrier wall, careful not to lose my footing on the rock pile, and return to Stellara. The lampposts along the roads in this part of the city aren't lit—no need, since Rune, Evander, and Gianna marked this section as dangerous because of all the debris and unstable structures. I've walked through here many times and know exactly where to step and what to avoid.

Drawing my cloak out of my pack, I shake it out before putting it on, making sure to secure the hood over my horns. The plan is to stay close to the building walls and move within the shadows until I reach Rune and Elijah's home. I'll change clothes and restock my food rations before searching for the sunstone. Rune has to have it somewhere. An important key like that would've meant something to her mother. I'm going to guess she keeps it close, like at home or in the citadel where the Star councils would often meet?

As I shuffle through a tight alley, disappointment presses on me. Finding that key might take longer than I hoped. Emerging from the darkness, I veer left and smack right into Elijah.

I try to sink back into the darkness, but he reaches out and grabs my arm. "Aleksandra! Where have you been?"

"Sorry, uh… I went for a walk, and uh… well, now I need to go wash up." The words tumble out in a babbling mess. It's ridiculous that I have to make excuses for myself, yet I don't have time to answer his questions or listen to another one of his lectures.

I try to pass him, but he swings his arm out, blocking my path. "Hey, have you seen Cameron?"

I shake my head and push a curl of hair from my eyes. "Nope. I haven't seen her since yesterday. In the garden." I try to sidestep, but he keeps his arm in place.

"So, where have you been? You weren't home last night."

"Well, since you guys said I could get my own place, I thought I'd go scope out the abandoned homes. Time got away from me, and it got late, so I camped out in one up on the northeast corner. This morning, I picked up where I left off, browsing old homes, searching out the one I liked best."

Elijah keeps his arm up, preventing me from going forward. His eyes search my face as if he's trying to decide whether I'm lying or not. "You shouldn't be this far from the community, Aleksandra."

Anger simmers in my gut. He speaks to me as if I were his child. That parental tone has me wanting to dig my fingers into his skull and force him to listen to the wails and screams of all those I've brought suffering to.

"Did you end up finding a home you liked?" he asks, diverting my thoughts about inflicting pain on him.

"Not yet. But I'll keep looking."

He still doesn't drop his arm, so having had enough of him in my personal space, I slam both hands into his chest, forcing him to stagger back. Fury blooms in my core, and if it were daylight, he'd see how flushed and annoyed I am. I throw the front of my cloak back over my shoulders, freeing my arms and hands, and lunge at him, grabbing the sides of his face.

"I'm done being nice."

His eyes go wide, and he tries to scream, yet no sound is permitted to leave his gaping mouth without my say. Dark tendrils snake out from within my hands and find their way into his open mouth. The darkness reaches his mind, and I bind his will to me.

Once done, I command, "Close your mouth and be still while I figure out what to do."

He does as instructed, standing there like one of those garden statues out in the courtyard in front of the garden area—silent, still, soulless.

But what can I do? I can't just leave him here, frozen. And I can't drag him across the city like a puppet on a string.

I glance toward the road, and—damn it—I hear a familiar voice. Rune. And someone else.

I grab Elijah by the arm and lead him into the alley's deeper shadows with seconds to spare as Rune and Gianna walk past the mouth of the alley.

"I'm sure they're out exploring and just lost track of the time," Gianna says, walking in step beside Rune.

Rune stops way too close to where we hide. My breath catches. She's scanning the road, but her eyes are unfocused, distracted. Still, one wrong move and we'll be seen.

"What if they're hurt?" the overprotective angel says, concern threading her voice.

"They're not hurt. They're out having fun. Aleksandra has been locked up her entire life. I think letting her roam the city and explore will be good for her."

I silently hope Gianna can convince Rune to ease up and focus her attention elsewhere.

"Why didn't they take Jordana with them?" Rune's eyes narrow with skepticism, and she crosses her arms over her dark blue tunic. Brown feathers trail behind her like a royal cape. Gianna's wings are hidden, tucked away. "If they were going exploring, why not invite her?"

"I don't know. Girls will be girls—whether they're an angel, human, or part whatever Aleksandra is."

Gianna's words sting deep, and I want nothing more than to sink my nails into her smug little face and show her exactly what I am.

I've accepted that I was born from evil. But not knowing the origins of the demon part of me has been eating at me since I could remember. What I do know is that Merigoth was an angel before she became Queen of the Under Realm. And the Bocnite are the source of the darkness. They are my true bloodline, and they have the means to amplify my power.

A rush of wind stirs the treetops, followed by a fluttering sound overhead. A winged figure circles once and then lands beside Rune and Gianna.

"There you two are," the messenger says. "Evander's at the realm gate. He and Sara need to speak with you. They say it's urgent."

"Go," Gianna tells Rune. "I'll head to your place and see if Elijah's heard anything from Aleksandra or Cameron."

"You sure?" Rune asks.

Gianna nods. Rune and the messenger take off, flying toward the realm gate.

Gianna, unfortunately, heads in the exact direction I was going.

Of course she does.

"Great. Just great." With one hand clasping the fabric of Elijah's shirt, I drag him out of the darkness and into the street. Daylight is fading fast, and I need to decide what to do next, and quick. Frustrated, I grumble, "How am I going to find the sunstone now?"

"You're looking for a sunstone?" Elijah mutters, his voice low and monotone, as if speaking while sleeping.

Pivoting to face him, I command him to answer my questions. "Do you know where Rune's mother kept important sunstones?"

He nods.

A vigorous burst of hope fills me. "Where?"

Again, in a low drawl, lacking any emotion, he explains, "In her mother's private study. It's above the old council building, north of the citadel."

I grab his shirt and tug him to follow. "Well, let's go get us some sunstone keys."

After compelling Elijah to lead the way to Rune's mother's private study, I feel confident the sunstone will be in my hand within the hour, maybe even sooner. And if it's not, I swear I'll tear this entire city apart until someone tells me where it is. I've worked too hard, for too long, to be stopped by something as simple as a locked door.

I shut the study door behind us and follow Elijah into the center of the long, narrow space. The air is thick with the musty scent of aged furniture and dust, making my nose twitch. I light a few candles, their flames flickering weakly, and blow out the match.

"Let's hurry up," I mutter. "I don't want to be in here longer than we have to."

Elijah walks to the hearth, moving methodically like a man in a trance. He reaches for one of the square, decorative wood carvings and presses it gently. It pops open with a soft *click*, swinging outward on hidden hinges.

"There," he says, stepping aside, eyes glazed and distant as he stares at the now-revealed compartment.

I push him out of the way and reach inside. My fingers brush against three smooth stones stacked atop each other. I pull them out and shut the hidden latch, cradling the sunstones in my hand. Like the other sunstones here, these feel cool, slightly rough, and oddly squishy.

I squeeze one, and its center glows faintly, as though a firefly has been trapped inside. Another squeeze extinguishes the light.

"Well, we'll have to take all three since I don't know which one's the right key."

"One goes to a safe," Elijah murmurs, voice distant, "but the safe is empty. Another unlocks Rune's mother's private holding cell." He turns slowly and points to the wall adjacent to the fireplace.

I follow his gaze, then step past him to examine the wall.

"Where's the door?"

Without a word, Elijah shuffles over to the large statue, a carved tree perched atop a pedestal, and gives it a push. It glides with surprising ease, the stone base scraping against the floor. As the statue slides aside, a dark recess in the wall is revealed. It's small enough to fit one arm and sits at waist height. The candlelight behind me flickers, casting a soft glow into the hidden nook.

Bending, I look inside and see a shallow bowl.

It's a keyhold.

I squeeze one of the sunstones to activate it and nestle it into the bowl.

Nothing.

I remove it with a deep, frustrated sigh. "Okay… let's try this one."

The moment the second stone clicks into place, a string of gears deep inside the wall stirs to life. *Click-clack… click-clack…* The sound of ancient machinery waking from slumber fills the room like a slow heartbeat.

Giving the door space, I step back as a section of the stone wall groans and grinds, then gradually pushes out into the room before sliding along the stone floor with a deep, scraping rumble.

"Stay here," I snap at Elijah, wanting a better look at the passage beyond.

With caution I step through. Inside is a large circular cell. A sizable gap carved into the wall follows the lines of the ceiling. Stars from the night sky twinkle beyond the opening. A single torch casts a warm glow into the room.

In the center is a long stone bench, and lying on it is a woman, her back to me.

"What do we have here?"

I circle around, the torchlight barely making out her features. But the second I'm on the other side of the bench, I take in the full appearance of the prisoner. The sleeping woman's complexion is a sickly gray, and her skin is dry with thin cracks cutting into her cheeks. My gaze drifts up to her wiry white hair, then halts at the sight of two black horns curling from either side of her skull.

Horns—like mine.

Only larger.

This is Merigoth.

I stare for what seems like forever, taking in the woman who created my existence. I've never been this close. I saw her once, from a distance, hidden while Master Ebenus met with her. It was one of the few times she summoned him.

Now she's vulnerable. Motionless. Caged like a dying rabbit.

A part of me wants to end her, thinking she deserves peace over whatever prison she's been trapped in. Sighing, I assume this is the work of mother's favorite child, trapping Merigoth in this state.

"Maybe I can help," I whisper, brushing a few brittle strands of hair from her forehead. I press my fingers gently against her skin.

And release the darkness.

It slithers out at a slow pace, working its way into her mind, and then with an abruptness, the dark tendrils are caught on something. I fall to my knees, whimpering in pain. My fingers remain stuck to the side of her face. I can't pull away. Something within the demon queen yanks at my power like a hooked fish on a line.

It's Merigoth. She's—she's ripping the darkness out of me!

"Ah!" I cry out as invisible claws sink into the tendrils, claiming more of my darkness. I try to escape, but her grip is stronger—hungrier—than I imagined.

"Stop!" I shout. I can't break the link. The darkness trying to fight within me is weak and being pulled by a power too formidable.

Screaming, I try and catch the tail end before its gone.

All of it.

My hand breaks free from her body, and I fall backward onto the stone ground. A hollow, deathly emptiness washes through me.

"No!"

A wicked laugh erupts inside my head, echoing from nowhere and everywhere at once.

"What have you done?!" I scream at her unmoving body, getting to my feet and seizing her face in both hands. "Give it back!" I close my eyes and search inward.

Nothing.

The place where my darkness occupied is silent. A vacant hole in my mind.

Behind me, Elijah's voice is small, groggy. "What's going on?"

I whirl around.

He's rubbing his eyes, blinking like a child waking from a dream.

This can't be happening.

This is *not* the end of my legacy.

I run toward him and drive my fist into his gut. He doubles over, gasping, hands clutching his stomach. His confusion doesn't matter.

The Bocnite will restore what was taken. And then… they'll give me more.

I spot some iron manacles hanging on the cell wall and make haste to grab a set. The chains clank together as I twist my fingers into his curls and yank him upright.

He groans, disoriented. Before his senses clear, I clamp the manacles onto his wrists.

"What are you doing?" he whines, panic growing. "Aleksandra?"

He still doesn't understand.

But he soon will. With a violent tug, I grab the chains connecting the shackles on his wrists and force him to get up and come. "Be silent or I'll end your life, and then Rune's." I stop and bring my face inches from his. "Are we going to have a problem?"

Giving me the saddest look of disappointment ever, he shakes his head.

"Good. Now, let's go."

CHAPTER 19
RUNE

The shimmer of the realm doorway casts a soft glow across the cobblestone courtyard, pulsing faintly against the night. I decided to keep the location close to the community, but not directly within it. As our community grows, we can decide if the doorway between realms needs a better location, but for now, here it sits.

The cool air of the Starlight Realm brushes against my feathers as I descend, wings wide, feet poised for an easy landing. The moment my boots touch down, I tuck my wings against my shoulder blades.

"Evander said to meet him and Sara behind Goslings, on the Green," a young angel says. She's perched on a stone bench, reading a book.

"Shouldn't you be heading home?" I ask, already veiling my wings in a shimmer of concealment as I exhale a slow breath. It's always easier to blend in when visiting Bricen.

"I like reading by the doorway. The lighting is nice. But also…" She glances at the shimmer between realms, a pleased smile on her lips. "I like watching the activity in the Human Realm. It's entertaining."

Before stepping through, I tuck a wavy strand of hair behind one ear. "Don't stay up too late."

She nods, and I pass through, over into our neighboring realm.

Stellara's serene sounds fade behind me, replaced by the distant hum of music spilling from the tavern and the howl of wind rustling through the treetops. The temperature drops immediately, and I tense, not from the cold, but from the memory it stirs.

The tunnels in Noviska. My angelic abilities blocked by the imbued magic of the cult leader, Master Ebenus, had almost resulted in Elijah's death. That moment stripped me bare—emotionally, physically. I won't allow myself to be that vulnerable again.

I follow the melody of singing and instruments toward the village tavern. When I told Sara I was going to open a permanent doorway between our two worlds, she only had one request—distance. She didn't want the portal too close to Bricen's front gate, giving travelers an easy way to sneak through. Sara also requested that Evander stay close to the doorway, ready to speak with anyone who wished to travel into our city. She kindly offered him one of the abandoned houses closest to the doorway.

I wish he said no. I wish he came home with the rest of us. But I understand why he didn't.

I'm about to climb the steps to the back door of Goslings when I hear my name.

"We're over here!" Evander calls, lifting a hand from across the open, grassy stretch. He and Sara stand outside the second home in the short row of small houses. It belongs to Elijah and Kit.

"It's a nice night," I say, glancing up at the clear sky, stars twinkling brighter amidst the new moon. Then, looking to my friends, I ask, "What are you two doing out here?"

"It's Kit," Sara answers. Her mouth is tight, her expression pinched with concern.

"What about Kit?"

Before she can answer, Evander steps between us, his broad shoulders blocking my view of Bricen's leader. "Where's Elijah?" Evander's hair has grown out since I last saw him. A few strands blow across his face, but his expression stays stern, unreadable.

Stars above—please don't let this be about Elijah and me.

I fold my arms. "Why?" I can already feel the annoyance blooming behind my ribs. Evander needs to get past these feelings he has for me.

Sara steps around him, her voice calm. "Because his sister's in trouble."

Any thoughts of our meeting having to do with my relationship with Elijah vanish. "What's wrong with Kit?"

"She's returned from Fayatin," Sara continues, "alone."

I blink. "Is Adele or Nathaniel in trouble?"

Sara shakes her head.

"Then… what's wrong with Kit?"

Sara's next words settle in my chest like ice. "Merigoth has done something to her. She's using Kit as a vessel to see and hear the outside world. The Queen of the Under Realm has been watching and listening to us for months."

I face the small cottage where they must be keeping Kit. "That's not possible." But even as I say it, the words taste like denial. After everything we've seen, I know better. "Is it ever going to end?"

"Rune," my friend says as he closes the distance between us and wraps his arms around me. His embrace is strong and comforting. I miss his presence. Despite my affection for my childhood friend, my feelings for Elijah are far deeper.

He steps back, holding my gaze. "We can end this tonight."

"He's right," Sara cuts in, breaking the moment. Evander steps aside to give her room to speak.

"But," she adds, "if we kill Merigoth, we hurt Kit. Maybe even kill her. Merigoth has somehow linked herself with Kit in mind and body."

A knot tightens in my chest. My thoughts scatter. "How do we help her? Did Adele send word?"

Sara nods and pulls a small piece of parchment from her pocket. She hands it to me, and the ends curl as I unroll it. A short message in Adele's familiar handwriting: *Check on Merigoth.*

"From what Kit told us," Evander says, glancing toward her cottage, "Merigoth also paid Adele a visit through a daydream. We need you to check on her state."

I hand the slip back. "Her state is that she's locked up. No one knows the location." Then, stuttering my words, I clarify, "Well, except Elijah and me. We've checked on her a few times."

At Elijah's name, Evander lets out a quiet groan.

I ignore him. "Merigoth's trapped in two places—Adele's mental prison and my mother's secret cell in Stellara. There's no way she's escaped."

"You may be right," Sara says softly. "She might still be physically trapped, but it appears she's found a way to free herself from her mental imprisonment."

She reaches for my arm, her fingers curling over it. Her voice lowers. "Please, Rune. We need to know she's still there."

It's not hard to open a doorway into my mother's old study, and a quick glance should be enough to put them at ease. So, to ease their worry, I oblige.

But the moment we step through, my heart plummets.

My gaze flies to the hearth. The hidden compartment is wide open.

"Rune!" Evander's voice cuts across the room.

He's standing in the doorway to the secret cell. I rush to him, weaving between the furniture, and stop cold at the threshold.

The stone room is empty.

The long stone bench in the center, where Merigoth's sleeping body was laid, is empty. The demon queen is gone.

"This isn't possible!" I shout, my voice echoing through the open ceiling.

Sara's eyes are wide, scanning the walls of the cell. "We have to find her."

The clatter of metal draws my attention. Evander's holding one of the shackles from the wall beside the door. He lets it fall. The sound bounces off the stone in sharp, jarring echoes. He then gestures to the empty hook. "It appears a set of shackles is missing. Maybe someone shackled Merigoth?"

"No. She was incapacitated. It can't be her—" My thoughts race about the danger I've put Stellara in. My heart slams in my chest. Panic floods every part of me. "We need to alert the community. She's out, and loose somewhere in the city. Who knows who she's already hurt?"

"Where's Elijah?" Sara grabs my shoulders. "If he's the only one who knew she was here, then you need to find him. He may know what happened."

I stare blankly at the empty hook where the shackles should be.

"Rune!" Evander shouts with urgency, and when I meet his eyes, his tone softens. "We'll find her. I swear by it. But right now, we need to evacuate the community. Angels and humans—everyone goes through the doorway tonight."

"We'll start moving them," Sara says. "You go find Elijah." She points toward the door.

I nod once, hard. Then, shoving every ounce of fear down deep, I run. The second I'm free from the building, I spread my wings and take to the sky.

After flying around and searching Stellara, I return to the doorway, where Evander is ushering angels and humans over to Bricen. I land and weave through the parade until I reach him. He asks an older angel to help keep everyone moving, then steps aside to speak with me.

"Did you find him?"

Shaking my head, I say, "I can't find him, Cameron, or Aleksandra."

Evander purses his lips and stares off at the procession of people. I can only imagine he's trying to solve the mystery of what's going on and how he can fix the problem and save everyone. The role of protector has always been his calling.

I'm about to ask him what the plan is once everyone's out of the city but get distracted when I hear someone shouting my name. Both Evander and I turn to see Gianna pushing through the crowd, towing Cameron behind her.

"Look who I found." Gianna wraps one arm around the girl. "Go on. Tell them what you told me."

Cameron grabs a flat gray stone hanging around her neck and holds it up.

Evander's eyes go wide as he asks, "Where did you get that?"

"You know what it is?" I ask.

He nods. "Don't you remember how Marcellus put one of those things on me so I could walk past the wards keeping angels out of the Noviska village? Then later, that Ebenus guy did something to the stone—bound my free will so Marcellus didn't have to use compulsion on me."

"I do," I say, recalling the moment Adele freed him from the imbuing power the stone held over him.

"Well, my free will was taken, but not by this necklace." Cameron drops the stone, letting the small pendant rest against her chest. "Aleksandra did that. This thing keeps me from using my wings. And I can't take it off."

"Here, let me," Sara says, stepping through the doorway from Bricen. She pulls out a small dagger, pierces the tip of her finger, and rubs the blood on the front of the stone. The symbol carved into it vanishes. She then slips the twine over the girl's head, removing the stone pendant.

Immediately, Cameron steps back and unfolds her wings. "Oh, thank the stars."

"Where is Aleksandra?" I ask, the sinking realization of her betrayal settling in. If Elijah is with her, it can't be good.

Cameron shrugs as she tucks her wings behind her back. "She left me in the woods. I don't remember much after she compelled me to stay. And when I woke and she wasn't nearby, I took the opportunity to run."

An angel approaches our small circle and, after excusing herself, says, "That's everyone. Though… they're all wondering what to do over in the human village."

"Tell them to sit tight. Someone will be there in a moment," I reply, then turn to Cameron. "Is there anything you remember that could help us find Aleksandra?"

"She dragged me out to the Shadowlands. She's looking for a cave that will take her to the Bocnite."

Dread washes over me. The Dark War lasted decades between the angels and the Bocnite and was the reason the Star Leaders built the wall surrounding the city. I look over and lock eyes with Evander. His pensive expression mirrors the dread swelling in my gut. It's evident we're both fully aware of how dire the situation has become.

Cameron continues, "I bet that's where she's headed, to the cave out in the Shadowlands."

"Why does that name sound familiar?" Sara mutters.

"The sunstones," I say, remembering the open secret compartment in the hearth of my mother's study and how the sunstones inside were missing. With a quick jerk of my shoulders, I stretch my wings wide. "We need to go to the Shadowlands."

Evander grabs my wrist, stopping me. "Wait! You can't just fly off without knowing what's out there. If Aleksandra is trying to open the Bocnite door, then we're in more danger than we thought."

I yank my wrist free. "She lied to me—to all of us! And who knows what she's planning to do with Elijah!"

"We need answers," Sara interjects. "About the Bocnite and about Merigoth. Aleksandra might have lied, but Merigoth is still out there. And we already know she wants to rule the Starlight Realm. If Aleksandra's traveling on foot, then we have a little time. You can open a doorway out to the Shadowlands if needed."

"What are you suggesting?" I ask, already dreading the answer.

"We need to talk to Marcellus. He's the only one who knows the full extent of Merigoth's plan."

That's the last thing I was expecting her to say.

"No. There's got to be another way." Evander crosses his arms over his chest, as if his say is the final decision on the matter. "You can't trust him."

I rest a hand on his arm. "Stay with Gianna and help keep everyone safe in Bricen. Sara and I will visit the Under Realm and speak to Marcellus. We can handle him. But with Kit being some kind of vessel for Merigoth, our community is still at risk, here and over there. I need you and Gianna to protect our people."

He drops his gaze to the ground, lost in thought.

"Rune," Gianna calls to me. "I'm taking Cameron over. She needs to find her family."

"Yes, please help her find them, and then stay with her and everyone else. Reassure them that we're handling the situation," I say, then look back at Evander. "Go with her. They'll have questions."

Eventually, he nods. "I don't like it, but if Merigoth is using Kit to see and hear everything… then she already knows more than she should. I'll keep everyone safe, and I'll watch Kit."

"Thank you." I pull him into a hug. He hesitates for a moment before giving in and wrapping his arms around me.

Once he's through the doorway, I sweep my arm wide, closing the portal between our two realms.

Now it's just me and Sara. She ties her long blonde hair back into a low tail and says, "All right, I'm ready. Let's go talk to my son."

CHAPTER 20
ADELE

The demon spirit is close. I can feel it. The royals are safely tucked away up here, but Nathaniel's still out there alone, and possibly unaware of the threat.

I have to find him.

"Is there another way out?" I frantically ask the room.

Victor's only been king for less than a day, and already his plate's overflowing with problems. He doesn't respond, too deep in conversation with Commander Pavik. Frustrated, I turn to Lord Stolkin and Lord Caldridge.

"Well? I need to find my friend."

Lord Stolkin clears his throat, dragging out his words as though he's not sure how to answer. He shoots a sharp glare at his son. "King Victor will dismiss you when he's done speaking to you."

I roll my eyes. Every second counts. I look to Selene instead.

"I'm going to look for Nathaniel, and I'd rather not have to leave through that door," I say, pointing to the only visible exit.

"Adele, I'm sure he's fine. Can't you wait it out? The guards are already dealing with the demon spirit."

"No, Selene, I can't." My voice is sharp, decisive. "They won't slay it. This one is smarter than the others." I storm toward Victor and Pavik. Their hushed conversation falters as I approach. "I need to leave!"

"And where might you be going?" Victor lifts his chin and glares down his nose at me.

"Do you know how to kill the ghostly thing?" Commander Pavik asks.

I don't know whether blades or arrows will work as they did when Kit and I faced the others in Goslings—but I tell them what they want to hear. "Yes. I can."

Victor and Pavik share a look. Then they both step aside. But just as I'm about to pass, Victor grabs my arm. "Commander Pavik will accompany you."

I shove his hand off my arm, and it's my turn to stare him down. "No, he won't. He needs to stay here and protect you and Selene." I turn to the commander. "Swords or arrows through the center have worked before. But again, this one's different. Be careful."

He nods, then opens the door for me.

I don't hesitate. Sword in hand, I race down the stairs two at a time.

The spirit's shrieks echo through the castle, piercing the corridors. Yet it has not crossed paths with me, as if it knows to avoid me. Smart little demon spirit.

I keep alert, blade in hand, as I move past the great hall toward the kitchen. Inside, I continue straight out into the bailey. Chickens and goats roam free, unaware of the danger lurking in the vicinity. The sky is clear, late-morning sun shining down on rows of regional soldiers camped along the hills leading up to Castle Helve. I weave past a flock of loose chickens and hurry under the stone archway, leaving the castle grounds behind. Careful not to be noticed, I jog down the hill toward the first encampment.

Nathaniel couldn't have gone far.

If I were him, I'd stay close to the perimeter or the forest's edge. It's the best place to eavesdrop on the soldiers' conversations. Nathaniel might be doing some recon to determine whether they're here in peace… or preparing to resist the new king's command to unite. That's why I would've snuck down if I could.

Keeping to the trees, I maneuver down the line of tents. The second I step out of the forest, a man in dirty brown-and-black clothes calls out to me. "Oy!" His blond hair is tied back at the nape of his neck, exposing a thick scar that curves beneath one ear. Looks as though someone tried to take it from him.

I stop, tightening my grip on my sword's hilt. "I'm searching for someone. Taller than you. Hair like yours—only washed."

He ignores the question, voice sharp. "No women allowed in camp. Too much of a distraction to the men."

As he approaches, I spot the capital *F* on his grimy shirt, pale yellow stars circling the emblem. He's from the western region—the wheat and barley growers of Fayatin.

"I won't be here long," I reply, already turning away.

"Your funeral!" he shouts after me.

Keeping an eye out for Nathaniel, I pass tent after tent. Men lounge by campfires, trading stories, or gather around makeshift tables, playing dice and card games.

From yellow stars to green, then orange—I move quickly between the camps. It's only when I reach the pale-blue-star encampment that I draw my hood up. These men serve Lord Houfston—the same imbecile who tried to seize Gailstein in Harvesgrove just weeks ago.

If anyone recognizes me, it'll be here.

There's one tent in particular that stands out from the others with its official banners posted outside the entrance. They bear the mark of Castle Nautica. Lord Houfston's command pavilion.

There's a heated exchange filtering out through the canvas walls. Their voices are indiscernible from where I stand. Curiosity gets the better of me, and I circle to the back of the tent, out of view of the soldiers, where I can hear more clearly.

"Bernard, we cannot wait until he unites the regions. We must act now." That scruffy voice is unmistakable and belongs to that pompous Lord Houfston. "He's already gone too far with this whole 'making himself king' debacle."

"You're not wrong," a second voice replies, unfamiliar but tense. Bernard, I presume. I don't recall him from my time under the general's thumb. He must be new. Bernard continues, hesitation edging each word, "But we can't—"

"No excuses!" Houfston snaps. "The other lords agree with me. I'd *strongly* consider where your loyalty lies."

I can practically picture the bloated fool with his arrogant sneer. The way he looms over people like a swelled tick, and now he's trying to bully Bernard into obedience.

Temptation flares. I could march in right now and end his threats for good. Make him *stop* being a problem. This thought has the darkness stirring in the pit of my mind, slowly rising with anticipation.

I take a step forward, ready to give in and let the darkness have its way with them, but someone grabs my arm and yanks me backward. I don't hit the ground. Instead, I collide with a solid chest, and it stops me from falling.

A voice hisses in my ear. "What do you think you're doing?"

The bite in his tone has me second-guess who it is, and I'm surprised when I twist around and meet Commander Pavik's hard glare. Of course, Victor sent him to follow me.

I reel in my reach pulsing at my fingertips. It, too, thought we were being attacked and was ready to lash out. I doubt torturing Victor's second-in-command would help my position as not being a threat.

"I need to find Nathaniel," I say, urgency tightening my voice.

Pavik nods, adding a subtle eye roll. "Yes, I know. Except you being down here doesn't exactly help Victor's efforts to unite the regions."

When the two lords exit the tent, Pavik grabs me and pulls me into the cover of the trees, tugging my sleeve with more force than necessary as he crouches low. I blink at him, confused. Why is the second-in-command of the most powerful regional army hiding from two insurgents? He should be out there ordering them to fall in line or face the consequences.

I shift beside him, making no effort to stay hidden as I lower myself to his eye level. "What's going on? Why are you hiding from them?"

Pavik's gaze flicks from the older men speaking in hushed tones back to me. "If they realize we know they're plotting a revolt, they may act rashly and attack the castle now."

"So?"

His lips press together. "Do you know how many men would die in that pointless assault? These regions will unite, whether the lords want it or not. Change is already in motion. There's no need for bloodshed."

He's not wrong. It's a valid point, and him trying to avoid bloodshed makes me like him a little more.

"So you're staying out of sight to avoid provoking them into doing what they're already considering?" I ask.

Pavik nods once. "Victor has a plan in place that will force the regional lords to concede and unify the armies."

"And you trust this plan?" I ask.

He doesn't hesitate. "I trust you."

My hands flex, the leather of my gloves rubbing against my skin. "What do I have to do with any of this?" Then it clicks. I realize what he's implying. Why he believes the lords will eventually concede, and why they'll fall in line with the new king's command to unite the armies.

Because he thinks I'll be the general leading them. I have little faith in the idea that these men will follow because they fear what I'll do if they don't. I wish Victor could see that. I bleed and die just as they would. I'm not as powerful as he thinks I am. Maybe against a small battalion, but not an entire army. I would be bested and killed.

With that in mind, I tell Pavik, "I haven't agreed to anything yet."

Pavik's smile holds an unexpected confidence, as if he knows something I don't. "You will."

Out in the encampment, the two older men part ways. Lord Houfston retreats into his tent while the other lord walks off, flanked by two guards. Pavik watches them for a beat, then says, "We should go. Before we're seen."

"I'm not leaving until I've found Nathaniel."

He exhales sharply, clearly trying not to lose his patience. "What if I send two men to search for your friend? They'll draw less attention than you skulking around down here."

Reluctantly, I nod. "Fine. But if they come back empty-handed by supper, I'm returning and I won't be hiding who I am."

"Understood."

We skirt the edge of the hillside, keeping to the forest's shadow as we ascend toward Castle Helve. Just beyond the bailey, a young woman comes sprinting toward us, panic in her eyes.

"Oh, thank the stars! I've found you both!"

Pavik steps forward. "What's wrong?"

A bone-chilling scream echoes from within the castle. The woman flinches and clutches his sleeve. "It's in the kitchens. That evil spirit thing is attacking the servants. Please, come help them!"

We don't hesitate. Pavik and I draw our swords and run.

I won't let another Reborn claim an innocent life.

CHAPTER 21
RUNE

Like the cool winds that sweep through Bricen and stir up memories of Noviska, the dry, hot air around us now drags me back to the days when Merigoth seized control of my mind and forced me and the other angels into becoming her Shade soldiers. All because she'd lost two of the three Shade babies she'd helped create.

What would my life have been like if Sara hadn't escaped with Adele and Aleksandra? It would be easy to blame the woman walking beside me for the tragedies that fell upon me, my people, and our city, except at the root of it all, she's not to blame. Merigoth is.

My gaze fixes on the pile of bones, stacked crudely into the shape of a throne. I can almost see her sitting there, barking out orders. *More! Bring me more sacrifices! I cannot take back what is mine without an army behind me.*

Back then, we obeyed her without hesitation. We kidnapped humans from their homes, ripped them from their families, and delivered them into her hands. Now, as Reborns, they'll spend eternity buried beneath the frozen caves of Noviska.

A hand waves in front of my face, snapping me back to the present. Sara's voice sharpens as I refocus. "He's not here. Let's search outside the mountain castle."

I don't move. My eyes are still locked on the bone throne.

She steps closer, her voice softer now. "Are you okay?"

"I just want this to be over." My words come out low, hollow. "There's so much to do to rebuild Stellara and get it back to what it used to be. And we'll never get there if we're always stopping to fight her."

"You're not wrong," she says. "She will always be a threat."

Anger and regret churn inside me. I should've ended her when I had the chance, right after I broke free of her enchantment. Instead of leaving her in her mental prison, I should've ended the threat for good.

"You can't change the past," Sara says quietly, as if reading my thoughts.

I follow her out of the throne room, silently hoping it's the last time I ever have to look at that grotesque monument to Merigoth's madness.

Outside, the torches staked into the ground have all been extinguished. That is, except for one. It burns far from the rest, flickering near the edge of the mountain castle entrance. It's planted in dry, cracked black soil beside the first of many sleeping holes—hundreds of them dug into the earth like unmarked graves.

The gravel crunches beneath our boots as we silently walk along the path toward the light source. The second we reach it, a voice floats up from inside one of the sleeping holes. "Took you long enough."

Sara and I move to where the voice comes from. Standing at the edge of the second hole from the torch, we stare down at Marcellus. He's removed his winter coat, which lies beneath him while his bony hands are clasped over his stomach. One hand is missing four fingers and has stubs right above his knuckles. Dark-rimmed eyes stare up at us. Pale skin clings to his skeletal frame.

"We left him with no food," Sara whispers.

Then louder, so he can hear her, she asks, "Did you not have anything to eat?"

Marcellus shifts slowly, too weak to do more than lift his shoulders in a feeble shrug. Each word comes with effort, broken by shallow breaths. "Food was… never replenished."

"Merigoth might have been a monster," Sara mutters, "but she still made sure I had meals three times a day while locked up in the Idle Tombs." She faces me. "We can't leave him like this."

But I already know what I have to say. "This hole is now his grave."

Sara's brown eyes go wide. A motherly instinct, I can only assume. Even though I don't have any children myself, I do know the weight of being responsible for others. And Marcellus is a threat to those I care about, regardless of his connection to Sara.

Tears break free and trickle along her cheek. Stepping away from the hole, to avoid him seeing her, she says, "I can't stand by and let my son die. Yes, he belongs locked up—we made that call—but I can't sentence him to death."

I glance down. His body is all bone and sunken skin. A man barely hanging onto life. A part of me wonders if mercy now would only lead to vengeance later. Could he recover? Could he pose a threat again?

"Rune," she says gently. "I'm not asking to bring him with us to Bricen. But we are responsible for him. We should've been sending food and water."

"You mean *I* should've been sending food and water," I snap. "Because I'm the only one who can open a doorway to the Under Realm."

She nods. "Well, yes. Though I wouldn't ask you to be the one to *deliver* the supplies."

Frustration buzzes beneath my skin. But she's right. If we want this place to be his prison, then I am his warden.

With a flick of my wrist, I open a doorway to Bricen. "Fine. I'll stay here. You go get him something to eat and drink."

"I don't want your pity," Marcellus says, voice rasping. He lifts a trembling hand, holding up a small black beetle pinched between his fingers. "I don't need you." He swallowed it whole, his defiant glare mirroring many occasions I've spent with Adele's frequent stubbornness.

Sara hurries through the portal. I crouch at the edge of the hole, staring down at the dying man. "How does it feel to be forgotten?"

His smirk falters. His gaze drifts upward.

"There are no stars in this world. No moon. Nothing. I just lie here and stare into the void. Some days I don't even know if I'm dead or alive."

I scoff and say, "I have no sympathy for you."

"And I, none for you." His voice is weak but bitter.

"What does that mean?"

A hint of a smile pulls at his cracked lips. "If you've come to ask about my queen, I can't help you. I was never privy to her plans."

"But you were. You *knew* she wanted to rule the Starlight Realm."

He nods slowly. "And *you* brought her there." He wheezes a breath. "You know… it took lying here in silence to realize that Merigoth's power is beyond anything Adele or I ever imagined."

He's referring to Adele's attempt to trap Merigoth in a mental prison.

"Everything that's happening now…" He coughs, then takes a few deep breaths. "It's all because… she planned it that way."

I stand, rejecting his words. Refusing to believe they're true.

"You've lost her, haven't you?" he says with a sick grin. He coughs again, struggling to laugh. "You've already lost Adele."

Before I can respond, Sara returns through the portal, arms straining to carry three potato sacks stuffed with supplies. She drops them into the hole, near Marcellus's feet.

"Pace yourself," she says, breathing hard. "I don't know when I'll return with more."

She glances between us. "Uh… what did I miss? Why is he laughing?"

Without answering, I grab her arm and guide her back toward the portal. Behind us, Marcellus begins shouting, voice climbing into madness.

"She'll come for me! She'll come for me, you wait and—"

I snap my wrist and close the doorway, sealing off the Under Realm and his broken voice.

Turning to Sara, I say, "We need Adele. She's the only one who can help us track Merigoth down and end this. For good."

CHAPTER 22
ADELE

Commander Pavik and I burst into the open kitchen, swords swinging as the demon spirit flits past us, circling up along the ceiling in a swirl of dark smoke and shrill sound.

"Get everyone out!" I shout to my armed companion, pointing to the group of cowering servants huddled in the corner.

Sword raised like a shield, he hurries across the room and ushers the whimpering women out. Meanwhile, I scream and shout to draw the creature's attention. It's mostly smoke with beady red eyes glinting like embers. I remember the first time I encountered one of its kind, back when I first returned to Bricen. The village was under attack, something that supposedly happened often. Kit and I took out a few with steel blades and sharp arrows, but this one—this one is different.

This one, formerly inhabiting Alister, is faster. Smarter.

Commander Pavik returns to the fight, cautious and guarded, his eyes tracking the dark plume circling above us. "Now what?" he calls from the opposite side of the room. Smart. He's taking a flanking position.

"I'll draw its attention. When it comes at me, strike from behind."

He gives a small nod.

Waving my arms, sword swinging through the smoky air, I yell, "Hey! Over here! Looking for a new host? I'm right here, come and get it!"

I curse under my breath, hoping it's dumb enough to take the bait.

It locks its beady red eyes onto me before circling around the room with a shriek. The darkness within my mind wakens and reacts, blanketing my insides like a protective shield. I fear my darker side knows something I don't—a survival instinct of some kind kicking on.

The spirit swoops lower. Commander Pavik ducks his head as it comes at him. And this time, when it comes my way it meets my gaze. Something more than just its evil glare hits me—something unseen rips through my mind like a blade through flesh.

Pain explodes behind my eyes.

I scream. The sound rips from my throat, raw and endless—but even as my mouth hangs open, I can't hear it anymore. My vision blurs. My arms drop limp at my sides. The hilt of my sword slips from my grasp, steel clanking against stone.

My throat aches from screaming, yet I can't hear the cries any longer. And now, my jaw is locked. I can't close my mouth.

Pavik's muffled voice shouts from the other side of the room, and I barely make out his form coming closer. But it isn't him that I'm staring at anymore. It's a strange, yet mesmerizing dark spot in the center of my vision that has my attention. The tiny circle grows wider and wider, as if taking up more and more of my sight.

I've decided that there's nothing more I can do. My fight is over. The darkness within my mind is finally claiming my body as its own or the demon spirit is on its way into my body. Either way, this is my end. No goodbyes or final words.

My body sways, a numbness taking root, causing me to fall hard against the edge of a nearby table. There's no pain, no sorrow. Only a sense of displacement, as if I'm lost and can't remember where I'm supposed to go. So I lie still, crumpled up on the cold floor, waiting for someone to find me.

When one dies, what familiar solace comes to carry the soul to the stars? Would I even be accepted for final rest among them, or would the guardians at the gate turn me away? I fear the time I spent trying to redeem the souls I tortured wasn't enough. Not enough for forgiveness.

The void in my thoughts stretches on, timeless and silent—until a voice breaks through. A familiar voice. At first, I think it's Mum. But as it draws closer, a lump forms in my throat.

"You need to wake up," the voice says gently. "That was a close one, but it's not your time to join me in the stars."

I fight back the wave of emotion rising in my chest and manage a whisper. "Aunt Lauren?"

"Yes, my dear. It's me. I'm always with you, even when you can't see me."

A shimmering white form emerges from the void just as the darkness recedes. It's replaced by a memory—the riverbank near the cave that leads to the Under Realm. The light fades, and there she is. Aunt Lauren, arms open. Somehow, I have my body again, and I don't hesitate. I run straight into her embrace.

"I miss you so much." My voice comes out in a whisper. I try to sound strong, but seeing her again breaks every wall I've emotionally constructed to keep people from getting too close. My nose sniffles, and I try to hold back my tears. "I should've told you more about how much I appreciated you. Back when I was a kid and now…especially now."

My aunt runs a hand down my braid, her other arm wrapped tightly around me. "Shhh… I knew," she says softly. "I always knew you loved me. Even though you don't always show it, compassion is one of your strongest qualities. Not only for me, but for everyone you care about."

She steps back, brushing a stray blonde strand from my face. "Adele, you may not realize it, but your actions have always spoken louder than words. Everything you do to protect your friends and family tells us exactly how much you care. Even those you live among, in the village, you protect them too. That's your true nature—to protect."

I didn't think about it like that.

"You've come a long way from the sweet little girl who used to lie in the grass with me, listening to stories about the stars." She smiles warmly. "Don't ever doubt your choices. Trust your instincts. You always know what needs to be done. The only thing left," she pauses, "is to open your heart. Let yourself feel the other kind of love, too."

I sniff and nod. "Nathaniel."

"Yes, and with others. But especially Nathaniel. He has a good heart, Adele. Like you, he's trying to make things right."

I don't know how she knows about his past, and hearing her say he's one of the good ones… It shatters me to think if I die now, I'll never experience love.

"I'm going to find him," I say, voice trembling. "I'm going to tell him."

There's no need to say what. She knows.

"I love you, Adele."

I tighten my grip on her shoulders, desperate. "No. Please stay. Just a little longer."

But the river fades. The trees. Her face. All of it dissolves with an iridescent glow, and then—darkness again.

Blinking, I open my eyes to a stone ceiling above me.

A low groan escapes my lips as I try to sit up.

Many hands reach beneath my arms and back, helping me upright. Blinking through the blur, I see Commander Pavik standing over me.

"Adele, are you okay?"

I turn to my left and see Mum kneeling by my side. "What are you doing here?"

"I brought her," Rune says from my other side.

Facing my friend, I immediately notice her wings are concealed. "What of the demon spirit?"

"Rune threw a gust of air at it, veering it away from its intent to inhabit you." Mum looks me over again, one hand gripping my chin as she inspects my face. I'm too exhausted to pull away, so I let her survey the damage. "I swear, half of that thing was already in your mouth and down your throat," she adds, letting go of my face and standing with a hand out to me. I take it, and she helps me to my feet.

Rune stands close behind Mum and asks, "How do you feel?"

I take a moment to assess how I feel inside. "Normal, I think."

"I tried to find you," Mum says, eyes tearing up. "But you were too far gone." Her voice cracks, and she struggles to finish.

Rune's expression mirrors Mum's—deeply concerned. "We thought we lost you."

Pressing the palm of my gloved hand to my forehead, I explain, "I think I was dead—or on my way to being lost forever." I look at Mum. "Aunt Lauren saved me. She found me and led me back."

Mum presses a hand over her mouth, as if to hide the emotional pain of knowing her dear friend has helped me from the other side. Then she wraps her arms around me and whispers in my ear, "I'm so happy it was her who intervened and saved you. That sounds just like Lauren. She's only ever wanted to help people."

"I hate to break up the moment, but we have another problem to deal with." Rune clears her throat, as if to shake off the emotional moment to focus on whatever news she needs to share. "The reason we've come to see you."

Reaching out, I cup Rune's shoulder and then give it a gentle squeeze. "Your timing couldn't have been better. So, thank you. I owe you one."

"Well, good. Because we need you to come with us," Rune says, turning away and flicking her wrist across the kitchen. A giant oval doorway appears, her home world visible on the other side.

"Is that what I think it is?" Commander Pavik approaches the realm doorway, holding one hand out. Without asking, he slips it through, then back out. "Amazing." He looks to Rune. "Is it dangerous—"

She cuts him off. "No. Perfectly safe."

He shuffles his feet and faces her with brows pinched. "I was going to ask if it's dangerous for extended travel. Like if one is going back and forth through it often."

"The answer is still no." Rune turns away from him and awaits my answer.

"What's happened?" I ask, needing to know because there's definitely something off with my angel friend. Her tone's too sharp, her stance too tense. "Is Kit okay?"

"She's fine," Mum explains. "Evander's watching her back in Bricen."

"The problem is Merigoth has escaped." Rune doesn't even try to soften it. "And we think she's working with Aleksandra."

"What? That can't be." My attention darts between the two of them. "You're serious." When they both nod, I shake my head. "But I bound Merigoth to one of the strongest mental prisons I've ever constructed."

Rune throws up her arms. "I'm not saying you didn't. I'm telling you what we know. Merigoth's body is gone. Whether she's awake or not is still unclear. But Aleksandra has been compelling others, and she's been sneaking out of the city and venturing to dangerous parts of the realm."

There's something else she's not telling me. She's too angry, too eager—it's not just Merigoth. "What else aren't you saying?"

It's Mum who answers. "Elijah's missing."

A chill rushes through me.

This time, Rune reacts. A tear trickles down her cheek. She quickly wipes it away.

"I can't leave without finding Nathaniel first," I say.

Commander Pavik steps away from the doorway and stands outside our little huddle. "I can help with that. After I know the king and queen are safe, I will personally lead a team to find him. You have my word."

There's not much more I can do here that Pavik can't handle.

I take one last look at him, trusting him to do what I can't right now. Then I turn back to Mum and Rune. "Let's go. It's time to find out exactly what my dear sister is planning—and where Merigoth's hiding."

CHAPTER 23

ALEKSANDRA

She's gone. That insolent girl *left*.

"What are you looking for?" Elijah asks, leaning against a tree. Pale moonlight filters through breaks in the forest canopy, casting fractured light across the forest floor.

When I don't answer, he asks again, more forcefully, "Aleksandra! Answer me. What are you—"

"*Be silent!*" I snap, scanning the nearby woods for any sign Cameron might still be close. But there's nothing—no tracks, no aura, no hint of her presence. I drop my pack to the ground and hunch forward, resting my hands on my knees. My head has been pounding ever since I left the study. It's like a pulse behind my eyes, echoing my frustration.

Elijah pushes off the tree and steps toward me.

I rise quickly, too quickly. Pain lances through my skull, but I don't let it show. "Keep your distance."

He halts, shaking his head. "What happened, Aleksandra? Things were going well. You were making friends. Living a normal life. And—"

"Do you think I enjoyed *playing house* with you and Rune?" My voice turns sharp as a blade. "We are not family. I don't belong there. I don't belong *anywhere*."

The weight of my horns feels heavier than ever.

"Did you know," I add, quieter but colder, "that when I was a child, I tried to saw them off?"

His gaze lifts, searching for them even in the dim moonlight. "I didn't know that," he says gently. "No one should have to change themselves to fit in. You can't help how you were born. And I'm sorry you were mistreated."

"Mistreated." I taste the word like something rotten. *What a gentle, inadequate term for what I endured.*

A bird calls into the night, snapping me out of this meaningless exchange. Elijah is not my friend. He is not my confidant. Not anymore.

He's my *sacrifice* now.

Cameron's gone. So Elijah will have to do.

I grab the chains of his manacles and yank hard. "Come on. We need to move. I want to put distance between us and Stellara before the entire city comes searching."

Stumbling after me, he asks, "Where are we going?"

"To the Shadowlands."

There's no point in hiding it. Cameron stayed because of her curiosity. I can only hope Elijah's relentless need to protect others will keep him from trying to escape.

I just need to get him to the Bocnite. Then he can serve his true purpose.

The rest of the trek through the forest is grueling, but by dawn, we've reached the edge of the Shadowlands. The land stretches before us, bleak and dreary, with the sun at our backs. With the sunstones safely tucked in my pack, and my sacrifice at my side, a purr of anticipation thrums through me at how close I am to victory. We just have to make it through the jagged rock formations… and their deadly shadows.

Still rubbing my temples, the headache relentless, I explain the dangers ahead to Elijah.

Not wanting him to be harmed by these bothersome rock pillars, I explain, "Don't touch them. Somehow the stones immobilize a person while the shadows claim the soul. Or something to that effect. Cameron explained it, but I don't remember the details." Huffing out an exasperated sigh, I exclaim, "Just don't touch the damn rocks, okay!"

We stand there for a short moment, giving him time to observe the threat before us.

Elijah raises an eyebrow. "And you still want to go out there?"

I shrug and tug on his chains. "Let's not find out what happens if the shadows actually reach someone."

We step out from the field of ankle-high dead grass, and the brittle stalks crunching under our feet become dry dirt. This time, I watch my footing more carefully since I'm not sure Elijah would be as valiant as Cameron was in saving me.

An hour or two later, we reach the entrance to the cave.

"There," I say, pointing to the dark hole carved into the earth. "Go ahead."

Elijah peers into the darkness, hesitation clear in his posture. "There's a cave down there?"

"Yes. Slide down on your bottom. It's not that far."

Still bound, his metal chains clank as he sits awkwardly at the edge, trying to balance without full use of his hands. "Could you at least unlock these? I kind of need my hands."

"I didn't bring a key," I say before shoving him.

He yelps as he slides, twisting onto his side and absorbing the impact with his shoulder. I follow after him, sliding down the smooth rock until my boots touch the cave floor.

"That hurt," he mutters, pushing himself upright. "And seriously… Why wouldn't you bring a key?"

"It wasn't exactly a priority," I say, pulling a sunstone from my pack. The moment I squeeze it, the stone glows to life. "Come on. Keep up."

I lead the way, retracing the path Cameron and I once took, until we reach the stone door embedded into the cavern wall.

Elijah's eyes widen. "Whoa. What's behind *that*?"

Lifting the glowing sunstone, I reply, "We're about to find out."

I slide my hand into the nook embedded in the wall and set the sunstone into its place on the keyhold. I pull my hand back, watching closely. I brought every sunstone, unsure which one would work—but luck's on my side. This one responds.

A deep grinding echoes from behind the stone door. Elijah and I both step back as dust bursts from the seams, the mechanism unlocking with a slow, ancient groan.

When the grinding finally stops and the dust settles, I grip the massive iron handle and pull the door open. A rush of stale, cool air sweeps over us, carrying with it a low, haunting wail.

"I don't like this," Elijah whispers. "Let's get out of here. Whatever you're after… I don't want to be part of it."

"Too late," I say, yanking on his chains and dragging him into the darkness.

The moment we cross the threshold, a torch flares to life on the wall beside us. Then, in perfect rhythm, others ignite one by one, illuminating a carved stone tunnel stretching deep underground.

Elijah resists, but I pull harder on his shackles, dragging him like a stubborn goat.

"What exactly are you looking for down here?"

I ignore him as I study strange symbols carved into the wall at eye level. The markings are continuous, intertwining with one another in a straight, narrow path. "This way," I say.

"This way to what?" His footsteps scuff against the stone. "Aleksandra! Where are we going?"

"I need power." No reason to lie. Not anymore. We're here, at the edge of everything I've worked for. "I'm done being mistreated. Done being ignored. It'll be me who'll be commanding obedience from others."

"You don't have to do this," he says, voice low. "We can talk. Let me help you."

I spin on him, chains rattling. "There is no *we*, Elijah. You don't get to erase decades of pain in a few sweet words. You don't get to *fix* this."

I reach up, grab the base of one of my horns, and tug until pain shoots through my scalp. "You see this? This is what people fear. What they mock. My whole life has been about serving others—giving them power, bowing in humility while they stand above me."

Straightening my posture, I let the fire rise in my voice. "Well, it's my turn now. The Bocnite will give me everything I deserve."

He stares at me, sorrow carved into every line of his face. "You did have an awful upbringing," he says quietly. "But that's all in the past. You can choose to—"

"I don't want to hear it, Elijah!" I cut him off. "There's only one choice, and I've already made it." Something inside of me snaps, and my hand whips out, striking him across the face. He stumbles, catching himself with his bound hands.

His gaze, when lifted to me, shows hurt in his glistening eyes. "If you think that'll stop me from helping you, you're wrong," he says, standing tall. Then, unexpectedly, he steps past me. "I won't give up on you, Aleksandra. And if this is what it takes to prove that…" He looks back over his shoulder, the torchlight dancing in his eyes. "Then let's go."

CHAPTER 24
ALEKSANDRA

We continue at a steady pace forward, following the markings carved into the smooth walls of the tunnel lit by iron torches. The perfectly detailed chiseling where the walls meet the ceiling and floor is remarkable. It's almost as though we're inside a structure or building, but deep underground.

Elijah walks ahead, his chains clinking softly, his mumbling persistent. Words like *hope* and *friendship* bounce uselessly off the walls. I've stopped listening. My thoughts are with the sphere.

Bring me a sacrifice and I shall give you all the power you desire and more.

It's not only the power I want, but answers. Merigoth created me and my Shade siblings with hopes that we would do her bidding. But was that her plan from the start? The journal holds all the answers to my questions, yet I can't decipher her words. Cameron—I should've had her read more of the journal to me while I had her in my custody. It doesn't matter. Because once the darkness has been restored and I've been granted ultimate power, I won't need the journal.

I don't notice Elijah has stopped until I walk straight into his back. He barely moves, but I stumble slightly.

"Oomph. Watch it," I mutter, stepping around him.

Then I see why he's frozen.

The last torch flickers behind us, and ahead there is only darkness, swallowing the end of the tunnel.

"Please tell me we're not going in there," he says.

I reach into my pack and pull out one of the extra sunstones. With a firm squeeze, it comes to life, casting a warm yellow glow that pushes back the darkness around us.

"You're not scared, are you?" I ask, a smirk tugging at my lips.

"Yes," he says, without hesitation. "Yes, I am most certainly scared of whatever's waiting for us in there." No shame. Just truth.

He sighs, defeated. "Look… if you say whatever you're looking for is down there, then I'll go with you. I want to help you get past whatever it is you *think* you need. But don't lie to me anymore, Aleksandra. I need to know what to expect."

He turns to face me fully, his eyes catching the sunstone's light. "Now, tell me… Who or what are these *Bocnite*?"

Ever the father figure. Relentless, as always.

Staring into the endless dark, I adjust my pack on my shoulders and say, "I don't know anything about the Bocnite.

What I do know is they turned Merigoth by tainting her blood, turning her into the demon she is."

"I know that part," Elijah says. "But why come looking for them?"

I exhale, slow and deep. No more circling. "Power."

The chains of his shackles clink softly as he cups my shoulder. "It wasn't the Bocnite who took your abilities. It was Merigoth."

Dismissing his gesture, I approach the tunnel entrance, welcoming the cool air against my flushed skin. "They will give me what Merigoth took—and more."

"And more?" he questions.

I pivot sharply and face him head on. My glare cuts through the dim glow of the sunstone. I'm done playing the sweet, shattered girl. Done hiding behind a mask people find more palatable.

"Do you think I care what happens to you?" I snap.

He doesn't get a chance to answer. I let the rage swell up from the corners of my mind. From the places where I bury the truth, the real me, whenever someone expects a softer version.

"There isn't one person alive I care for," I hiss. "No friends. No attachments. No—"

"Family?" he finishes.

Untamed laughter bubbles out of me. It feels almost good, that rare taste of honesty. "I don't need a family. I need *allies*. And only those who devote their lives to serving me qualify as allies. People who *see* my potential and those who *fear* the consequences of denying it. I will rule. Not just one realm. *All* of them."

Elijah takes a small step back, chains rattling. "Why would anyone follow you?" he asks, quietly. "You hated how

Master Ebenus treated you. You hated how Sara left you. Why would you choose loneliness over the one thing you've always wanted? Happiness."

Enough.

His words cling like spider silk. Annoying. Sticky. Fragile.

I raise my arm and slap him—hard. The back of my hand strikes his cheek with a sharp *crack*, sending him stumbling. He catches himself against the tunnel wall, hand to his face.

"The only reason you're still breathing," I say coldly, "is because you serve a purpose. But test me again with your little speeches about 'a better life'—and I'll end you without a second thought."

He stares at me, eyes full of hurt he doesn't voice. Just nods, solemn and slow.

Wordlessly, he falls into step behind me.

And we enter the darkness, the sunstone's pale yellow light our only guide.

I've lost track of time. Could be an hour. Could be half a day since we entered the tunnel.

All I know is the air keeps getting colder. There's also this strange, musty, damp smell in the air, tinged with something sharp and acidic.

Elijah noticed it first. He pressed his nose to the wall like some kind of bloodhound and confirmed the smell was seeping out of the stone. He also pointed out the slick, viscous coating lining the tunnel walls, something that hadn't been there when we still had torches.

"For stars' sake, that rotting smell is getting stronger." He coughs, the sound echoing forward into blackness. "By the sound of it, this tunnel goes on forever."

I roll my eyes and counter, irritation slipping into my tone. "I *highly* doubt the tunnel goes on forever."

A strange chittering reverberates in the dark, high-pitched and too close.

We freeze. The sound comes again and Elijah ducks behind me, raising his shackled hands over his head.

He wasn't exaggerating about being scared.

"What's that sound?" he whispers, voice tight. His fingers are digging into my shoulder.

Slipping from his grasp, I say, "Come on." I doubt he'll turn back now. He's too scared to face the dark alone.

The chittering comes again, louder this time, and it's not ahead of us, but *all around* us.

"Stay close," I say, then start running. Elijah's boots are moving fast, right behind me. With the sunstone leading the way, I follow the curves of the tunnel, descending deeper and deeper underground. When I know we've put some distance between us and whatever was making that chittering sound, I slow.

"The rotten smell. It's gone," Elijah points out.

I hold my sunstone out, taking a few slow steps until the glow reaches beyond the tunnel walls. My breath catches. The tunnel opens up into a spacious cavern.

"Do you see that?" Elijah asks, inching forward. Chains rattle softly. He points ahead.

A pinprick of white light appears, piercing the dark. It grows slowly, pulsing brighter with each dragging sound, like someone pulling themselves along the dirt.

"We've not had visitors for some time," a gravelly voice calls out as more tiny lights flicker to life. The cavern blooms with a soft glow from hundreds of miniature sunstones, no larger than pebbles, scattered like stars across the walls and ceiling.

The cavern is comparable in size to the courtyard outside the garden area in Stellara. The ceiling, on the other hand—that rises well over three stories high.

"Hello?" I call out. "Are you the Bocnite?"

A pause. Then the voice answers. "Mmm. We are."

The white glow reveals the speaker: a hunched creature dragging a limp body. With a grunt, it drops whatever it's holding, a *thud* echoing through the cavern before it pockets its light source. Then it nudges the unconscious figure with its foot, rolling the body off the edge of a ledge.

I tense instantly. I didn't even notice the ledge. Only when I step closer and lift my sunstone do I see the chasm below.

Elijah notices too. His hand clamps around my arm with a grip like iron.

My gaze focuses on the underground creature.

I can't be sure, it appears to be a he but could also be a female. It stands just over half our height, its gray skin mottled and wet with inky trails that streak from its forehead down one cheek. Horns curl out from either side of its head, dark and ridged, framing pointed ears that jut out beneath thick curls of black hair.

Its clothing is torn along the edges. Rips along the sleeves and pants suggest long wear or rough battles. It finally turns its full attention to us, head tilting as if assessing.

Sizing us up.

"Who was that?" Elijah blurts.

"Doesn't matter," I snap, brushing off the question. I've got more important answers to find. With urgency, I retrieve the onyx sphere from my pack and hold it out to the creature. "Were you the one speaking to me through this?"

It reaches with a trembling hand, its slender gray fingers tipped with long, sharp nails. But I pull the sphere back before the Bocnite can touch it. The creature's hand retreats, but its dark eyes stay locked on the object. "Where did you get that, child of Loralai?"

"Loralai?" I echo, frowning.

Elijah leans in to whisper, "That was Merigoth's name… before she became the demon queen."

Of course. That makes sense.

"I am her descendant, yes," I say firmly. "That makes me your descendant too." I gesture to its horns, then to my own.

Its gaze lifts briefly, then returns to the sphere. "We are Bocnite. We do not live above—only below. You come from"—it points a gray finger to the cavern ceiling—"up there. You… are not Bocnite."

"I *am*!" I bellow in frustration, my voice carries up into the cavern. "Listen here, shorty… I've brought my sacrifice. I want what's owed to me!"

"Your *sacrifice*?" Elijah echoes behind me, his voice uncertain, a nervous laugh slipping through. "Aleksandra… what are you talking about?"

I ignore him. Right now, I only want to hear from the Bocnite. With all the confidence I can muster, given I've lost the darkness within, I demand, "Take me to the source. *Now!*" My voice booms through the cavern, making a few of the lights overhead flicker.

The creature raises its chin high, and repeats, "You are not Bocnite." Deep wrinkles crease across its pasty skin, signaling its age. It wipes the back of its hand across its forehead, smearing dark, sticky liquid down its face. "What you ask will only end with suffering. Now, *go away!*"

"You're absolutely right! I will make everyone suffer!"

The Bocnite slams its foot on the stone bridge we stand upon, and the entire cavern shakes from its powerful stomp. "You will not pass!"

And then I realize something. The limp, the smear of blood, the lifeless body dropped over the ledge. There was a fight. A brutal one, and this creature survived. It won.

The Bocnite's shoulders sag under the weight of exhaustion. With a weary sigh, it turns and walks away, leaving us standing in the flickering gloom.

It stops, nearly lost in the tunnel ahead, when a voice rises from the darkness behind us.

"I don't think so, old friend."

Spinning around, I squint into the passage we came from but see nothing. The voice is unfamiliar to me, but not to Elijah. He grabs my arm, his eyes wide, fixed on the void.

"Aleksandra," he whispers with urgency. "We need to go. *Now.*"

"Who is it?" I demand, frustrated that he knows what I don't. He doesn't answer. He just pulls me toward where the Bocnite was heading.

Then the Bocnite limps past us, its posture now straighter, renewed with a kind of desperate purpose. It plants itself between us and the voice, standing guard. "You are not welcome here!" it growls.

"Oh, sweet Oric," a woman coos from the shadows, her voice like warm silk. "There was a time you *enjoyed* my company."

My breath catches.

Merigoth.

"You've done enough, Loralai!" Oric snarls. "Leave this place now, or I'll—"

"You'll what?" Her voice is soft, lulling almost. Like a bed after a sleepless night.

My muscles relax and a haze takes hold of the corner of my vision.

Why was I so tense?

Elijah rubs his temples beside me, murmuring under his breath. "Not again… no, no, no." Then he pushes away from me and takes off, disappearing down the tunnel from where the Bocnite had emerged. "Aleksandra!" he calls. "Come on!"

But I don't move. Everything feels… safe here. Warm. Calm. What was I worried about?

I try to focus and remember. There was a conversation… a reason I came here…

Oric's voice cuts through my thoughts. He sounds extremely angry. "You're not welcome. *Go away!*"

He turns to leave, but then quickly whirls and faces the woman again, trembling with rage. "Get out of my head, you vile nuisance! Your mind games won't work on me!"

The Queen of the Under Realm steps out into the soft glow of the ceiling lights. She wears a wicked grin while her hands curl up against her chest. Her thin white hair falls around her horns and pointed ears. Her gray skin mirrors Oric's.

Merigoth glides past me without even a glance. She approaches Oric, who stands his ground, protecting the passage from her, though I don't understand why. We're all family. This is a wondrous reunion. I feel so much for both of them.

"Leave, Dark Ally." Oric withdraws a long dagger the length of his forearm. "That was my only warning."

Merigoth's voice drifts into my mind: *"Be still, child. I'll be with you in a moment."* She never looks away from Oric.

I nod and remain where I stand. There's no need to resist. I don't want to. She is family, and I would do anything for family.

I watch as she moves with an uncanny speed, too fast for the eyes to catch. In a swift, fluid motion, she snatches Oric's blade and drives it into his side. The Bocnite falls to his knees and then onto his other side, clutching the blade protruding from his body.

Then she gestures for me to follow with a simple wave.

And I do—because everything feels right.

CHAPTER 25
ADELE

Since we couldn't find Merigoth in the city, we've shifted our focus to Aleksandra and Elijah, assuming they're still together. Now, Mum and I trudge through dead grass in an open field, following the direction Rune gave us while she scouts from the sky above. At first, Mum thought our angel friend could open a doorway to the Shadowlands, but it turns out Rune can only create doorways between two places that she has either seen herself or been shown. Since no one has ever traveled beyond Stellara's borders, we're stuck making the journey on foot.

"I'm not saying it was your fault," Mum repeats, her tone weary with repetition. "But what if she found a weak spot in how you formed the mental prison?"

"It was fortified. The strongest bind I've ever created." I almost miss the forest trail we walked earlier, strange as it was. The trees there shimmered with a soft golden dust that rose into the air with the slightest touch. It was beautiful in a haunting way. Unlike the Under Realm's barren, molten landscape, that forest reminded me of the forest surrounding Bricen.

Mum takes a sip of her water before offering me some. Accepting the leather waterskin, I thank her, and she continues, "Well, her ability involves giving someone bliss, not doing what we do—manipulating the mind. That was…" She pauses, and I can only imagine the heartache she feels whenever she thinks about the son she abandoned.

"Mum!"

She blinks several times before looking my way.

"Marcellus might have helped her with trapping a person's will, but I don't think it was all him in doing so," I say. "Our abilities come from the same poison that infected her, which means maybe she can do more than just enchant people with bliss."

Mum reiterates the information out loud. "If she shares our mind-control abilities… maybe she freed herself." Then, narrowing her gaze, she whispers as if we're trading secrets, "You think Merigoth wanted you to entrap her?"

I shrug, then nod. "It's a possibility we have to consider."

After a moment of deliberation, she sighs. "Maybe."

No. It has to be the answer, because now that I think back, it was all too easy. Merigoth could've used her bliss on me to stop me, but she didn't. Instead, she chose to show me the moment the angels turned their backs on her. She'd been poisoned by something out here, and the leaders of the Starlight Realm banished her and left her to suffer and die.

I'm torn between feeling sorry for the demon queen and hating her for what she's done to my family and friends.

Mum seems to be deep in thought, too, when she whispers more to herself than to me, "We brought her to the one place she's been after from the start."

I rest a gloved hand on her shoulder, and when she looks at me, her inner turmoil shows in her glossy eyes and tense expression. "We couldn't have known. Not you, me, or Rune."

She nods, wiping the tears collecting under her eyes. "I just want us to live in peace. To never have to deal with Merigoth or any evil ever again."

Dropping my hand from her shoulder, I avert my gaze and search the sky for Rune while saying, "There will always be evil. It's all a matter of to what degree."

"How did you become such a wise girl at such a young age?" She offers me an unconvincing smile, then cups my cheek with her hand, drawing my attention from the sky to her. Her skin is soft, and I hold onto this moment, since I rarely feel anyone else's touch.

A shadow passes over the ground, and I look up again to see Rune circling above. "Let's not focus on what can't be changed. We need to find Aleksandra and Elijah. And then we'll search every inch of Stellara for Merigoth."

"We can't injure her without hurting Kit," Mum reminds me.

"Yeah. I know." The idea that my friend's life is on the line troubles me. I hate that we have to be careful about not hurting the demon queen to protect Kit. I can only hope a solution presents itself soon, because apparently, my mental prisons aren't as fortified as I thought.

With a forceful gust of air, Rune abruptly lands in front of us, crushing more than a few stalks of dead grass.

"Whoa!" She regains her balance and then faces us. "I almost missed the mark on that landing."

"Are you okay?" Mum asks.

Rune nods. "I'm distracted, that's all. Trying to figure out what Aleksandra's up to, where Merigoth went, the safety of the Stellara community, how we're going to save Kit, and poor Elijah." Her expression shifts, and I fear she's going to break down and cry.

"Hey!" I shout, cutting her off from continuing her doom-and-gloom list. "Let's focus on one thing at a time, okay?"

She rustles her feathers before tucking them behind her. Standing tall, more composed, she says in her leadership voice, "My apologies. I'll do better to control my emotions."

"Rune, it's okay to be upset," Mum chimes in.

My thoughts are contradictory to my mum's. Now is not the time to be letting our emotions get the better of us. We need to be prepared for anything, and that means keeping our wits sharp and attentive. While searching the Shadowlands, I ask, "Did you see anything?"

"They're not anywhere I can see," Rune says, standing by my side. "But I did spot a trail in the dry dirt. It was a clear path through the Shadowlands leading to a tunnel that goes underground. I'm going to guess it was left by Elijah."

That's great. More caves. Why are we always ending up inside a cave? After groaning in frustration, I ask the question I already know the answer to. "You think that's where the Bocnite live? Underground?"

Rune nods, adjusting the sword strapped at her waist and the bag slung over one shoulder. I'm not sure what's in the bag, but I saw her grab the blade before we left Stellara. As she touched the weapon, my hand moved instinctively to the hilt of my dagger. Silently, I wish I'd brought my bow and quiver.

Rune starts walking while saying, "If we keep a steady pace, we can reach it within the hour."

We fall in line behind her, letting her lead us toward the Shadowlands.

Less than ten minutes later, the Shadowlands come into view. The horizon is dotted with jagged black rocks that jut from the ground at strange angles. Their smooth sides glint faintly in the fading sun from behind us, and I can't help but wonder if they were carved and placed with intention rather than formed by nature. Then again, this isn't the Human Realm—what counts as "natural" here might follow rules I don't understand.

As we get closer, Rune warns us, "Don't touch the rocks."

Mum steps across the boundary, eyeing the nearest black pillar. "What are they?"

Rune points to the long shadow cast by one of them. "It's the shadows that are dangerous. I don't know how exactly, but my mother's old journals said they *consume* you."

"Consume, like… eat you?" I ask, pulling Mum back a step. "Or cover you like a blanket?"

Rune shrugs. "Let's not find out. Just don't touch the stones and stay out of the shadows."

Mum glances over her shoulder. "The sun doesn't reach this part of your world?"

Rune shakes her head. "No, not directly. The sun's path circles the northern hemisphere of our realm. There's a short stretch of the day where daylight reaches this part of the Shadowland, but the sky during those hours will never be any brighter than a hazy gray. For the rest of the terrain, it's covered in endless night, with only the stars twinkling above producing a slight overcast of light. But, you should know that the shadows from the spires aren't there because of sunlight. They're there because they're part of the curse of this land."

"Was the curse always there?" Mum asks, still examining the rocks.

"Stay close to me, and step where I step," Rune instructs. "My angel sight allows me to see better in the dark. And no, Sara. This land wasn't always cursed. Something poisoned this land, seeping deep within the earth. Now, if we want to get to the cave, we need to hurry and be careful."

"This keeps getting better and better," I say, following Rune out into the Shadowlands.

It doesn't take long for us to find the cave entrance Rune saw from the air. If Elijah is down there, we aren't far behind.

Without hesitation, Rune slides down the smooth rock slope into the dark. Mum follows right after her. I pause for just a moment and listen. I can't see into the dark, but I want to make sure no one is planning to sneak up behind us. When I'm sure we're not being followed, I lower myself onto the rock and slide into the unknown.

"Did anyone bring a way to see down here?" Mum's voice echoes faintly from my right.

There's a brief rustle as Rune digs through her shoulder bag. A soft yellow glow blooms in her hand, revealing a small, smooth orb.

"I brought a sunstone," she says. "They're usually used as keys—but they make decent torchlight too."

The light expands just enough to illuminate the landing beneath the cave entrance. We slowly turn in place, taking in the carved-out stone chamber around us. It's not large, but the precision of the cuts in the rock is unmistakable—this place was made, not formed.

Rune gestures for us to follow as she spots a narrow opening ahead.

The tunnel is tight. Rough edges of the rock brush my arms through my cloak as I squeeze through. Eventually, the tunnel opens into another small chamber. Rune raises the sunstone, casting its light on a towering stone door etched with symbols and grooves.

"I believe this is the doorway my mother sealed off, trapping the Bocnite from spreading the curse," Rune explains, running her fingers over the carvings.

There're torches already lit on the tunnel wall ahead. "I'll take the lead now," I say, and step through the doorway. The corridor's walls are smooth, every surface carefully chiseled.

From behind, Mum's voice echoes through the tunnel. "I hope Aleksandra and Elijah aren't in any trouble."

"Let's just hope the Bocnite haven't found them yet," Rune says, and I'm not sure if it's meant to reassure Mum or prepare her for what we might find." She then shares, "Stories of their kind were told to scare angels with hopes they wouldn't leave the city. Anyone who did leave and ventured too far… was never seen again."

"But there's no way to know what really happened to them, right?" Mum asks. Given everything she's witnessed in her lifetime, I don't blame her for entertaining other reasons they didn't return to Stellara. "Maybe they found a new place to live. Another hidden community."

We stop talking and focus on our path. The tunnel continues to slope downward, pulling us deeper underground. The torch lights end, and we continue in darkness, the only light coming from the small sunstone in Rune's hand. It isn't until we've cleared the horrible stench of something rotting that Rune stops cold.

We stand still and listen. A groan echoes up from somewhere ahead. In a panic, Rune takes off, rushing through the dark tunnel toward the aching moans.

A faint white glow greets us as we enter the cavern, the ceiling rising as high as a pine tree. I reach for Mum's arm, pointing toward the ground.

"It's a bridge—watch your step."

She kicks a few pebbles without realizing, sending them skittering off the edge. "Good to know. Thanks."

Rune and Mum rush ahead to the figure lying on the stone floor. I hang back, my eyes fixed on the creature, and judging by its shape—and its stillness—it must be a Bocnite. The walls and ceiling are speckled with glowing dots of light, just enough for me to see that it's definitely not human. Or angel.

"I think it's dead," Mum says, crouching near without touching it.

"No," the creature groans. "Not dead. Angry, yes. In pain, yes. But not dead."

Rune drops to her knees beside it and helps it sit up. The creature scoots backward, clutching its stomach until its back hits the wall.

"You mustn't follow," it begs with a heavy gasp. "Not allowed. Leave this place."

"Not until we find our people," Rune says firmly.

The Bocnite shakes its head. "Too late. She claimed one. Will find the other. Go. Live. Not die."

"Who is she?" I ask.

The creature, a halfling figure with gray skin and small horns protruding through tangled hair, doesn't respond. It stares blankly at the ceiling, groaning.

Mum gently lifts its hand from its side. Its skin is soaked in dark blood. She looks up at me and shakes her head. There's too much. We can't save it.

Rune pulls a dagger from inside her leather vest and slices the tip of her finger.

"We can't let them die down here," she says. "And if that means saving this demon creature, then so be it."

She presses her bleeding finger to the creature's lips, letting her blood drip into its mouth. "I don't know if this will work," she whispers, "but we have to try."

"We'll find Elijah," Mum says, resting a hand on Rune's shoulder.

Rune watches the wound on her finger close, already healed. "Can you tell us where they might be?" she asks the creature.

There's a long silence before it coughs and narrows its dark eyes at her.

"You're one of them," it rasps.

Rune says nothing but nods once. The Bocnite exhales, as though recognizing something. Its eyelids drift shut.

"Aye. Don't hurt us. Your kind… have done enough." Its voice is faint now, heavy with pain. "The Bocnite aren't your enemy. Wardens. That's all. Know your true enemy, and leave us Bocnite in peace."

"What does that mean?" I ask Rune.

She stares at the creature for a long beat before answering. "I will consider your words… but make no promises."

The Bocnite gives the faintest nod. "Oric. My name is Oric. And the gatekeeper room is where you will find her."

Mum rises and scans the shadowed tunnel ahead. "We need to find this gatekeeper's room."

I glance from Rune to Oric. "What does that mean—the Bocnite are wardens? I thought you said they were dangerous."

Rune gets to her feet, sliding her dagger back into its sheath. "Well, it appears there's a lot I don't actually know."

With a frustrated sigh, she strides past us and disappears into the dark tunnel. Her voice echoes behind her:

"Come on! We need to figure out what's really going on down here, and where Elijah and Aleksandra are!"

"Go. Find your friends," Oric mutters, waving us off weakly. "Be wary of the dark ally. My fate lies in the battle between shadows and stars."

The phrase catches me off guard. *The battle between shadows and stars.* I glance upward. The ceiling glitters with embedded sunstones, casting a soft, scattered light, like stars in a night sky.

"You two coming?" Rune calls, farther ahead now.

"Good luck," Mum says to Oric, then gestures for me to go first.

I don't hesitate.

We disappear into the dark, heading deeper underground, toward the Bocnite city.

CHAPTER 26

ELIJAH

Kit would be disappointed in me, knowing I ran, and worse, that I didn't wait to make sure Aleksandra was following me. Then again, my sister would also be the first one to remind me that being scared doesn't mean I'm weak.

But against Merigoth?

The trauma of the Under Realm still causes Kit to wake up screaming. I'm confident that she would've run too.

The metal edges of the shackles bite into my wrists as I shift behind the rock, trying to stay low. My breath comes fast, too loud in this deathly quiet. The pinpricks of light sparsely dotting the ceiling guide the way through the tunnel, but they don't do much to help me see the ground. Recalling how the Bocnite rolled its dead off into some unseen abyss, I'll have to be careful where I step.

I need to go back. What if Aleksandra needs me? I start to stand, but then an idea occurs to me… Maybe she doesn't need me to intervene. She's clearly more powerful than we initially believed. The struggle of what to do makes me want to scream.

Shaking off the annoyance of the girl's betrayal, I focus on what's important—making sure she's okay. My knees wobble as I try to rise from my crouch. I drop down, pressing my forehead to the cool rock. Breathe in. Out.

If Adele or Rune were here, they wouldn't hesitate. They'd charge in. Brave. Fearless.

But they're not here.

"Be strong. You can do this," I whisper, trying to believe my words. "Aleksandra may be in danger."

I shift again, about to make another attempt at moving, when Merigoth's voice slices through the silence of the tunnel. Every ounce of borrowed courage slips out of me, and I freeze.

"I don't blame you, my deary," the Queen of the Under Realm purrs. Her tone is soft, almost loving, but it drips with menace. "It's all about survival and control for you, isn't it?" she asks.

Then I hear Aleksandra's voice. "Yes. I want to control those who hurt me."

It sounds like her… but the edge is gone. It sounds like her, yet it doesn't. Aleksandra's words seem flat, missing the sharp wit and energy I know she possesses. And when Merigoth's silhouette glides past and I finally dare to peek out, I understand why.

Aleksandra follows with slow, meandering steps, her arms limp at her sides, her eyes unfocused—as though she's being led on an invisible leash.

A stone lodges in my throat.

Normally, I'd jump out, grab her, and make a run for it. But I can't. Not when I'm not sure she'd come willingly. Not when her mind might already belong to Merigoth.

My thoughts race, frantic. What can I do? What should I do? The questions spiral, but there's only ever been one answer.

I have to save her.

Still, my body remains rooted to the ground.

I stay motionless until their figures dissolve into the darkness ahead. My fingers tingle, a wave of pins and needles washing through them as I shake them awake, uncurling them from fists I didn't realize were clenched so tightly. The tension in my chest loosens just enough to let me breathe.

I stand, slow, shaky.

The cuffs rattle.

No one else is coming. There's only me.

And I refuse to abandon Aleksandra to Merigoth's control.

Keeping my distance, I follow Merigoth as she leads Aleksandra deeper into the tunnels. The ground slopes downward, pulling us farther underground. Every so often, a sharp clattering, like stone striking stone, echoes through the dark, startling me into stillness. I press against the rocky wall, listening. I have to assume Merigoth knows I'm following. I'm nowhere near as stealthy as Adele or Rune. Pebbles scatter beneath my boots, and these shackles aren't exactly quiet. But the queen never turns around or acknowledges my presence.

For now, I'll take it. Whatever game she's playing, I'm still in it. Still behind them. But the deeper we go, the more certain I am that neither Aleksandra nor I are getting out of here alive.

We round a bend, and the tunnel opens onto a ledge that overlooks a massive cavern. Below us, stone structures rise from the rock, carved directly into the earth. They're shaped like perfect boxes with small windows and narrow doors, the structures lining winding paths that snake through the underground city. Above, the faintly glowing rocks that dotted the tunnel ceiling now speckle the cavern roof in clusters. They're larger here, casting a pale light over the tops of the rectangular buildings. But their reach ends there. Everything below the rooftops lies in shadow.

I duck back into the tunnel as Merigoth and Aleksandra descend a staircase carved into the cavern wall. Once it's safe, I ease forward and watch from the ledge. Merigoth leads Aleksandra through the boxlike buildings, their figures slipping deeper into the gloom.

As soon as they vanish into the shadows, I hurry to follow. My footsteps are loud, echoing off the stone steps, but I don't care. I can't lose Aleksandra.

The strange rectangular shapes I'd seen from the ledge above were too vague to make sense of. But now, walking among them, I see the dark stone blocks are dwellings. What's even more unsettling is how empty the city is. Where are the Bocnite?

I keep moving, staying alert. If these creatures decide I'm a threat, they may ambush me from wherever they're hiding. As I walk deeper into the city, I notice more oddities.

There's no color. No decorations. Nothing lining the fronts of the homes. Not even curtains or coverings over the window holes. The same with the doorways. No actual doors. Anyone could come or go freely.

It's an eerie way to live. Too exposed for my liking.

A part of me wants to understand them. To know if they're a danger to Stellara now that the surface gate has been unlocked. Will they escape and try to enter the city? There must be a leader among them, someone who should be notified that the door has been opened. Maybe Rune and I can offer some guidance to those who want to live on the surface.

That's if I make it out alive.

I follow the path deeper into the stone city and stop at a wide staircase carved into the rock in the shape of a semicircle. It descends to a dark opening beneath the main city floor. A warm flicker of torchlight spills out.

Outside the door, I crouch low and peer inside. It's a large room with a low, concave ceiling. Merigoth stands at the rear, her back facing me, while Aleksandra stands a few feet from where I hide. I'm tempted to reach in and grab her, except Merigoth calls the girl forth.

"Kneel here, child." Merigoth's voice echoes through the chamber. From within Aleksandra's pack, she pulls out a black sphere.

Immediately I recognize that trinket from Aleksandra's dresser. She told me it was an old toy she and Sayen used to play with. What a fool I was to believe anything she said.

Aleksandra obeys and kneels at the center of a wide circle etched into the stone, its outer edge marked by a deep, deliberate groove that traces the boundary.

When Merigoth turns away again, I slip inside, clutching my shackles tight against my chest to keep them from giving away my position. I settle into the snug space behind one of the thick pillars that encircle the room. Each one is built from the same dry, dark stone as the rest of the city—except for the one Merigoth now faces. That pillar is smooth and glossy, like the black stones jutting from the ground in the Shadowlands above. She places the black sphere into a small carved-out space at waist height of the pillar.

I also note how there's not a single thing in here that I can use as a weapon.

"I bring you a gift," Merigoth calls while pressing both hands to the sleek pillar. A long pause follows before she speaks again. "I wish to finish what we started over a century ago." Another pause, then she speaks as if answering a voice I can't hear. "All of it. Drain yourself into me, and I shall give you what you want—and take what I am owed."

I need to help Aleksandra. The girl hasn't moved from where she kneels, unaware of what's about to happen to her. What would've happened to me if not for Merigoth intervening.

Shoving the thought aside, I focus on how to save Aleksandra. If I can just reach her, and then drag her away before she's offered up like some sacrificial prize…

Yes. It'll work.

Coming out from behind the pillar, I stay low, but as I approach the deep groove of the circle cut into the stone ground, inky strands of liquid rise up from within, floating into the air around Aleksandra. The tips eventually move inward, forming a spiral ring around her. The poor girl has no awareness of what's happening a mere breath away. The ends of the black strands snake up from the ground and fully encase Aleksandra.

Merigoth doesn't turn and keeps her hands pressed to the glossy, onyx-like stone, utterly focused.

I *have* to reach Aleksandra.

Creeping closer, I cross over the circle's threshold, and I'm immediately met by a rush of wind from the inky turbine. Using one hand to shield my eyes, I struggle to step closer.

Then, a commanding voice floats into my head. *"Leave now or be accepted into the offer."*

I shout into the rushing air, "No! I won't leave her!" My eyes strain to remain open as the air grows fiercer.

Merigoth turns to face me. The gusting wind lifts the thin white strands from her shoulders as her laughter echoes through the cavern. Her frail, bony arms stretch outward toward the carving that encircles the floor, and she shouts, "Take my offering, Shadowrock of the Starlight Realm! I shall give you your freedom, and you will give me the power to do so!"

Her laughter is cut short by the sickening sound of bone rattling against bone. I gasp as her enormous bone wings unfurl. The sight is both magnificent and horrifying.

My gaze snaps back to Aleksandra. The dark tendrils spiral faster, a vortex of inky chaos closing in on her where she remains kneeling in the center of the circle. The moment the black whirlwind makes contact, her head jerks back—and she screams.

Crawling forward against the force of the unnatural wind, I inch closer. The slick tendrils whip from the swirling dark and lash against Aleksandra, coating every inch of her exposed, pale skin.

"No! Please, stop!" I cry, reaching for Aleksandra with both hands, the metal chains of the shackles clanging in the wind. I'm not thinking about the consequences of touching her while the unnatural liquid coils over her skin. It doesn't matter that she betrayed us. No one deserves this. Her wrist is slick, coated in an evil substance that clings like icy clay beneath my fingers. I ignore the sensation of something crawling up over my skin. If I can save her, I'll endure it. I'm not leaving without her.

With a hard tug, I try to pull her away. Nothing. She won't budge. It's as though her body has been welded to the stone.

And then... her screams stop.

She goes still. Statue-like, with her head tilted back and mouth gaped open in a silent wail.

"Aleksandra! Can you hear me?" I rise to my feet and move closer, then crouch beside her. "Fight it! Whatever's happening, you have to fight it!"

Merigoth laughs. "Foolish boy. You cannot take back what has been offered!"

Her soulless gaze bores into mine, and for a second, panic claws at my gut. I want to run. To save myself from whatever is about to unfold. But Adele wouldn't run. Rune wouldn't run. Kit wouldn't run. And neither will I.

Shoving the fear down, I plant my feet.

"Take me instead!" I shout, my voice barely cutting through the winds that rage around us.

Aleksandra's body convulses. Her eyes are wide, locked on the stone ceiling. I stumble away, clutching my chest as the icy sensation recedes from my skin.

"The offering has been accepted!" Merigoth cries, voice rising in triumph. She throws her head back, mouth stretching unnaturally wide. Cracks split across her pallid skin, reopening old wounds. Black blood weeps from the seams, but she doesn't care.

The inky tendrils that burrowed into Aleksandra's skin twist their way out of her open mouth and into the air. They coil into a thick, writhing rope and drift toward Merigoth.

Scooting backward, I drag myself across the stone, desperate to put distance between me and whatever horror is unfolding. I tried. I *really* tried to save her.

After retreating to the pillar nearest the doorway, I cower and watch.

Merigoth sways, struggling to hold her footing as the darkness forces its way inside her body through her mouth. She braces herself, arms splayed wide—until the wind turns on her.

Her frail body is hurled backward, and it slams against the cavern wall before crumpling to the ground. A force I can't see flips her over, then pins her down as the tendrils continue pouring into her open mouth.

The last of the darkness escapes from Aleksandra's body, and she collapses to the ground. The remaining tendrils vanish down Merigoth's throat.

The room falls silent.

I leap to my feet and rush to Aleksandra's side. Brushing damp strands from her face, I pause. Her hair—once golden—is now gray, like that of an old woman. Thick curls have thinned into wiry strands, revealing the pale scalp at the base of her horns. Gently, I turn her face toward me. Wrinkles and age spots mark her skin, making her nearly unrecognizable—but I know it's her.

Behind us, Merigoth stirs. I don't have much time.

After sliding my hands under Aleksandra's arms, I drag her across the cold stone floor to the pillar farthest from the doorway, careful to avoid the strange onyx pillar a few feet away. Once we're securely hidden, I keep watch.

Merigoth is standing.

What I thought was a cloak draping her shoulders unfolds to her newly restored wings. A powerful, healthy laugh echoes through the chamber as she admires them. They still resemble angel wings in shape, but now they're covered in smooth, leathery skin, like those of a bat.

She gives her head a little shake, admiring the long golden waves of thick hair that spill over her shoulders. Her once-cracked gray skin is now healthy and flawless. She looks… restored. Something between angel and demon. The black horns remain, but they're no longer brittle or sickly.

"I will leave you to the Bocnite," she says, retrieving the onyx-like sphere from the pillar and carrying it off in both hands. I don't realize she's speaking to me until her black-filled eyes lock onto mine, finding me in the shadows.

"Tell Rune I'm coming. Tell her this realm is mine, as it always should have been. I'm sending the Bocnite to Stellara to hunt down anyone still living in the city. Tell her to leave this realm as it now belongs to me."

She strides across the room with determination, her confidence unwavering, and leaves us behind. I cradle Aleksandra in my lap, careful not to let the shackles or my chains touch her fragile form. "Oh, Aleksandra… What are we going to do now?"

CHAPTER 27
ADELE

We've been running up and down the narrow roads of the Bocnite city for over thirty minutes, and we still haven't found the gatekeeper's room. Rune even tried flying above the city, but the glow from the sunstones embedded in the cavern's dome barely reaches the tops of the structures. Everything below is shrouded in darkness. On foot, though, we have just enough light to make out the outlines of buildings and roads. It feels like that moment of the day when night threatens to fall at any second.

Rune says her vision can only pierce so far into the shadows, and her hearing picked up a strange sound earlier, something like strong wind, but it vanished just as quickly as it came. Now, Mum and I trail behind while Rune leads. All three of us are attentive, listening for any sign that might point us toward Elijah and Aleksandra.

Mum jogs ahead to speak with Rune, leaving me to take in the eerie stillness of the Bocnite city. The buildings look carved straight from the cavern stone, probably once part of the surface floor. The only illumination comes from above. There's no glass in the windows, no doors in the doorways. Just empty openings. We haven't seen a single Bocnite… or the dark ally.

But I have a suspicion.

If the dark ally is who I think it is—Merigoth—then maybe we've played straight into her hands. Maybe Mum's right. Maybe that mental prison I crafted for her wasn't as impenetrable as we believed. Maybe she let us think we'd won, only to guide us exactly where she wanted us all along.

"Psst."

The sound hisses from inside one of the nearby structures.

Rune and Mum don't seem to notice and continue moving farther down the road. I, on the other hand, stop cold and turn toward the open doorway. My hand moves to the hilt of my dagger, ready to draw.

"Hello?" I call quietly, peering into the dark.

"You shouldn't be here. Bocnite no like strangers." The voice is young, childlike.

"Come out," I demand, drawing Rune's and Mum's attention.

They both turn. Rune immediately stalks toward the building's entrance while Mum hurries over to my side.

"What is it? Did you see something?" Mum asks.

"I'm not sure. One of the Bocnite, I think." I inch closer as Rune peers through the dark entryway. "Anyone in there?" I call.

Rune shakes her head and returns to the road. "It's empty." With her enhanced vision, she'd see better than Mum or me.

"Go. Must leave," the Bocnite whispers again.

And now I see it.

A small figure stands against the back wall. Its pupilless black eyes gleam, even without the trace of light. Short, stubby horns poke through a thick mop of curls, and its gray skin blends almost seamlessly into the stone surroundings. The features are strikingly similar to Merigoth's, except this child's skin is smooth and healthy, not cracked or dried out.

I draw my dagger, then level the tip at the underground creature. It appears harmless. A girl, small and frail, but I know better. Appearances lie. None of the Fayatins who came to me for questioning ever guessed I was the infamous Interrogator.

"Come here," I say. "We need to see you better."

Both Rune and Mum draw their weapons. Rune's broad shortsword gleams, while Mum holds the Fayatin dagger I retrieved after chasing a guard through Bricen's hazy morning some time ago.

"I don't see anyone," Rune whispers.

"Oh, it's there," Mum says, peering through the open window. "You can't see her?"

"Oric will not be pleased," the Bocnite murmurs. She steps out of the shadows into the soft gray twilight. "Close the door. Don't let it out."

"You're not making any sense," I snap, glancing around to double-check if a door has somehow appeared—still nothing. Just the same open entryway. Irritation tightens in my chest at the girl's cryptic warnings. "There is no door!" I growl, scowling as I jab the tip of my dagger toward the empty doorway.

We're wasting time. We need to find Elijah.

Rune turns to me, tense. "Who are you talking to?"

Mum answers for me. "You don't see her? The Bocnite girl?"

"No." Rune tightens her grip on the hilt of her sword. "Why can't I see it?"

The Bocnite lifts a small hand and points at Rune. "Angel. Her kind is not welcome inside the city. Protection from the dark ally."

I relay the message to Rune, and she groans in frustration. Then I turn back to the Bocnite. "We need to find the gatekeeper's room. Can you show us? We'll leave as soon as we find our friend. He's not supposed to be here."

The creature's gaze flicks between me, Mum, and Rune before settling on me again. "You carry the blood of the dark ally." It's not a question. More like a quiet observation. I can only assume she's guessing based on why Mum and I can see her.

"The dark ally… is that Merigoth?" I ask.

She stares, motionless. After a pause, she slowly shakes her head.

"What about Loralai? Does that name mean anything?" Mum tries, keeping her voice calm.

The girl's black eyes widen, and she clasps her hands at her waist, wringing them as panic creeps in. "The dark ally! The dark ally!" she chants in a frantic singsong.

"Okay, settle down," I say, sliding my dagger back into its sheath. "Yes, Loralai's blood runs through our veins, but we're not her allies. We're here to stop her."

"Send Loralai away for good?"

I hesitate. I want to say *yes*. I want to promise her that. But how can I, when killing Merigoth could mean losing Kit too?

"We'll do everything we can to make sure she never returns to your city," I say, the words feeling both honest and uncertain.

The girl's fingers stop wringing. She lifts one hand, a signal to wait, then scurries across the room. Without hesitation, she starts digging at the base of the stone wall.

"Can someone tell me what's going on?" Rune mutters behind me.

"She's digging," Mum answers, watching closely. "Looks like they bury their belongings in the walls."

When the Bocnite girl returns, she holds a small stone box. Its lid sticks, but she eventually pries it open and sets it gently on the floor. From inside, she pulls out a flat stone carved with strange markings and holds it out to me.

"See Bocnite," she says, gesturing toward Rune.

An imbued stone. It must be enchanted to help Rune see what she otherwise can't. I accept it, then turn to Rune. "She says this will let you see the Bocnite while we're inside the city."

Rune sheathes her shortsword, eyes locked on the small black stone in my palm.

"We don't know what else that thing will do to me," she says. "Marcellus used one on Evander… and Aleksandra says the magic in these objects can vary depending on the carved symbols. So I'd rather not. We don't know if seeing Bocnite is all it'll do. I won't risk it."

She's not wrong. We have no way of knowing what other instructions are hidden in those etchings.

Trying to offer reassurance, I say, "Mum or I can take it off of you if anything goes wrong."

Rune stares at the stone for a long moment. Her fingers twitch toward it—then she draws back. "No. I don't want any magic clouding my judgment."

"Fine. For now." I pocket the stone and turn back to the Bocnite girl. "Where is the gatekeeper's room?"

The girl drops to her knees and stretches her hands out, palms down. Her eyes close, and her face settles into focus. Mum and I watch as the ground in front of her trembles, changing from hard stone into fine black sand. Then the sand begins to move, sculpting itself into a miniature version of the city surrounding us.

It's stunning. Controlled not with tools or words, but with thought.

"This is amazing," Mum whispers.

"Rune, you should really take the imbued stone. You're missing this." I offer it again.

Rune shakes her head, stepping away, and focuses on surveying the road behind us. "Just figure out where we're going. And hurry."

A tiny ball of sand forms. "We here," the Bocnite girl says, pointing to the ball.

On its own, it rolls down a street, takes a right, then a left, then continues straight before stopping at a semicircular stairwell descending toward a doorway.

"There," she says. "Gatekeeper's cavern."

"So—right, left, then straight," Mum repeats. "Got it. Let's go."

Before following, I crouch beside the Bocnite girl. "Thank you."

She looks up at me, face serious. "Run from Shadowrock. Shadowrock true enemy. Not Bocnite."

"I understand."

Then I rise and hurry to catch up with the others.

CHAPTER 28
RUNE

There's no way I'm putting one of those imbued stone charms anywhere near my body. My mind is my own. If that means I can't see the Bocnite, then so be it. Adele and Sara can. If there's a threat, they'll warn me. They'll be my eyes in this cursed underground world.

"Rune!" Adele calls, and I turn to face her. She and Sara have veered left, taking a narrow path off the main one. "This way."

My eyesight adjusted the moment we stepped into the dark tunnels above, but something about this place is different. The shadows here don't shift as they should. They linger unnaturally along the ground and hug the bases of buildings, thick and unmoving, as if the darkness is part of the stone itself.

"How much farther?" I ask, eyeing the walls. Smooth rock, etched with scattered symbols. They're not decorative. I'd say the symbols are more for identifiers meant to mark different buildings.

"Well, the last time I visited, it took me about ten minutes to reach," Adele says dryly.

"Now isn't the time to finally be cracking jokes, Adele," I say with a groan. Elijah could be injured or worse… but I don't want to think about the worse scenario.

Sara skids to a halt, raising a hand to warn us to be careful. "I think we're here."

Adele and I hurry to her side and peer around the corner.

An open space stretches out before us, nearly the size of the Green behind Goslings. Towering buildings ring the area, creating a fortress-like wall. One of the larger sunstones embedded in the cavern ceiling shines directly overhead, casting a pale glow that highlights the center of the courtyard.

"Are there any Bocnite here?" I ask. No point in searching the area myself.

Sara studies the shadows, then shakes her head. "None that I can see. Adele?"

Adele doesn't answer at first. She's focused on the open space, her eyes locked on the center of the courtyard. "No," she finally says. "But that's where we need to go. It's exactly what the Bocnite girl showed me in her map of the city."

We step out and approach the top of the broad steps that lead down to an open doorway. The stairs arc in a wide semicircle, almost like tiered seating in an amphitheater— built not just for descent, but for gathering. For watching.

The instant I hear a faint voice, I redirect my internal tethers to heighten my hearing.

"Hold on, okay? We'll figure this out. I'm not going to let you die."

I freeze.

His name slips from my lips. "Elijah."

Without hesitation, I bolt down the steps. "It's Elijah!" I shout over my shoulder. Adele's and Sara's footsteps thunder after mine.

Inside the carved circular chamber, stone columns line the room like silent sentinels. In the middle of the room, Elijah sits on the floor, holding someone in his arms.

We cross the chamber quickly. I drop to my knees in front of him, not even registering the Bocnite features of the person he cradles.

"Are you hurt?" I search his face. It's dirt-smeared, tear-streaked only, no injuries.

"You came," he whispers, voice hoarse. His gaze flicks to Adele and Sara, then returns to mine. "You're too late."

Sara covers her mouth, then moves closer. "Is that—?"

"Aleksandra," he says, the chains rattling as he gently lowers her to the floor.

I didn't recognize her. Her skin is a sickly gray, her once-sharp features dulled and sunken. Deep scratches mar her cheeks, and the horns atop her head have begun to peel—bits of them dry and brittle, flaking away like old bark.

Sara hurries and sits beside her daughter and immediately begins examining the damage. She pries open one of Aleksandra's eyes. She lets the lid fall shut again, then places her hand against the girl's face, focusing.

"She's still alive," Elijah says quietly.

Sara nods, removing her hand. "She is. But just barely."

Adele stands, scanning the room with guarded eyes. "What happened?"

Elijah doesn't answer right away. His expression reveals so much of his heartbreak, guilt, and exhaustion.

"I'm so sorry, Rune," he says, voice shaking. "I wanted to believe Aleksandra wasn't the villain. That if she could just see a better life, if someone believed in her…" His gaze falls to the girl lying on the floor. "I thought it would be enough. That her anger would fade."

He drops his head. "But this was her goal," he continues bitterly. "Well—not this exactly. But getting here. Gaining more power through this… Shadowrock."

"She had us all fooled," I say gently, tilting his chin up so he'll look at me. Our eyes meet. I want him to know he's not alone. After retrieving a small metal key from my pack, I release him from the shackles. They fall to the ground with a final *clank*. I love this man with every part of me, and seeing him shattered like this—hurt, betrayed, and carrying the weight of it all—it breaks my heart. That someone as kind as him was taken advantage of.

Going forward, if she survives, I will not allow Aleksandra to live in or visit the Starlight Realm. I'm done with being betrayed.

"Where is this Shadowrock now?" Adele asks, stepping around to stand behind her mother. "And what happened to Aleksandra?"

"Merigoth," Elijah seethes. "She caught up with us on the bridge before we entered the city. I…" He pauses, swallowing hard, clearly struggling to go on.

"What happened on the bridge?" Sara presses gently. "We saw a Bocnite lying there."

"I don't know." His voice drops, thick with shame. "I ran from the bridge, leaving Aleksandra to face Merigoth alone." Voice trembling, he barely gets out his next words. "I was a coward."

"No, you weren't!" I snap, sharper than intended. The man I love is anything but a coward. The things he's done for those he cares for aren't the actions of a weak man. Searching his kind eyes, I reassure him with a firm declaration, "Aleksandra did this"—I gesture to her afflicted form—"to herself. Had you'd stayed, you might be lying there bleeding out as well."

Adele sighs and uncrosses her arms. "Elijah, you did what you had to do. Now, come on. What happened next?"

Her impatience needles at me, stirring a quiet dread. We're already too late. Just looking at Aleksandra with her withered body and those peeling horns, it's evident Merigoth got what she came for. And if she was after power here, then Stellara is next. I silently thank the stars the city was evacuated. The angels that remain are safe in the Human Realm.

Elijah continues, his voice hoarse. "I followed them here. I didn't realize Merigoth had already taken control of Aleksandra's mind… not until it was too late. The poor girl didn't have a choice."

"What was Merigoth after?" Adele asks, her voice taut with restrained fury.

He points to the stone floor, where a circular seam cuts deep into the ground. "Merigoth had Aleksandra kneel in the center. And then she…" He turns his pointing finger toward the only pillar that stands apart from the rest with its smooth onyx surface. A round hole is carved into the stone at waist height.

Adele crosses the room and places a gloved hand inside the dark cavity. After feeling around the inside, she looks over and tells us, "There's nothing in it."

"Merigoth took the sphere that fit inside," Elijah explains. "I don't know what it was, but Aleksandra brought it here. She's had it with her this whole time."

"That black orb she keeps on her nightstand?" I ask, recalling the item Elijah's speaking of. "She said it was a toy she and Sayen used to play with."

Adele scowls and her gaze shifts to her sister's body, lying unconscious on the floor. "She lied to us all."

I move to the onyx pillar and inspect the hollow space. "This is a keyhold. Like the ones for our sunstones, except different. Merigoth must've known the sphere stone is a key."

"So if it's a key," Sara says, still on the floor by Aleksandra's side, "then it must unlock something."

"This *is* a gatekeeper's room," Adele adds. "Which means, whatever Merigoth unleashed was locked up here by the Bocnite."

Elijah rubs his wrists, the skin bruised and cut. "Merigoth called it 'Shadowrock.' It moves like black water… floating in the air."

Stretching her gloved hand, Adele grabs the hilt of her dagger and softly says, as if speaking to herself, "That's what the Bocnite child meant." She looks to me and clarifies, "The Bocnite aren't your enemy. Your mother had it wrong. This Shadowrock thing is your true enemy."

The room falls silent. Adele moves away from the pillar and heads to the main door we entered through, then surveys the Bocnite city beyond. Elijah returns to help lift Aleksandra, while Sara rises, staying close to her sick child.

Then, Adele's voice carries from the doorway. She's speaking to someone in a hushed conversation that I can't see. I'm assuming it's a Bocnite.

"Who is Adele talking to?" Elijah asks, craning his neck.

Sara glances toward the door. "There's an older Bocnite man with a long dark beard. He's standing outside the door. You can't see him. There's an enchantment over the city. Adele and I share Bocnite blood, so we're able to see them. Or at least… that's my guess."

While Adele speaks in private, I turn to Sara and Elijah. "We need to get back to Bricen and strategize how to save Kit and Stellara. We can't risk anyone else dying. We can't underestimate whatever power Merigoth has gained from this Shadowrock."

Adele returns, her expression grim. "The Bocnite man says the keystone can absorb the Shadowrock from Merigoth. Once it's contained in the keystone, we can return it here."

"Easier said than done," Elijah says, clear doubt etched into his face.

"Agreed," I say, because he's right. It may sound easy, but we'll have to figure out a way to get close enough to her without her enchanting all of us and claiming our wills for her own purpose.

Sara stands, wiping her hands on her pants. "We need to regroup and form a plan."

"We do. But first, there's more," Adele says with a sigh. "He told me the Shadowrock is nothing more than a phantom demon without a body."

"Did he say where it came from?" Sara asks.

Adele points toward the ceiling. "Somehow, Merigoth freed it from one of those Shadowland rocks we were trying to avoid touching."

I clear my throat, thinking about what my friend is saying. "So, the Bocnite messenger is telling you that Merigoth… back then, Loralai… Somehow withdrew the essence from one of those death rocks and—"

"And brought it down here. The Bocnite man explained that she didn't want to bring it back to Stellara, so she asked them to keep it here so she could study it. Something went wrong, and well, whatever happened next inflicted Merigoth with its poison. The Bocnite were able to lock it up here." Adele shifts her hand to point to the ground, in the circle. "He said when they went to speak with the Star Leaders of Stellara, they were met with hostility. The angels thought the Bocnite were going to attack and poison them like Merigoth."

"The Dark War," I whisper. "I remember those awful years. The many battles fought beyond the city borders. I was just a child."

"Well, the Bocnite lost. The angels locked them down here, and they've been in the dark ever since."

My insides feel as though they want to scream and cry all at the same time. The pain we caused these Bocnite wasn't justified. My mother jumped to conclusions without hearing their cause. Standing straight, I tell my friends, "We must make this right. Fix what the angels of the past did to these creatures."

Sara places her hand on my forearm. "We will. But first, let's get Aleksandra out of here and regroup with Evander and Gianna. We need to figure out what our next move is."

"Rune," Elijah says, cradling Aleksandra in his arms, "we can still save Stellara, but we need to regroup back in Bricen."

I nod and open a new doorway to Bricen. Evander and Gianna are there talking with a few of the villagers.

Before we even cross over, a tall broad-shouldered man wearing a long-sleeved tunic and a thick leather apron steps toward the doorway. The scowl on his face reflects the angry tone in his voice as he demands, "Where is my brother, Adele? Where is Nathaniel?"

CHAPTER 29
ADELE

Nathaniel. I hope Commander Pavik was able to find him. I won't let the guilt of leaving him in Fayatin consume me now.

I ignore Brandulf and move to the edge of the Green, pointing to my small cottage.

"Put Aleksandra in Selene's bed."

Elijah shifts her weight, cradled in his arms. "Once she's settled, I need to check on Kit."

Brandulf steps between us, his glare as sharp as his voice. "Where is my brother?"

His concern is justified, but he can wait two more seconds.

"Step aside," I say, jaw tightening. The darkness stirs, slithering down my arms like an old friend roused from sleep. My hands flex at his impatience. He doesn't miss the gesture and responds with a groan. I close the distance between myself and the towering man. His nostrils flare with every breath. When he opens his mouth to speak, I raise my bare hand mere inches from his face, ready to silence him.

His breath hitches.

I hold his gaze. "I don't think Nathaniel would like hearing how I had to restrain you because you have the patience of a child."

I have no intention of actually subduing this oaf, so I lower my hand and then slip my glove on. "Don't think I won't do it," I add, in case he thinks I'm getting soft. "Now step aside and let me finish speaking to Elijah."

After a few more seething breaths, Brandulf steps back. Tension still radiates off him like heat.

I return to Elijah. "Be careful with Kit. Merigoth—"

"I know, Adele." He exhales, shifting Aleksandra to a more comfortable hold. "She sees and hears everything."

Without another word, he turns and heads toward my home.

Mum appears beside me. "I'll go with him. I want to see if there's anything I can do for her."

"There might not be anything we can do," I admit, instantly regretting it.

She gives a quiet nod. "I know." In moments like this, when she's worn and deep in thought, I see the older version of myself reflected in her. She walks away, leaving me alone with the angels and one agitated blacksmith.

"What now?" the shorter angel asks, her name slipping my mind for a moment. Her wings are hidden, but I remember them being black, like her long, straight hair.

"We can't return to Stellara," Rune answers. "Merigoth has taken the city. She's sent an army of Bocnite into the city."

Evander reaches over and wraps his hand around the angel's fidgeting fingers. "It'll be okay, Gianna. We'll figure this out. All is not lost. Not yet."

Gianna. That's it. I've seen her enough times that I *should* remember her name.

"Adele." Brandulf's voice slices into my thoughts, my name laced with rising impatience.

"Your brother is fine," I say, barely looking at him, silently willing the stars to pull him back to his smithy. When he doesn't move, I spin to face him with more force than intended.

He straightens. His arms fall to his sides. If he's thinking of challenging me… The darkness within pulses again, eager to be unleashed.

"Adele," Rune warns. "Restrain yourself. People are nearby."

I glance to the left. She's right. One public misstep will undo all the effort I've put into earning their trust. Closing my eyes, I focus on my breathing and shove the darkness back. Before the moment gets awkward, I open my eyes, and with a calmness, say, "Listen, we've got a situation on our hands. Nathaniel is safe. He's with Selene at Castle Helve. So if you don't mind, we need to focus on stopping the evil that's happening over in the Starlight Realm."

"You speak the truth?" His voice is softer now. "My brother's unharmed? No danger in that ruthless country?"

I nod, firm. "I'll be returning to Fayatin soon."

He grumbles something under his breath and stalks toward the crows' shed, then leans against the wall. Still watching. Still *there*.

My insides teeter on the edge of fury. Just as I'm about to snap, Evander interrupts. "Brandulf, your help has been appreciated," he says, tone even. "We could use more eyes at the front gate if you're caught up with your work at the smithy."

Brandulf folds his thick arms across his chest and grunts a low, stubborn, "No." He doesn't move from the shed, eyes locked on us as if he's waiting for someone to push him.

"Leave him be," Rune cuts in, sharp. "We're wasting time."

She's right. As much as I want to let the darkness loose and show Brandulf what happens when someone challenges me, I rein it in. A few deep breaths, and I drag my focus back to the real threat.

"So," I say, turning to the group, "how do we get past the Bocnite?"

Evander glances at Rune, then at me. "I have an idea." He pauses, brows furrowing as the plan takes shape in his mind. "What if we *act* like we're going to fight our way in? Gather as many villagers and angels as we can. Make it *look* like we're launching an attack."

"Set up a camp outside Stellara," Rune adds. "Far enough to stay hidden, close enough to be seen. Create a distraction."

Gianna's expression tightens. "You want to use frightened villagers and weary angels to face the Bocnite from the Shadowlands?"

It's a bad idea. She's right. The villagers can't fight, and the angels are barely past their trauma from the Under Realm.

"No," Rune says before I can. "We won't risk them like that."

I nod and pivot the conversation. "Let's think ahead. How are we going to remove the Shadowrock from Merigoth? Once we have that figured out, we can work backward to the infiltration plan."

"You *can't* get to Merigoth without getting through the Boc—" Evander starts, but I raise a hand.

"I know, I know," I say. "But *if*—just if—we did get past them, then what? What happens *next*?"

Rune steps closer, her voice steady as she recalls what the Bocnite told me back in the gatekeeper's room. "Either you or Sara will need to make physical contact with Merigoth while holding the Bocnite keystone."

"Where is this keystone?" Evander asks.

"Hopefully with Merigoth," I say, my uncertainty a little too apparent. "Once we find it, I'll force the Shadowrock from her body and back into the keystone."

Rune holds up a hand and adds, "We still need to sever the connection between Merigoth and Kit before we end her once and for all."

"I can help with that," Mum says, coming up from behind me. We make room for her in our little circle, and she continues, "I can enter her mind and block her sight and hearing."

"You can do that?" I ask.

She nods. "It's quite similar to how I heal people with trauma or excessive fears." She then narrows her eyes at me and points out, "You would too, if you would show up more often for your training on healing people."

I can't help the eye roll and smirk that follows. "It doesn't come as naturally to me."

"Regardless," Rune cuts in, "Sara, you can make it so Merigoth can't hear or see through Kit?"

Mum nods. "But against Merigoth, I can't say how long the blocks will hold."

"It's a good advantage," I say. "Once I've removed the Shadowrock, and hopefully Merigoth is left in a weakened state, I can sever the connection between the two."

"You think that'll work?" Evander asks. "If you touch both Merigoth and Kit at the same time?"

I nod, even though I have no idea if it'll work.

"She's lying," Brandulf mutters from behind us.

"Ignore him," I mutter. "I'm sure it'll work. I just need my reach to be inside both of their minds in order to find the tether that connects them."

"Great," Gianna says with a heavy sigh. "Can we jump back to the part where you want us to *pretend* we're going to fight the Bocnite?"

Rune, Evander, and Gianna volley ideas back and forth, alternative plans because none of them seem eager to send innocent villagers or recovering angels into what could easily become a bloodbath.

Because let's be honest. If the Bocnite sense a threat, they may strike.

We need an army.

An army…

And then it hits me.

"Rune," I say, stepping forward, heart pounding with sudden clarity, "I think I know where we can get a *real* army."

All three angels turn toward me, curiosity flickering across their faces. Rune raises an eyebrow, voice cautious but intrigued. "And where might you be hiding an army?"

I can't help the small smile that curls at the edge of my mouth. "Let's just say someone recently offered me a position of power… one that *conveniently* comes with command over an army."

CHAPTER 30
ADELE

Castle Helve waits on the other side of Rune's doorway. It still amazes me how easy it is to go from Bricen to Fayatin by simply walking through a mystical portal.

"Should we come with you?" Rune asks, one hand drifting to the hilt of her sword.

I shake my head. "Thanks, but no. I don't plan on staying long. The goal is to find King Victor and Queen Selene—"

"Selene is a queen now?" Rune cuts in, clearly surprised.

"I wasn't expecting that," Evander adds. "She was here, not long ago. Helping Lau…" His words trail off. He sighs and looks away.

"It's okay," I say softly. "And yes, Selene was recently here helping Aunt Lauren."

"Sorry," he says, his voice sincere. "It's all still so soon—"

"Evander," I interrupt before the conversation takes a detour down an emotional rabbit hole. "It's fine. Can we please focus on getting an army?"

I turn back toward the doorway. A small cluster of Castle Helve guards move in on the Fayatin side, clad in leathers trimmed with midnight blue, staring at us with awe and uncertainty.

"Great," I mutter. "We've got an audience."

Rubbing my temples, I glance at Rune. "Your call if you want to leave the doorway open or close it. It shouldn't take me long to find the king, accept his offer, and gather the guards."

But the more I think about it, the more I realize this could take longer than I'd like. Rune's raised eyebrow tells me she's thinking the same thing.

"You sure about that?" she asks.

I groan and drop my shoulders. "No. Best to close the doorway."

I step through, and the guards on the other side jump back, gasping and muttering curses under their breath.

"Give me an hour, then come find me," I call back to Rune.

Brandulf steps up beside her. For a second, I think he might follow me through. "Bring Nathaniel home," he says.

I nod. I've learned not to make promises, especially ones I might not be able to keep.

With a fluid circular motion of her wrist, Rune closes the doorway behind me. The guards around me resume their gasps and whispers, as though I've brought a ghost into their midst.

My cloak flutters as I stride toward the stairwell. "Show's over!" I shout. "Get back to your posts!"

It doesn't take long to reach the tower's upper floor. The one with the locked chamber where I left the new royals and Fayatin lords. Two guards stand at attention on either side of the heavy wooden door. Muffled arguments filter out from within.

"I need to speak with King Victor," I tell them.

They remain still for a moment, until one finally nods and disappears inside. The other steps in front of the door, blocking my path.

The voices hush. A moment later, the door swings open and Commander Pavik greets me with a broad sweep of his arm. "Adele. You've returned."

The guard moves aside, and I step in. Inside, everything looks just as I left it—Victor, Selene, Lord Caldridge, and Lord Stolkin, all gathered in a tense cluster.

Selene stands by the window, a white handkerchief clenched in her hand. She rises the instant she sees me, her pale blue dress catching the light, a delicate crochet shawl draped over her shoulders.

"Adele! Oh, thank the stars someone is here to settle this debate."

She glides across the room, loops an arm through mine, and pulls me toward the center of the chamber.

"Please explain to these fine gentlemen that we need to focus on mending Fayatin's morale *before* crossing the Yasmin Sea to Noviska for trade talks."

Politics have never been my strong suit. That's why Mum stepped up as village leader after Trevor's death. She and Aunt Lauren made a strong team for Bricen. Now, with quiet grace, Evander has stepped in to lead alongside her, and I'm grateful he has.

From an outsider's perspective, what Selene says makes sense. "I agree with Selene."

My friend gently squeezes my forearm, her fingers pressing firm enough that I can feel them through my tunic's sleeve.

King Victor leans against a writing table, the center part lifted and propped into place, as if someone were in the process of writing a letter. He rests against the front edge, arms crossed over his loose tunic. The collar ties are unbound, hanging open so a good portion of his chest is exposed. "So, you'd rather see Fayatin's farmers and fishermen keep feeding the entire country, like they have for the past century?" He pushes off the table and strolls forward, tsking softly and shaking his head. "No, I'd think you, out of everyone in this room, would understand the condition of those farmlands and fishing posts."

He's not wrong. I've visited many of Fayatin's farms and fishing depots while under General Onica's command. The working and living conditions were worse than those in the desolate lands of the Under Realm—locals forced to labor in crumbling buildings and collapsing fields. The boats and docks along the marina are slimy and reek of rot.

"You're not wrong, either." I glance toward Lord Caldridge and Lord Stolkin. "And you have the counsel of those who are much older and wiser than we are. They've seen far more of the world than we have. I'd take their advice under consideration over ours."

It's probably not what Selene wants to hear, but it's the truth. If we can bring in food and resources for a time while

Victor focuses on rebuilding the farms and marinas, it'll benefit the country in the long haul.

Maybe Victor's actually going to do good for this country.

Selene's pleading expression shifts into a pout. I rest a gloved hand over hers, still gripping my arm, and explain gently, "Victor is thinking of the people. Signing a trade agreement with Noviska, and maybe even Harvesgrove, would temporarily alleviate the burden on the farmers and marinas. It would give them time to clean up, rebuild, and recover."

She glances between me and her husband. "Well, why didn't you explain it like that? I would've agreed with you if you had," she mumbles, releasing my arm. She folds her handkerchief into a neat little square and returns to her seat under the window.

The king looks to me. "I guess I not only need your skills as a general, but also as a translator." The lords sitting in their wingback chairs chuckle, amused at his playful poke at Selene.

The moment is short-lived, and Victor's gaze sharpens. The levity drains from his face. "I wasn't sure when you'd return. You left quite abruptly."

"My apologies. Something came up." My gaze finds Commander Pavik's for the briefest moment. He saw what happened in the castle kitchen—the demon spirit. He may not understand everything yet, but he's seen enough to know otherworldly threats exist.

Victor lets out a thoughtful *mhmm*. "And now you're ready to accept my offer of becoming my general to lead my army and be my trusted confidante."

Before stepping through Rune's portal, I decided to accept, because we need his army. But now that I'm here, I'm not so sure. Committing to this role feels too final. I'd be deceiving a man who seems genuinely committed to making Fayatin a better place.

"Can we come up with an alternative… a less permanent position?" I rush to continue before he can take offense. "It's not that I don't appreciate what you're doing for the country. I applaud your efforts and your goals. I truly do. But my home is with my family in Bricen."

I glance down at the stone floor, the weight of the moment settling in my chest. Accepting this role means more than leading his forces. It means choosing a kingdom, a ruler, a future… and possibly never returning home.

He waves a hand, gesturing for me to continue. "What kind of position?"

"Well," I begin, "as you just witnessed, I'm no good with political decisions. You clearly have a strong head on your shoulders for that. I'm willing to stay in Fayatin through the season and help your new general organize the guards for your united army."

Victor silently contemplates my offer, pacing the length of the hearth while rubbing his chin. When he stops, he asks, "And whom might you suggest I appoint to the general position?"

With a smirk, I reply, "I think you already know the answer to that."

We both turn to look at Commander Pavik. He's young, though older than me, but he's proven himself to be a capable leader these past few days. He's loyal, rational, and best of all, given their friendship, Pavik would speak honestly when it matters most.

Victor crosses his arms and counters by speaking his thoughts out loud. "I do worry that the regional lords won't see the union of guards for the good of the country if my man becomes their general." He stops pacing and looks at me. "They may see it as a power grab. Me wanting their men for my own self gain."

"If the only reason you wanted me as your general," I say, cutting in before Victor can respond, "was because of my abilities, then consider this—I no longer use my power to hurt innocent people. I won't ever be controlled like that again."

He understands what I'm really saying. If I agreed, he'd be getting me, the eighteen-year-old girl, not the infamous Interrogator. "I think you may need to rethink that, but I'll accept your conditions." Victor gives a slow nod, something shifting in his eyes. "What do you say, old friend?" he asks Pavik, his voice a mix of reluctant disappointment and hopeful enthusiasm.

Pavik crosses the room in two steady strides and stands at attention in front of the king. "It would be my honor to lead your army."

Thank the stars, I think, silently exhaling the tension I didn't realize I was holding. I escaped the commitment and can live my life with my family in Bricen.

The lords rise to their feet, offering congratulations to their new general. I clear my throat, drawing attention back to me. What I need to ask next… well, it's uncomfortable, to say the least.

I inhale deeply. "Now that all of that is settled," I begin, carefully choosing my words, "I need to ask a favor." I emphasize the last word, hoping they grasp just how reluctant I am to ask it.

All four men turn to face me. It's King Victor who speaks. "What is your request?"

"Commander—sorry, *General* Pavik—has seen firsthand the otherworldly threat my friends and I are up against. The demon spirit that forced you into hiding? That was only a glimpse… a very small part of something far greater."

Victor looks at his new general, who nods in confirmation that I'm telling the truth. The king turns back to me. "And how can we be of service to your cause?"

"There is," I pause, hoping I don't sound crazy, "an evil woman. Her name is Merigoth, and she's been infected with demon blood. Her power puts my abilities to shame." There's no lie there, as all this time I thought I'd constructed the most secure mental prison I'd ever woven. I shake the thought away.

"Anyway," I continue, "Merigoth, the Demon Queen of the Under Realm, has been ruling over a neighboring realm that's not of our world. It's where the demon spirit we fought off in the kitchen came from. A desolate world, without sun or plants. A dead realm."

Victor steps forward, curiosity flickering in his gaze. "And this demon queen—she's threatening *our* world?"

"Yes and no," I say. "She's escaped the Under Realm and is now invading a realm called the Starlight Realm, which is home to our angel friends. She wants to rule *their* world… and eventually, ours."

Victor glances at Pavik, then at his father and Lord Caldridge—before suddenly laughing. "Oh, Adele," he says with a shake of his head. "You *almost* had me believing you."

Selene shoots up from her chair beneath the window. "She's not lying! Some of the angels she speaks of… they're dear friends of mine, too."

Victor's laughter falters. He blinks, then stares at Selene with a wild mix of disbelief and dawning realization. Then his gaze finds me. "You're serious? You're saying there are other *worlds*, like beyond the seas, with mystical beings like demons and humans with wings?"

"Not across the seas," I correct him. "Not even in our world. These neighboring realms are only accessible through mystical doorways, opened by a power held by a single angel." I pause. "I know how it sounds."

"I've seen the doorway she speaks of," General Pavik adds, his voice steady. "She's telling the truth."

Victor studies us, the weight of everything hanging in the silence.

"What is your request?" he finally asks, standing tall with his chin raised high. He carries a tone that's tight with both impatience and curiosity.

"I need to borrow your army."

"*Borrow?*" Lord Stolkin echoes, eyes narrowing.

"The army you just denied leading as my general?" Victor clarifies.

"Yes. I only need to borrow them for a short duration. The demon queen has an army of underground beings guarding the angel city's entrance. We need your soldiers to act as a diversion, to set up camp near the outskirts and make it look like we're preparing a full assault."

Selene steps beside me, concern tightening her features. "Adele… that sounds dangerous."

I shake my head. "Not if we move quickly. The goal isn't to engage them. If we can reach the demon queen before she commands them to attack, there won't be a battle. The guards' only job is to appear threatening—to provide a distraction."

Pavik nods with approval. "It sounds like a well-thought-out plan."

Victor looks at his friend, dragging a hand through his disheveled hair. He's been hiding up here in this chamber for most of the day. "You think so?" he asks, voice low with uncertainty.

Pavik nods. "I've seen enough to know she's not lying."

"I have no reason to lie," I add quickly. "I'd give anything to be living a quiet life in a small village on the east side of Harvesgrove. Not fighting demon spirits or queens from dying realms."

Victor studies me a moment longer before saying, "I'll allow you access to the army—on two conditions."

Relief floods my chest. I'd braced for a refusal. "What are your conditions?"

"First, you must make your case to the men yourself. Only those who volunteer will join you. I won't force a single one."

That, I can work with. "I agree. And the second?"

A wicked smile spreads across his lips. "I'll need proof you can be trusted to bring them back unharmed."

"Proof?" I echo, not understanding.

"Well, not *proof*, exactly. A… task. One you'll complete for me before you leave." He leans in slightly. "There's a traitor to Fayatin. I want you to imprison him—in a mental prison."

I stiffen. "I told you, I won't use my abilities to harm or imprison anyone."

He raises a finger. "Ah—but what you said was that you won't use your powers on *innocent* people."

I hesitate. "That's… true."

"Good," he says, with chilling satisfaction. "Because this man is *far* from innocent. Deal with him, and you'll have your army based on those who willingly choose to follow you."

Victor and I lock eyes. I don't want to agree. But I'm running out of options—and time. Finally, I nod. "Who is this traitor you want me to incapacitate?"

Victor snaps his fingers at the guards. They bow and hurry out of the room.

Selene sits again, but something's shifted in her expression. The lines of her face are drawn tight with dread. Her gaze lowers, as though she already knows what's coming.

The door opens. Two guards step inside, dragging a beaten and bruised man between them.

They drop him into a chair in front of the fireplace.

My breath leaves me.

No.

I take a step forward, and my heart plummets while my anger rises. It's the man I love. Shattered. Bloodied. Barely conscious. And accused of treason.

CHAPTER 31
ADELE

Dropping to my knees, I search Nathaniel's bruised face. His head lolls to the side, and only when I grip his cheeks with my gloved hands does he stir, mumbling incoherently.

"You've got the wrong man," he whispers.

"Nathaniel, it's me. Adele."

He tries to open his eyes, but they're blackened and swollen shut.

I shoot to my feet, rage boiling through me. I'm about to lunge for Victor when one of the guards grabs my arm. In a fluid motion, I twist free, spin behind him, and toss one glove to the ground. My bare hand finds the back of his neck.

Sleep, I command silently.

His body crumples, sword clattering against the stone floor.

The second guard steps closer, uncertain.

"Touch me," I warn, "and you'll end up like your friend."

He halts, one hand hovering near his weapon.

General Pavik quickly steps between me and Victor. "Adele, it's not our fault you keep company with traitors."

"He's not a traitor!" I shout. I peel off my other glove and let it drop. "He was here as *my* guest."

Victor's voice cuts through the tension from across the room. "Ah, but did you know he was a Fayatin guard and betrayed his assigned post? He and his brother attacked the guards at the trading depot near the northern mines. It's all in the records about how they robbed the supply station and fled the country."

"That's a lie! Whatever's in your records has been falsified. Nathaniel told me about serving under General Onica and how he used *his own rations* to buy boots and clothing for the miners. And when his older brother—"

"Adele," Nathaniel croaks, voice thick with pain, "don't… it's fine."

"No. It's *not* fine," I say, turning to him. "You weren't the one in the wrong. You were trying to *help* those people."

Fury bubbles inside me, near eruption—until my gaze lands on Selene.

She's seated again, knuckles white around a twisted handkerchief.

"Did you know?" I ask, my voice cracking. "Did you know they were beating him?"

Selene's eyes brim with tears. "Adele… please. Think of Rune and Stellara."

Nathaniel groans. "Adele," he calls, more lucid now.

"He's not a traitor!" My heart pounds furiously, shaking my whole body. "Set him free, or I'll—"

"Adele, no!" Selene pleads at the same time Victor growls, "Or you'll what?"

General Pavik lifts a calming hand. "Adele, it's your word against our records. Using force won't help your cause. If you want His Majesty's army, you'll need to prove we can trust you."

I glare at him, clenching my fists. He's not wrong, but neither is Nathaniel.

"Adele," Nathaniel calls again, weaker now. I kneel beside him, brushing his hair from his forehead. "I'm in a lot of pain," he says, breath shallow. "If you don't do what they ask… the beatings won't stop."

Tears sting my eyes. "No. I won't torture you."

Victor's voice rings out, sharp and cold. "You will bind his mind if you want my permission to *borrow* my army."

There it is. The Victor I remember—the entitled, arrogant boy I met under General Onica's command. He may wear a crown now, may talk of unity and rebuilding. But this—this cruelty—shows he hasn't changed.

I rise to my feet. My voice is steady now. "Fine. I'll do it. But you *swear* to me that no harm will come to him while he's imprisoned. And when I return your army, you'll return *him*. Alive. Whole. Just as he is now."

Victor smiles. "Agreed. Now, get on with it."

I turn back to Nathaniel. "I'm so sorry," I whisper.

He tries to smile, but flinches from the pain. "Think of it this way… I'll have time to rest. You go save Stellara. I'll be here when you get back."

My hands tremble as I cradle his face—his beautiful, bloodied face.

Please, I beg the darkness within me. *Be gentle.*

The reach stirs, answering my call like a coiled shadow slipping forward. I guide it softly, carefully, pleading with it to treat Nathaniel as Mum would in healing, not in harm. I'll not let it show him nightmares or trap him in terror.

My heart is overjoyed with relief when my reach pulls forth a memory of Bricen. It's a warm spring day, and Nathaniel is lying in the lush grass of the Green.

"This is actually quite nice," he says, taking in his surroundings. "I don't feel any of the pain or the world outside."

I lower myself next to him, and he sits up so we're facing one another.

"I'm so sorry this is happening to you," I say.

"It's not your fault. Brandulf and I assumed the guards would tell a different story than what really happened. I mean, I probably would've too, if it meant avoiding trouble with our lead commander."

"That's not the point," I say. "And you know I would've fought them all for you, right? But—"

"But you need his men. I understand, Adele."

He raises his arms toward the warm, sunny sky. "This isn't so bad." He gives me a wink, adding, "It's like a secret hiding spot where no one can find us."

"Well, we're not hiding. We're still in the chamber room with everyone watching."

Then he does something that completely catches me off guard. He drops his arms and takes my bare hands into his. I flinch, about to pull them away, but he holds them tightly.

"Oh, no you don't. You're already in my mind. You can't hurt me—"

He suddenly winces. "Ouch!"

After pulling one hand away, he rubs at his forehead.

"Sorry," I say, then silently scold my reach for its subtle reminder that it can hurt him if it chooses. "The darkness in me sometimes has a mind of its own."

"Is that right? Good to know." He slips his hand back into mine. "Please go and help your friends. There's nothing more you can do for me. I'll be here when you defeat Merigoth and return with Victor's army."

"What if we don't win? What if the Bocnite attack and Victor's army actually has to fight?"

He smiles and leans in close. "I believe in you, Adele. You, Rune, Elijah, Evander, your mum, and Kit. You'll come together and win. I know you will."

"I've never felt this livid before. It's a different kind of anger than I've ever felt."

He squeezes my hand. "That's because it's not just anger—it's fear of losing someone you love. It feels heavier, doesn't it?"

The darkness pulses in agreement.

"Adele," he continues, "leave me here and go help save Stellara."

Sniffling, I close the space between us and kiss him. The moment our lips touch, I understand what it means to love someone. I'd do anything for him, because the hum of excitement within me from our mouths pressed together is something worth fighting for. And I want nothing more than to spend hours exploring this new feeling.

When we break apart, his smile warms my heart.

"I'll expect a real live kiss when you come to wake me up."

"Agreed," I say, getting to my feet. "And you're right. I do love you."

He lies back in the green grass, folding his arms behind his head. "See you soon." The sunbeams grow brighter, overtaking the scene and pushing me from the safe space in his mind.

I open my eyes and stare down at Nathaniel's unconscious body, slumped over in the chair.

Wiping my eyes, I turn to the others in the room. "It's done. I expect him to be kept in comfort until I return." I take two steps forward, General Pavik still standing between me and Victor. Locking eyes with the king, I say, "If you ever force me to do that again, I will come for you—and personally show you what the darkness in me can do."

He doesn't respond with words—just a solemn nod.

"Let's go see about getting you an army," General Pavik says, swinging his arm toward the door.

"Yes. Let's," I seethe, then storm out.

CHAPTER 32

Aleksandra

Why do I feel so weak? I'm supposed to be strong. Powerful. I was supposed to—

Ow. My head throbs. My arm feels so heavy. Too heavy. I can barely lift it. What's wrong with me?

"Careful. Don't move around too much," a familiar voice says.

"Elijah?" I rasp, struggling to open my eyes. "Where are we?"

"We're in Bricen," he replies. "You… you had an encounter with Merigoth."

A cold, damp cloth touches my forehead, and I flinch from the sudden chill.

"What are you doing to me?"

"Trying to clean you up."

"Why does my body hurt all over?"

He lets out a deep breath. "Were you really going to offer me to that Shadowrock spirit?"

"It's not a spirit," I murmur, attempting to roll away, but my limbs ache too much to move. "It's the essence of one of those rocks from the surface. They don't have bodies like us. Instead, they're created to live out their days in those stones spread out throughout the Shadowlands."

Silence falls between us. I brace myself for another chill from the cloth, but it doesn't come. Too much time passes, the quiet stretching unnervingly.

"If you're waiting for an apology," I say finally, "I don't have one. Yes, I was going to give you to the Shadowrock, even though I didn't know what it would do to you."

"I trusted you," he says, his voice catching. He quickly adds, "And before you bring up how you've been abused and mistreated your whole life, so you don't know any better, I just want you to know something. No matter what's happened to you, you *do* have a choice. We tried to give you that. But you've been so focused on vengeance, on proving to your abusers that you're more than what they said you were."

"Elijah…" I whisper. "I don't know any other way. You say I have a choice, but how can someone choose well when they're filled with anger and revenge?"

"I don't know," he says quietly. "I guess it's hard. But if you *know* your anger is leading your choices, if you can recognize that, then you have the power to stop and choose differently. That awareness means you're capable of more."

A knock on the cottage door saves me from having to answer.

"Come in," Elijah calls.

The door creaks open. A young voice says, "I brought fresh water and clean rags."

"Thank you," Elijah replies. "You can set them here."

There's movement, the sound of sloshing water.

"Can I stay and help?" the girl asks.

This time, I recognize the voice. *Magdala.* Tall, quick-footed, with long, light brown hair—one of the fastest kids in the village. I wish I could see her face, but I still don't have the strength to open my eyes.

"Of course," Elijah says.

Chairs scrape against the floor. Then the cool rag returns, brushing against my skin. A wave of embarrassment washes over me, but I remember how this child once showed me compassion. My horns scared her at first. But now… she doesn't see them. She sees *me*. Could it really be possible to be accepted here? To live a normal life among these people?

"Aleksandra?" Magdala's voice cuts through my thoughts. "My mum made some vegetable stew. Do you want a bowl? Are you hungry?"

Her kindness brings tears to my eyes. I can feel them slipping free, even though I still can't see her. "That would be nice," I whisper.

The chair scrapes back sharply.

"Whoa! Slow down, Magdala!" Elijah warns. "You're going to knock over the water bowl."

"Sorry!" she says, giggling. The door opens, letting in a cool breeze that carries the scent of the smithy's fire. "I'll be back, Aleksandra! I'll bring you a fresh roll too!" The door closes behind her.

"She really looks up to you, you know that, right?" Elijah says as he wrings out the rag, droplets pattering into the bowl.

"Well, she shouldn't."

"You're not wrong," he replies. The bitterness in his voice stings, but I understand it.

The door opens again, and I brace myself. Another visitor, come to gawk at the defeated demon girl. This voice I recognize immediately.

"I'm here to take over. Sara needs your help with Kit."

"Okay. She's out of danger, even if it doesn't look it," Elijah replies, stepping away from my side.

"Hey, Gianna," I say softly.

"Don't 'hey' me," she snaps. "What you did could've destroyed everything. I'm not as forgiving as Elijah. His heart's too good for his own sake."

I sigh, knowing she's right. "You don't have to stay."

"You're right," she says. "I don't. But I *choose* to. If Elijah's not giving up on you, then neither am I."

I don't deserve it. But I thank her anyway. "I have a lot to think about. About the kind of future I want to live."

She doesn't respond. I can't see her, so I have to trust that she won't take this chance to end my life before I've had the chance to change it.

She continues tending to my wounds in silence. I say nothing more. But inwardly, I pray to the stars that my sister finds Merigoth… and makes her pay for what she's done.

CHAPTER 33

ADELE

Whenever General Onica spoke to a large crowd or addressed her guards, I hid in the shadows, unwilling to be seen or bear the weight of so many eyes. She loved the attention and thrived on the bowing, the obedience, the applause for her battle cries and promises of victory. Hearing those lackeys cheer her on always turned my stomach.

And now, here I am about to do the same thing.

I'm supposed to give a speech. Rally the guards. Tell them we're off to save a realm. There's no way they'll believe a word I say. Doubt coils in my gut, and I'm starting to wonder if this entire plan was a mistake.

"You'll be fine," General Pavik says beside me as we descend the hillside from Castle Helve. He's exchanged his leather armor for the navy coat Victor had tailored. A formal garment with gold trim that signals his new rank.

"That's easy for you to say," I mutter. "You don't have to convince a bunch of disgruntled guards to fight something that sounds straight out of a children's fairy tale."

He chuckles. "You're not wrong, my friend."

The word *friend* hits strange. We're not there yet. But I let him keep his illusions.

As we walk through the encampment, soldiers turn to watch us. Some are sharpening weapons, while others are chatting or playing games. One by one, they fall in behind us, curiosity piqued by our unexpected arrival.

Word spreads fast. Soon we're met by the regional lords, all lined up with their advisers flanking them.

"The Interrogator has graced us again," Lord Houfston announces, arms wide, voice loud. "Have you come to put us in our rightful place? Force us to kneel to a king we didn't choose?"

"Whether you agreed or not—" Pavik starts, his voice booming, but I raise a gloved hand to silence him. He groans, stepping back.

Lord Houfston continues, his tone bitter. "We will not submit. Not to Victor Stolkin," he says the name as if it burns, "and not to you, demon-blooded Interrogator."

Around us, guards cheer and raise weapons, their cries echoing across the hill.

Then another lord speaks. This one I'm familiar with from my time under General Onica. Lord Bivven, I believe. The older man with hints of youthful red hair still clinging to his head focuses his gaze on Pavik and me. "Not all of us share Houfston's view. Our loyalty lies with our regions, not sides. We want only what's best for our people."

Pavik gives Lord Bivven a nod of appreciation. A quiet understanding passes between them, but I'm not one to guess at hidden meanings. I've heard enough.

I step forward, voice steady. "I'm not here as the Interrogator. I'm here to ask for your help."

That stuns them. Even the lords seem caught off guard, everyone except Houfston, who narrows his eyes at me.

"I know this sounds impossible," I continue, projecting my voice. "But there's a threat to a neighboring realm. I'm asking any able body, anyone willing to fight for something bigger than our petty wars, to step forward."

Silence answers me.

No one moves.

Disappointment sinks into my chest. I thought this would go better.

"Maybe I'm not explaining it clearly," I say, pushing forward. "There's a demon queen. She's commanding an army of underground creatures to invade a city that doesn't belong to her. It belongs to our allies, the angels."

The moment I say the words *demons* and *angels*, confused murmurs ripple throughout the crowd. Disbelief, suspicion.

"She speaks the truth!" Pavik shouts. "I've seen the magic doorway with my own eyes."

Still, the lords shake their heads, and shouts rise from the crowd.

"You're lying!"

"There's no such thing as angels!"

"What's your real agenda?"

A clear voice rises above them—Rune's.

"Angels are real!" she says loud enough for the men in the back to hear. "And we are not to be feared."

She moves to my side, Evander flanking her opposite. After a nod between us, she addresses the guards directly.

"My name is Rune. I'm one of the leaders of the Starlight Realm. What Adele said is true. Our home has been taken. We need your help, not to fight our enemies directly, but to create a diversion. A distraction. To make it *look* like we're preparing for battle while we sneak past and end this without bloodshed."

"You look normal!" a lord calls, waving toward her.

Rune glances at Evander, who nods. In one fluid motion, they both unfold their wings.

Gasps ripple through the crowd. Some men curse. Swords come free of scabbards.

Rune keeps her composure. With a flick of her wrist, a portal blooms open in the air above us, showing a luminous realm beyond.

"This is our world," she says. "The Starlight Realm. And it's under attack."

"You're the human bird who attacked Lord Houfston!" someone shouts.

She closes the portal and tucks in her wings, stepping toward Houfston. "Yes, I did. After he locked two of my friends in a cage. Would you not do the same if someone stole your own?"

That sobers the crowd. The shouting dies.

Rune walks right up to Houfston, who retreats behind a guard. "Nice to see you again," she says. "I hope you're done invading other people's homes."

"You don't scare me!" he snaps.

"I'm not trying to," she replies. "I'm asking for your help."

"The answer is no!"

Rune shrugs, glancing back at me. *Oh well.* Then she turns to the rest of the crowd.

"What about everyone else?"

There's a long pause. Then Lord Bivven shouts, "My men are free to choose! I won't stop them!" This prompts a few guards to move through the crowd, maneuvering to the front. Then more lords offer similar permissions.

"We thank you," I tell them. "Once this is over, we'll bring you back safely. Pack your tents, ready your weapons, and meet us here in one hour."

The crowd disperses, and we regroup, joined by a few of the supportive lords.

Pavik addresses them. "Victor doesn't seek to take your armies. But if a time comes when our regions must unite, he hopes you'll be willing. Like you are doing now, for the greater good."

"Moving on," I say, shifting the focus, "let's talk about how we save the Starlight Realm."

"The plan is simple," Rune explains. "We camp just outside the city, close enough for the Bocnite to notice. We draw their attention while Adele and the others sneak in."

"Who are the Bocnite?" Lord Bivven asks.

"They're the underground creatures being controlled by the demon queen," Rune says. "They're victims, like us. We don't want to hurt them. That's why the distraction is so important."

Pavik continues to speak with the lords while I look to Rune and ask, "Where's Elijah?"

"With Sara," Evander replies. "Helping prep Kit."

"Then let's move. We've got a queen to stop."

CHAPTER 34
ADELE

A few hours later, we have the Fayatin guards set up a safe distance from Stellara's front city gates. General Pavik had the smart idea to pitch extra tents, creating the illusion that our numbers are larger than they really are. Only fifty guards volunteered in the end, and it's less than I'd hoped.

We stand with a small group of them, discussing strategies for worse case scenarios if confronted by the Bocnite. When Evander lands abruptly behind us, the Fayatin men instinctively reach for their weapons. They're still trying to wrap their heads around demons, angels, and the fact that we're in a land that doesn't exist on any map they've ever seen.

"Sheath your weapons. There will be no blood spilled today. Is that clear?" As their acting general, they all comply, returning their weapons to their sides.

Evander reports on what he saw from the sky. "We've definitely caught the Bocnite's attention. Now that night's fallen, they're starting to gather along the city wall. Watching our position."

"Good," I say. "As long as we don't move toward the city, they'll likely hold their ground."

"Let's hope so," Rune adds, her gaze on the horizon. "Their numbers outmatch ours ten to one."

Pavik leans in, his voice low. "Please don't say that too loud. We don't want the men panicking."

"Where would they run to?" I ask.

He strokes his beard. "Anywhere but here. And in this magical land, who knows what they'd run into."

"It's not a magical—" Rune begins but cuts herself off with a sigh. "Never mind." She turns to Evander. "Stay alert. If they make a move, take cover in the forest."

He nods, then motions for Pavik to follow. The two of them step away, deep in discussion, while Rune and I move to return to Bricen.

I whistle, sharp and short. Within seconds, the crows appear, their silhouettes sweeping in from the trees above. They've followed us all the way here from Fayatin. Now they'll return home with me, back to their brother.

As soon as they get close, Rune lifts her hand. A portal shimmers open, revealing a quiet Bricen. Looking to Rune, I ask, "Where is everyone?"

She shrugs and says, while stepping through, "Let's go find out."

All is quiet... *too* quiet in the village.

The crows take off, scattering into the sky in search of Barclay while Rune and I make our way toward the tavern. Inside, we find Mum sitting at a table with Kit.

Mum rises to greet us. "Oh, good. You're back. Just in time." She gestures toward Kit, who sits motionless, her gaze fixed somewhere beyond the empty room.

"I've just finished blocking her sight and hearing. It won't hold Merigoth out forever, but it's a start."

I step closer and lightly poke Kit's shoulder.

She flinches, then yelps, "Ow!" Rubbing the spot, she adds, "Adele, I *know* that's you! I may be deaf and blind, but I'm not some vegetable you can just poke and punch."

Her unfocused eyes drift upward, scanning the space above us. It reminds me of how Trevor used to look at the ceiling when he spoke to someone. A small laugh slips out before I can stop it. I quickly shake the amusement off and apologize. Because none of this is funny, especially not what's happening to Kit.

Kneeling in front of her, I take her hand in mine, gloved fingers curling around hers.

"We're going to fix this," I whisper, even though she can't hear me. I squeeze her hand gently, hoping the gesture speaks louder than words.

"I know," she says softly, her voice strained but steady. "Everything will be fine. I trust you, Adele. I trust all of you. Because this… this isn't how I want to live."

I give her hand one more squeeze before standing and turning to Mum. "Good work."

The tavern door bursts open, slamming hard against the wall.

"Adele!" Brandulf storms in like a one-man army. "You said you'd bring Nathaniel home. Where is he?"

I stiffen. If I tell him what happened at Castle Helve, he'll go on a rampage.

"He's with Selene," I say. "I didn't want him anywhere near the fight."

"No. You *promised*—"

"And I will, you pain in my ass!" The words fly out before I can stop them. "Sorry. I'm sorry," I add quickly, exhaling. "There's a lot happening right now, and I promise your brother is safe. He means a-a-"—I stutter my words, saying them out loud for others to hear for the first time—"a lot to me."

Brandulf makes a *hmph* sound, as if he doesn't fully believe me.

"I swear. Please… go back to the smithy. Forge some metal. Sharpen farming tools. Anything. Just… give me until tomorrow."

For a moment, I think he'll plant himself against the wall like earlier. But instead, he nods.

"Fine. You have until tomorrow to bring him home." He turns to leave.

Elijah is about to enter the tavern just as Brandulf storms off. He flattens himself against the door frame, barely clearing the massive man's shoulders. Once Brandulf is past, Elijah hurries inside with a bounce in his step, making his way straight to Rune's side.

"Where are we at with the plan?" he asks.

"We're all here," I say. "And we need to go now before whatever Mum did to Kit wears off." I glance at Rune, offering a subtle signal.

She catches it and nods, lifting a hand. With a flick of her fingers, a shimmering doorway opens right inside Goslings, leading to her mother's private study over in Stellara.

As Elijah heads toward it, he hands me my bow and quiver. "Grabbed these for you after I got Aleksandra situated."

"Thanks," I say, slipping the quiver over my shoulder before stepping through the doorway.

Elijah follows, gently guiding Kit by the elbow. He helps her into a faded armchair, positioning her carefully. She sinks into the cushions with a small sigh.

The room smells musty, the kind of scent that clings to old books and forgotten places. Outside, the night is thick and moonless; no light filters through the grimy windows. I whistle, and before Mum and Rune walk through, two crows fly into Goslings and through the doorway. They land on the window bench, feathers ruffling as they take in the space.

"Do they have to be here?" Rune asks.

"Valor's our eyes. She'll let us know if it's safe. And we may need Serafina to find the keystone because she's good at finding treasures."

Rune sighs. "Fine." She flicks her wrist, and the doorway seals shut behind us.

She turns to face the room. "We're still unsure where Merigoth is. Evander did a quick survey from the sky earlier. Unfortunately, it was still daylight. Given that Bocnite are creatures of the night, they were almost certainly hidden, and Merigoth was somewhere in the city."

"We'll find her," Elijah says, placing a hand on Rune's shoulder.

She gives him a small smile, enough to hopefully satisfy him. But I see through it. She's not convinced. Not yet.

I tighten my grip on my bow and step closer. "Elijah, stay here. When we locate Merigoth, Rune can open a doorway and bring you both to us. That way, Kit doesn't have to navigate the city blind and deaf."

He nods. "Got it."

Rune steps over and gives Elijah a tight hug and a quick kiss before slipping out of the old study. Mum and I follow, careful to keep quiet as we move down the stairs and out of the building. My thoughts spin the whole time—about love, about Nathaniel. For the first time, I truly understand the emotions tied to loving someone. I *will* survive this. I *will* be victorious, because I want to kiss Nathaniel, again.

"This way," Rune quietly says, waving for us to follow. In a stealthy procession, we run through the dark, cobblestone streets of Stellara, the area looking more destroyed than I remember.

We duck into a shadowed alley. Rune slams a fist against the wall, teeth clenched. "What have they done to my city?"

Before I can answer, distant voices grow louder. We peer out to see a group of Bocnite gathering. They're child-sized creatures with loose black curls, dark horns, and skin the color of ash. They mumble words we can't hear. A few of them take the opportunity to raise their hands and turn nearby stone statues, flowerpots, and benches to sand. Then a sharper voice barks at them to come over. They continue mumbling, until eventually half of them break away and head for the front gates of the wall. The other half turn and walk in the opposite direction.

"Those four must be going to Merigoth," Rune whispers.

"How do you know that?" Mum asks.

I chime in, guessing the same. "Where else would they be going?"

"Right," Mum agrees. "So we follow them."

We keep low and in the shadows, my grip tight around my bow. The Bocnite lead us through the wreckage of the city until we reach a tall, looming building, much larger than any around it. Wide steps stretch across the front, carved from demolished stone.

"The citadel," Rune says. "Where the Star Leaders used to gather. A place of power."

"Fitting," Mum murmurs, drawing her shining Fayatin dagger. "Let's go find her."

I grab her arm before she steps into the open. "We need the element of surprise, remember?"

She nods. We follow Rune through a side entrance into the citadel's dark interior. The pale moon shines down, but it's not enough to see what's around us. We keep close to Rune, since her sight is better in the dark, weaving silently through a maze of cold rooms. Then, Merigoth's voice echoes from nearby, sharp and commanding.

"She's close," Rune whispers.

"Go get Elijah and Kit," I say. "We'll wait here."

She nods, flicking her wrist. A glowing doorway opens with a soft hum, casting light on the space around us. We're in a strange sitting room with long, oddly designed chaise lounges with arms on both ends.

Valor and Serafina fly through the doorway from their spots on the window seat into the room we're hiding in.

"I'll be right back," Rune says, and the doorway vanishes.

Mum and I inch forward, through a door that opens into an adjoining chamber. We press against the wall, listening. The crows hop after us, and I shush them with a quiet hiss.

Inside the room, Merigoth bellows, "I *don't care* if they're not advancing! The fact that they're out there at all is infuriating!"

I glance at Mum. "Sounds like our distraction is working."

She nods. "We need to act before she tells them to attack."

She's right. But we also shouldn't do anything until Rune returns with Elijah and Kit.

"Adele," Merigoth says, her voice smoother now, almost amused.

My heart drops when I hear my name.

"I *know* you're there. Come out and talk to me like a civilized person. It's been too long since we last spoke."

How does she *know* we're here?

She chuckles softly. "Come on, little one. I know you're listening."

Mum shakes her head, lips tight. But I already know—I have to go out there.

Somehow, she got to Kit. Somehow, she broke through the block Mum placed. She's using Kit to find us.

Mum's shaking her head, but I know I have to. It's time to face Merigoth.

CHAPTER 35
ADELE

The look on Mum's face tells me she's already convinced we've lost. Well, I refuse to accept defeat. We came here to end this once and for all, and that's what I'm going to do.

I glance at the pair of crows. "Serafina, go find the keystone. It's a smooth black stone, about the size of a loaf of bread." The well-trained bird responds with a soft *caw* and takes off silently.

"Oh, Adele. Don't keep me waiting," Merigoth calls again, her voice teasing.

If she's toying with us, there might be Bocnite nearby, waiting to strike. Mum and I exchange glances. My stare is firm and resolute, while hers wavers, clearly expecting the worst.

"We can do this," I assure her. "When Rune returns with Elijah and Kit, tell them to be ready. Once Serafina finds the keystone, we'll need to move fast."

"Be careful." She presses a hand to my cheek. "And whatever happens, you know I'm proud of you."

"Mum, this isn't the time."

"This is exactly the time—the only time we may have, if something goes wrong." She swallows hard, holding back her emotions. A single tear slips down her cheek.

I take her hand in mine, then lower it gently from my face. "Neither of us is dying today."

Then, just before stepping out into the grand room, I glance over at Valor, and whisper, "Wait until she's distracted. Then fly."

Out in the main chamber of the citadel, tall torches fixed to iron stakes rise from the stone floor. They're positioned around a wide platform in the center of the room. I assume the Bocnite used their abilities to turn stone into sand to force the torches into place.

Four throne chairs sit atop the platform, all but one knocked over. I imagine Merigoth throwing a tantrum, knocking each one down like a spoiled child denied her way. She now sits in the lone upright chair, hands resting on its carved arms, eyes locked on me.

"I owe you a thank-you, Adele," she says, her voice smooth and laced with mockery. As I slowly approach, she continues, "Without you, it might've taken me years— maybe decades—to get here." She spreads her arms wide, gesturing to the grand room. "You made this possible. And I thank you."

"I don't want your thanks," I snap. My voice shakes with anger. "I want you to leave Stellara and go back to the Under Realm where you belong."

She laughs, low and delighted, never looking away from me. "Oh, Adele. Is that what you really want?" She pauses just long enough to make me tense before adding, "Because from what I've seen, that's not what you and Sara have planned."

"How do you know what we have planned?" I ask, careful to keep her attention on me. A faint flutter of wings echoes from behind, barely noticeable above the echo of our conversation.

She offers nothing but a cryptic smile.

Buying Serafina more time, I ask, "You're looking much healthier. Was that the work of the Shadowrock?"

Her eyes gleam. "You've been speaking to the Bocnite, haven't you? They're the only ones who know about the Shadowrock's existence." Her gaze flicks briefly to the far-right side of the room, where the shadows retreat behind the torchlight. Then she looks back at me, voice taking on a lecturing tone. "The Bocnite are fascinating creatures, aren't they? So misunderstood. So… powerful."

I resist the urge to glance toward the dark side of the room where she looked. I hold her stare, not giving anything away. She goes on, rambling about their ability to turn solid stone into sand, something I already know, but I let her talk. Every second she wastes on her own ego is more time Serafina has to find the keystone.

Wanting the crows to investigate, I casually clasp my hands behind my back and subtly gesture toward the area with a shake of my hand, pointing to where I want them to go. It could be the keystone.

A faint rustling from the thick wooden beams above tells me they understand.

"Did you place an enchantment on the Bocnite city to prevent anyone not of their bloodline from seeing them?" I ask, keeping her attention locked on me.

"I can't take credit for that," she replies. "But if their goal was to keep me from seeing them, they chose the wrong imbuing incantation for concealment."

"You're not wrong," I mutter. Then, louder, I ask, "What exactly happened back then? I only know what happened when you returned to Stellara after being infected. That memory you shared with me right before I trapped your mind."

A snarl curls at the corners of her lips. "My compliments on the amendment you made to that memory—adding the mirror and having me appear as Merigoth rather than Loralai."

"I figured it was a good reminder of the wicked person you've become." Sometimes I even impress myself with how creative I can be when amplifying someone's nightmares or fears.

Merigoth shakes off the annoyance of what I did and rises from her seat. Her long leathery wings remain folded neatly against her back as she begins pacing across the top of the dais. Her skin is no longer sickly gray or cracked like dried clay. Now, it's soft and full of life, like flower petals. A wave of thick, shiny, golden-blonde hair cascades over her shoulders, a stark contrast to its former thin, brittle state. Even her eyes have returned to a normal color, rather than being consumed in blackness. Soft blue eyes stare down at me as she retells her misfortunes.

"I was a curious angel," she begins, her voice smooth and distant. "Even as a child. My mother would often say that my extensive curiosity would get me into trouble someday." She chuckles, the sound light but tinged with bitterness. Her leathery wings shift slightly with each step as she paces. "Fate led me to the Shadowlands. It was there that I met a Bocnite man studying the rock formations. That… was the beginning of the end."

I'm half listening, half wondering how the crows are doing. Then I hear it—a subtle, low chirp, exactly from the area she glanced toward earlier.

They've found it.

"But how did you get infected?" I ask, urging her to keep talking. The longer she rambles, the better. Aleksandra might care about our origins, but I don't. I am who I am. And these gloves… they may never come off. And even if they could, would I still feel like me?

Merigoth keeps talking, her story spilling out in dramatic, practiced waves. While she's distracted, I cast a quick glance over my shoulder and whisper a soft, sharp *psst* toward Mum.

The motion lasts only a second. I turn back to Merigoth as if nothing happened, keeping my posture casual. With my hands still behind my back, I point toward the shadows, then form a fist, representing the keystone before pointing again.

Please understand what I'm saying, Mum.

"Over time, I earned the trust of the Bocnite," Merigoth continues. "Eventually, my new friend invited me to their underground city, where I met others and learned about their community. Still curious about his research into the rock formations, I remained close to him, building up our friendship. At first, he was hesitant to share anything, but eventually, he confided in me."

She pauses, her gaze staring off into the distance, as if remembering.

"He told me there was an entity living inside the rocks, and how over time, he'd learned how to communicate with one of them. Eventually, with the guidance of the entity, my Bocnite friend successfully transferred the creature's phantom essence out of the jutting rock and into a smaller, temporary stone."

The keystone, I assume silently.

"The Bocnite explained during his studies of the Shadowrock, he'd learned that it exists as an intangible entity and required a *house* to survive. The stones of the Shadowlands gave its kind a place to reside without dying until a more suitable option came along. The problem was, once the Shadowrock beings found solace inside the rocks, they couldn't easily free themselves without help. My friend had multiple encounters where the Shadowrock tried to claim his body. Realizing his error in freeing the demon entity, he and other Bocnite built a room to contain the Shadowrock, using a keystone to keep it secure." Merigoth briefly looks my way, still engulfed in her own story. "Of course, after hearing this fascinating story, I needed to see it for myself. Supposedly, this dark entity possessed unnatural power that the Bocnite almost failed in containing."

Merigoth's voice lowers, as if she's confessing something sacred. "The Bocnite refused at first. Biding my time, I gradually won my friend's favor through repeated visits and small doses of bliss, which led to him finally taking me to the gatekeeper's room. It was at this point in time that everything would change. My curiosity, you could say, forged your existence."

I couldn't help but be enthralled by her origin story. For so long, I've wanted to know more about the demon blood coursing my veins. I stand still, attentive to Merigoth as she continues her tale.

"Once inside the gatekeeper's room, well… That's where everything changed. The memories are hazy, but somehow the Shadowrock escaped. I tried to keep it away from me, using the Bocnite man as a shield. But it didn't want him. It wanted me. I could feel its power the moment the shadow tendrils entered my body through my mouth. It was hungry and eager to thrive outside of its former stone existence. It wanted its kind to be flesh and blood rather than stone. I fought back, and thankfully, other Bocnite heard my screams and came to stop the Shadowrock from fully taking over. In the end, I *became* one with the part that merged with me, tainting my blood, altering my appearance. Its voice was always present, echoing in the depths of my mind to return—to help its kind thrive."

She stops pacing and looks at me with an expression full of gravity. "You see, child, it's not Bocnite blood in our veins. In fact, the Bocnite aren't even demons. The demon part of us comes from the *Shadowrock*. Its power and poison combined to make us what we are: Shades of the Shadowlands."

She stares at me as though I'm supposed to be awestruck. But I've had enough of this story time.

"I actually don't care," I say flatly. "Demon, Bocnite, or Shadowrock—there's no changing who I am."

"Ah, but there is," she replies, taking the few steps from the dais to ground level. "I can take the darkness from within you… just as I did with Aleksandra."

The thought stuns me. A life without my reach? My mind races with images: sparring with Kit, gardening with Magdala, shaking hands with Rune, and most of all, touching Nathaniel. Could I exist without the strength and power of the darkness?

"You're tempted, aren't you?" she coos, slowly approaching. "I can pull it from your mind, if that's what you want. It is *your* choice. I have no desire to hurt you."

Her last words jolt me back.

"You have *no* desire to hurt me?" I throw her words back at her like an accusation. "Are you serious? That's *all* you've done—to me, to my family and friends, to everyone in this realm and the next! You've been out for blood. You've never cared about the lives lost!"

From behind the throne chair, Mum suddenly appears, stepping out fast. She sprints toward us. Merigoth turns to strike, but Mum ducks low, sliding beneath one of Merigoth's unfurling leathery wings. In one smooth move, she stands and grabs the queen's wrist.

Merigoth freezes. Her body locks up as she trembles, struggling against whatever Mum just triggered.

I rush to help.

Mum thrusts the black stone sphere toward me. "One hand *here*!" she shouts.

I don't hesitate. I rip off my gloves, letting them fall to the floor. With one hand, I press my palm to the black stone. With the other, I grip Merigoth's free wrist, securing us all into place.

Inside Merigoth's mind, Mum and the evil queen are engaged in battle. Their arms are swinging, fists striking flesh and bone. I hurry to join, but just as I rear back to land a punch into Merigoth's side, she lashes out with a wing, knocking me hard in the chest and sending me tumbling across the grassy field where we stand. It *feels* real, each impact, each breath, but I know this isn't the physical world.

I scramble to my feet and charge back into the fray. This time, I call on my reach. It whips forward like a shadowy lash, cracking through the air with a thunderous *snap*. Each strike connects, drawing a hiss from the demon queen as she flinches under the blows.

"Enough!" Merigoth snarls. She raises a hand and a surge of energy slams into us, hurling Mum and me backward.

Mum is first to rise, hands up, body tense, ready to strike. I hurry to my feet and stand beside her, mimicking her stance. Both of us focused on the queen.

Behind Merigoth, a massive shadow blooms like an inky, swirling storm cloud. And it's roaring like a wild beast. Lightning flashes deep within it, illuminating the dark, growing mass.

Slowly, our hands drop to our sides in unison.

"Uh, Mum. Is that what I think it is?" I ask as we both stand there and stare at Merigoth.

No answer. Mum stares with intense focus at the threat.

"I was *hoping* you'd bring the fight in here," Merigoth booms, her voice reverberating through the air and into our minds. "Now you'll feel the full power of the *Shadowrock*!"

I inch closer to Mum. "Mum," I whisper, "we're not really here… but it feels real. If we die in here—"

"Our bodies die out there," she finishes grimly. "Get ready," she says, her breath coming faster now.

"What's the plan?" I ask, heart pounding as the shadow cloud moves toward us—thick, roiling, and vast.

"Well," she replies, voice low, "we came here to end this… so let's end it."

I blink. That's *not* a plan.

The Shadowrock looms, nearly on top of us.

"Right," I mutter, bracing myself. "We fight darkness with darkness."

That gets a grin from her. "Embrace the darkness, my dear. It's part of you and part of the Shadowrock."

I have no idea what she means… again. But there's no time to ask.

I reach inward. *Time to do your thing*, I command.

A surge of energy floods me. Here, inside Merigoth's mind, it manifests as black tendrils, snapping outward, striking the advancing threat. Beside me, Mum does the same. Her reach whips and weaves, meeting the Shadowrock head on.

We can't see Merigoth now. The Shadowrock cloaks her completely, veiling her in its dark clouds and lightning. But her voice echoes out into her mind.

"You thought you could *best* me?" she sneers. "I saw it all the moment you entered that fragile little human's mind— when you blocked her eyes and ears. You gave me access to *yours*, Sara. I *know* your plan!"

Her laughter rises, sharp and chilling. "You are such *weak* fools!"

"Now!" Mum yells, sending the tendrils of her reach to the outer edges of the Shadowrock.

I follow her lead, mirroring the movement but striking the opposite side. The winds howl as the pressure builds.

"We need to force it into a tight spiral. That will make it easier to control than if it hits us as one massive storm."

I nod, already feeling my reach adjust instinctively. The black tendrils herd the outer edge of the Shadowrock's billowing form, guiding the thick cloud of shadow into a narrow funnel toward us.

As it bears down, I shout, "What do we do when it reaches us?"

Mum doesn't respond. She just stares at the churning darkness.

"Mum!" I call again, louder.

Still nothing. Only Merigoth's laughter echoing through my skull, curling like smoke in my mind.

"Mum!"

"Hold your reach, Adele!" she barks, eyes flashing. Then she thrusts out her open palm, just seconds before the Shadowrock touches us. "Give me your hand!"

I don't hesitate. I press my palm to hers, and I feel the weight of the keystone even though I don't see it.

"Now!" Mum commands. "Use your reach—push it forward!"

The instant the dark cloud meets our hands, the air splits. The Shadowrock's force slams against us—but it falters. It *doesn't* know the keystone is there, between it and us. Mum hid the stone right in its path.

Wind tears around us, howling and violent, as the dark clouds of the Shadowrock are pulled into the invisible keystone.

"Hold it!" Mum shouts, even as Merigoth's laughter is replaced with agonized shrieks.

"We've got her now!" Mum says, smiling through the gale, her hair whipping in every direction as the last of the Shadowrock is pulled into the keystone.

When it ends, it's like a vacuum collapsing shut. Silence drops, heavy and absolute.

Where the storm once was now stands Merigoth—old, brittle, exposed. Her wings are skeletal, bones weathered and dry. She opens her mouth and wails—and the sound is so piercing I nearly double over, clutching my head.

"We need to get out of here," Mum says, already closing her eyes.

In a blink, she vanishes.

I turn to leave too, but before I retract my reach and pull out of her mind, Merigoth locks eyes with me.

"You will not end me," she growls. "My destiny is far from over."

I meet her glare. "We'll see about that."

Then I snap back to my body.

We're in the grand room of the citadel, on our feet and breathless. What we weren't expecting were the Bocnite surrounding us. Dozens of them. Each holding long spears carved from stone.

Mum and I are still clutching the keystone—and Merigoth's wrists.

"Don't let go!" Mum commands the moment I open my eyes. "We're not done yet." Then, lifting her head to the ceiling, she calls out, "Bring her, now!"

"Aren't you worried the Bocnite will attack?" I whisper, eyeing the stone-skinned creatures as they shift uneasily between the flickering torch stakes.

"No," she answers. "Merigoth's compulsion is either fading or gone. They're confused. All they see is the keystone. They don't know if we're friend or foe." She glances at me. "Let's finish this before dealing with them."

Just as I nod, Rune emerges from the shadowy passage of the adjacent chamber. Elijah is with her, guiding Kit forward. Rune's expression is all purpose and steel, while Elijah looks as if he's seen a ghost, his gaze locked on Merigoth.

"It's okay," I tell him. "As long as we've got her"—I nod toward the wrist I'm gripping—"she can't wake."

He swallows hard, then gives a stiff nod and helps his sister to the center of the circle, positioning her between Mum and me.

Mum says, "Rune, take the keystone. Elijah, help Kit get close enough for us to grab her wrists." Then she turns to me. "Are you ready?"

I meet her eyes. "Let's sever the bond between them."

Mum gives the signal.

Rune steps forward and gently lifts the keystone from our joined hands. Its pull lingers, like static in the air.

Elijah steadies Kit, guiding her forward. Just as she steps into place, Merigoth writhes in our grip, a last effort of her resistance. Our hold nearly slips, but at the last moment, Mum and I reach forward and grasp Kit's wrists.

The second our skin touches hers, Merigoth jerks and goes rigid, as if caught mid-scream. Frozen again.

"You're going to be looking for—" Mum begins, but I cut her off.

"I know what I'm doing."

This time, I don't dive into Merigoth's mind. Instead, I find my way into Kit's.

Darkness surrounds me. A void, empty and thick, as though I'm suspended inside nothing.

Kit is there. Standing in the middle of it all, still. Unaware.

Mum must've blocked her senses to protect her, which means this blank slate is all she has left.

"Kit," I whisper, stepping closer. "Can you hear me?"

No reply. Her gaze is unfocused. Hollow.

"Adele, hurry!" Mum's voice filters into Kit's mind—thin and echoing.

I turn toward the sound and see her, far in the distance, standing beside Merigoth.

She's in Merigoth's mind, while I'm in Kit's.

"What are you doing over there?" I shout across the void.

"In order to keep the tether severed, I need to stay here," Mum replies. "And *you* need to stay there."

She lifts a hand and grasps something that resembles a trailing rope. It stretches outward from Merigoth's chest, pulsing faintly. The longer she holds it, the more visible it becomes, emerging inch by inch between the minds.

It's the tether binding them.

It suddenly appears on my side, snaking out of Kit's chest. Up close, I see it's no ordinary rope. It's made of *blood*—glimmering red, swirling with a slow churn, sticky and alive.

I follow Mum's lead and wrap my hand around it. It's warm and slick, resisting my grip like a living thing. Every instinct tells me to recoil, but I don't. I *won't*. This is what's been holding Kit hostage.

I summon my reach again—not to torture, but to *dissolve*. To destroy.

The darkness stirs inside me, responding to the command with a sharper focus than ever before. A single tendril emerges, honed to a blade-like point. It slashes down on the blood rope in one swift motion.

The tether splits.

Kit gasps and opens her eyes. Her gaze finds the fraying rope, then me. Awe washes over her face.

"You saved me—again!"

"Hopefully for the last time." I wrap my arms around her. My reach recedes, pulling back into the depths of my mind.

When I look back across the void, Mum is gone.

"Come on," I say. "Let's go."

Kit nods, and together, we retreat from her mind.

Back in the citadel's grand chamber, Merigoth has collapsed to her knees. Her face twists in agony and rage as she mutters curses under her breath.

We all face her—Mum, Rune, Elijah, Kit, and me.

"You've lost," I say, stepping forward.

"You've taken everything from me!" the queen hisses, then spits at our feet. She tries to stand but falters, trembling.

Kit doesn't hesitate. She runs to a nearby Bocnite, snatches its weapon, and shouts, "There's one last thing to take!" With a cry of fury, she spins and swings the stone-bladed spear. It slices clean through Merigoth's neck.

The queen's head falls with a sickening *thud*.

We all step back, stunned.

Kit is breathing hard, tears glinting in her eyes. "She needed to be gone. *For good.* She's hurt me—all of us—for too long."

The spear slips from her hands and clatters to the stone floor.

Then, something unexpected happens.

The Bocnite erupt into cheers, raising their weapons high. The sound of their voices fills the citadel like a crashing wave.

Elijah rushes forward to hug his sister. Mum wraps her arms around me. When we pull apart, Rune approaches and hands me my gloves with a proud smile.

"It's over," she says softly. "It's *finally* over."

CHAPTER 36
ADELE

Walking over, I find him right where I left him—basking in the spring sun. His arms are folded behind his head, muscles flexing at the edges of his short-sleeved shirt.

Without opening his eyes, he says, "I was hoping today would be the day."

I sit beside him. He rolls to his side, smiling at me.

"How was it?" I ask.

He sighs as he sits up, then scoots closer until our knees are nearly touching. He crosses his legs to match mine, and we sit quietly, eyes locked. "Honestly? Relaxing."

"Good."

Then he asks, "How does my body look? Still bruised?"

I try not to let my smile falter. "You're healing well."

He huffs a soft laugh. "I guess I'll find out soon enough, huh?"

"I brought you back to Bricen before waking you," I explain. "Figured the journey wouldn't be comfortable if you were conscious."

He reaches for my hand, and I don't pull away.

"That was kind of you." He lifts my hand and presses a gentle kiss to the underside of my wrist. "I'm looking forward to being closer to you," he says, lowering my hand slowly. There's uncertainty in his gaze. "If you still want to continue our courtship."

My stomach flutters at the word—*courtship*. A new beginning. A new chapter beyond friendship. And a test of the boundaries I've always feared to push.

Since the battle with Merigoth, something has changed between me and the darkness. An understanding of unity. I was fearful to live without it, and it apparently didn't want to be ripped from its home within my mind. To be able to touch people like Mum and Aleksandra without the constant worry of hurting them would be a wonderful feeling. That's all I'd asked of my reach, and in return I promised to release it every now and then, even in ways like this—where Nathaniel and I can escape the real world and come for some privacy.

"Are you ready to leave?" I ask.

He stands quickly, raking a hand through his overgrown hair. "Yup. Let's go!"

After rising, I take his hands in mine.

"Close your eyes," I whisper, "and when you open them, we'll be home."

When we open our eyes, he's lying in my bed, smiling as he looks around the cottage. I'm sitting beside him on the edge of the mattress, our hands still clasped.

He glances down, his tone soft but curious. "Your gloves?"

He doesn't pull away, and that comforts me.

"It'll take some getting used to," I admit. "But… I don't think I need them anymore."

He sits up, wincing slightly as he pulls me into a hug. His arms wrap around me anyway. "That's wonderful news, Adele."

I let him hold me for a long moment. And just as he begins to shift away, I lean in and kiss him.

My first *real* kiss.

The sensation is unlike anything I've ever known. Warm. Whole. Real. *This* is the life I've fought for. A life where I am free.

Free of fear.

Free to choose.

Free to be happy—on *my* terms.

**THANK YOU FOR READING
SHADES AND BLOOD OATHS
BOOK THREE IN THE THREE SHADES TRILOGY**

If you enjoyed this book,
please consider sharing your thoughts in a review.

And if you really, *really* enjoyed this series, please consider sharing
your thoughts on your social media pages and with your friends and
family.

To learn more about my books, where to find me online, sign up for my
newsletter, visit my author shop, and more visit:
KimberlyGrymes.com

ACKNOWLEDGMENTS

Thank you to everyone who read all three books in the Three Shades Trilogy series. This was a fun story world to write and I'm already missing these characters. Found family and strong female protagonists seem to be my go-to tropes, and I look forward to writing more stories with those strengths in mind.

Before I thank those who directly helped make this book the best it can be, I'd like to express my deepest gratitude to my husband, Jim, for his unwavering support and encouragement. He's been there for me since I decided to write and publish my own stories. I'd also like to thank my three kiddos, Kayla, Abby, and Chloe, for their constant love and support. They're always there to celebrate with me or give hugs when I'm burned out from writing or marketing. I couldn't do what I do without their love and encouragement.

I'd like to thank Nikki at NAM Editorial for another round of amazing copy and line edits, waving her magic wand and fixing all my grammar and sentence structure flops. Her talent for identifying inconsistencies for character details and world-building continues to amaze me.

No story would be complete without a final pass over by a proofreader. And I'm so happy that over the years Aime has continued to proofread my stories, but also become a good friend. So, if you didn't know—I tend to be an underwriter before sending the manuscript to the copy/line editor. Then, after I get it back, I apply all the feedback AND do what I call 'add fluff' to the story. And this is another reason why it's important for the manuscript to go through one final round of professional editing. I appreciate everything you do for me and my stories, Aime at Red Leaf Word Services.

The last step was sending the finished manuscript to my audiobook narrator, Amanda Davidson. Amanda's ability to bring a story to life with her exceptional storytelling and diverse voices was the perfect finishing touch for the project.

I'd like to thank Angeline Trevena at Step-By-Step Worldbuilding for hand-illustrating the map of the *Three Shades Trilogy* and Yves Muench for the character illustration artwork on the cover.

I also want to extend my sincere appreciation to all of my writer friends, who have been with me throughout this journey. We proudly cheer each other on as we follow the yellow brick road together in reaching our dreams. Stay strong and stay in touch, because it's no fun doing this author gig alone!

Last, I'd like to thank you, the readers, for sticking it out and reading the final book in the series. I'm always brainstorming new story ideas, so I hope you'll return to enjoy whatever adventure I end up writing next. Happy reading until then!

Kimberly Grymes is drawn to the imaginative realms of science-fiction, fantasy, mystery, and the paranormal. Her passion lies in crafting original tales within the young adult fantasy genre, where she explores worlds of magic, adventure, and the supernatural. In addition to her storytelling, Kimberly supports fellow writers through her author shop, where she provides a range of checklists and worksheets designed to guide writers through the brainstorming, outlining, and writing process.

When she's not immersed in creating resources or weaving narratives, Kimberly enjoys spending time with her family, indulging in movies or TV shows, and delving into captivating books. She and her family reside on the outskirts of Wichita, Kansas, accompanied by their two lively miniature pinschers, Cori and Jubilee.

To learn more about my books, where to find me online, sign up for my newsletter, visit my Etsy shop, and more visit:
KimberlyGrymes.com

www.ingramcontent.com/pod-product-compliance
Lightning Source LLC
Chambersburg PA
CBHW020125310726

48970CB00006B/1729